I0637638

Black Forest Souvenirs

Henry W. Shoemaker

Black Forest Souvenirs

HENRY W. SHOEMAKER

CATAMOUNT
PRESS

an imprint of Sunbury Press, Inc.
Mechanicsburg, PA USA

CATAMOUNT
PRESS

an imprint of Sunbury Press, Inc.
Mechanicsburg, PA USA

Copyright © 1914, 2023 by Henry W. Shoemaker.
Cover Copyright © 1914, 2023 by Katharine H. McCormick and Sunbury Press, Inc.

Sunbury Press supports copyright. Copyright fuels creativity, encourages diverse voices, promotes free speech, and creates a vibrant culture. Thank you for buying an authorized edition of this book and for complying with copyright laws. Except for the quotation of short passages for the purpose of criticism and review, no part of this publication may be reproduced, scanned, or distributed in any form without permission. You are supporting writers and allowing Sunbury Press to continue to publish books for every reader. For information contact Sunbury Press, Inc., Subsidiary Rights Dept., PO Box 548, Boiling Springs, PA 17007 USA or legal@sunburypress.com.

For information about special discounts for bulk purchases, please contact Sunbury Press Orders Dept. at (855) 338-8359 or orders@sunburypress.com.

To request one of our authors for speaking engagements or book signings, please contact Sunbury Press Publicity Dept. at publicity@sunburypress.com.

FIRST CATAMOUNT PRESS EDITION: January 2023

Set in Adobe Garamond | Interior design by Crystal Devine | Cover by Lawrence Knorr | Cover art by Katharine H. McCormick | Edited by Lawrence Knorr | Headpiece and tailpiece by Katharine H. McCormick | Illustrations from photographs by W. T. Clarke.

Publisher's Cataloging-in-Publication Data
Names: Shoemaker, Henry W., author.
Title: Black Forest Sourvenirs / Henry W. Shoemaker.
Description: First trade paperback edition. | Mechanicsburg, PA : Catamount Press, 2023.
Summary: Henry Shoemaker compiled these folk tales set in the Black Forest of north-central Pennsylvania. Shoemaker's stories recall the decline of big game in the region and the exit of the native peoples as the European settlers advanced westward. This collection of tales has been modernized for 21st-century audiences but maintains the charm, wit, and suspense of the originals.
Identifiers: ISBN : 979-8-88819-038-8 (softcover) | 979-8-88819-039-5 (ePub).
Subjects: FICTION / Fairy Tales, Folk Tales, Legends & Mythology | FICTION / Cultural Heritage | FICTION / Small Town & Rural | FICTION / Short Stories.

Product of the United States of America
0 1 1 2 3 5 8 13 21 34 55

Continue the Enlightenment!

BY THE SAME AUTHOR:

Wild Life in Central Pennsylvania (1903)
Pennsylvania Mountain Stories (1907)
More Pennsylvania Mountain Stories (1912)
The Indian Steps (1912)
Tales of the Bald Eagle Mountains (1914)
In the Seven Mountains (1913)
Susquehanna Legends (1913)

* * *

Immaterial Verses (1898)
Random Thoughts (1899)
Pennsylvania Mountain Verses (1907)
Elizabethan Days (1912)

* * *

Legend of Penn's Cave (pamphlet) (1907)
Story of the Sulphur Spring (pamphlet) (1912)
Stories of Pennsylvania Animals (pamphlet) (1913)
Stories of Great Pennsylvania Hunters (pamphlet) (1913)

CONTENTS

Foreword by Lawrence Knorr   ix

Explanatory Preface   xii

CHAPTERS

I.   John Decker's Elk   1
Locality: Centre County, Clearfield County, Potter County;
Told by John Decker, Lewis R. Miller.

II.   Why the Senecas Would Not Eat Trout   12
Locality: Potter County; Told by Billy Shongo, Jacob Fenstermaker.

III.   Young Woman's Creek   21
Locality: Clinton County, Potter County; Told by William Patterson.

IV.   Conquering Fate   32
Locality: Potter County, Mifflin County;
Told by W. R. Wagner, J. R. Ramsey, George Gast.

V.   In the Rafters   42
Locality: McKean County; Told by Thomas G. Simcox and others.

VI.   The Winter of the Wolves   53
Locality: Potter County;
Told by James Dougharty, Samuel L. Wallize, Mrs. Anna Stabley.

VII.   The Three Rivers   65
Locality: Potter County; Told by Thomas G. Simcox.

VIII.   A Story of Regina   77
Locality: Tioga County, Schuylkill County, Lycoming County;
Told by Jacob Portzline, Thomas G. Simcox.

IX.   The Death Shout   98
Locality: Clearfield County, Potter County; Told by Jacob Quiggle.

X.   The Healing Spring   108
Locality: Clinton County; Told by Thomas G. Simcox.

XI.   A Hunter's Daughter   118
       Locality: McKean County, Potter County;
       Told by James Dougharty, C. W. Dickinson, P. L. Webster.

XII.   The Moment the Lights Were Lit   130
       Locality: Clinton County; Told by John Q. Dyce.

XIII. Hugh Mitcheltree   141
       Locality: Pottery County; Told by George Mitcheltree.

XIV.   George Shover's Panther   151
       Locality: Lycoming County, Clinton County;
       Told by Charlie Crawford, M. Button.

XV.   The Tramper   162
       Locality: Potter County; Told by D. A. Kohler and others.

XVI.   Little Red Riding Hood   172
       Locality: Lycoming County, Potter County;
       Told by Charlie Crawford, F. Lanks.

XVII. The Cursed Woods   183
       Locality: Potter County; Told by George Gast.

XVIII. The Screaming Skull   195
       Locality: Potter County; Told by George Gast, H. Shurr.

FOREWORD

THE YEAR leading up to the publication of this book was an eventful one for Henry Wharton Shoemaker (1880–1958). While writing the book, Shoemaker married his second wife, Mabelle Ruth Ord (1878–1967), in 1913. He also lost his beloved maternal grandmother, Cordelia Mayer Quiggle (1828–1914), in January 1914. Shoemaker's preface was signed in June 1914. Thus, by the time he was signing off on this volume, Shoemaker had inherited the mountain estate he dubbed Restless Oaks from his grandmother. It is very likely this elderly connection to the region—Cordelia was born and raised in the region around McElhattan—was the inspiration for many of his tales. The darker turn taken by this book, with its several ghost stories, a couple of which are as macabre as a good Poe yarn, may have been influenced by this event.

One story of particular interest for its unusual horror is titled "In the Rafters," about an alcoholic couple who, rather than raising their son, dispose of him and then collect sympathy from the community. Here is a section of it:

> Meanwhile, all plausible causes for its absence could be spread abroad. Chuckling over their evil intentions, the couple staggered to their feet and went over to the crude wooden trestle which served as the child's bed. The little fellow was sound asleep, and the father, with his huge, bony fingers, strangled him to death where he lay. Then the mother dressed the child and doubled the body into a soap box which had served as a receptacle for stove-wood. The woman laid some boards loosely over the top. Then the couple started up the rickety stairs to the

attic; Sweek went ahead carrying a small kerosene lamp. At the next to the top step, he slipped, dropping the lamp. Luckily, as it fell, it went out, preventing an explosion that might have incinerated the murderers, victim, house, and all. Mrs. Sweek dropped the box containing the little corpse, and it rolled out in a heap on the floor at the foot of the stairs.

Sweek swore long and loudly, ordering his wife to go down and get another lamp. She protested that she had broken the other lamp the day before; in reality, she was afraid. Sweek was just as scared as she, so he compromised by lighting numerous matches in his trousers' pockets. By this uncertain light, the woman could pick up the child's body and put it in the box, and the trip to the lonely garret was resumed.

This story stands out for being unusual among his many tales. The recent exit of his own son to the West Coast with his first wife may have been on Shoemaker's mind. Does this story betray some feelings of guilt for this situation? Did Henry lament having the young lad raised by his mother and not Henry and the stepmother?

Meanwhile, Shoemaker continued his relationship with his mistress, Hilda Herlacher. There are hundreds of letters in possession of this publisher to that effect. Interestingly, Shoemaker refers to a character, a famed hunter Clem Herlacher, in the story "Conquering Fate":

"That critter lives in there now," said one of the mountaineers. "He's got a lot of nerve with lumber wagons and fishermen passing by every day. Surprisingly, the panthers hang on in this valley; there always is one here. They have followed me several times, and none have been killed since Clem Herlacher went in the caves and carried off a nest of cubs about twenty years ago."

A Clemens Franklin Herlacher (1856–1937) was born in Loganton, Pennsylvania, near McElhattan. According to the 1920 Census, Hilda was the daughter of Elmer E. Herlacher, 58, a telegraph operator for Western Union. This Elmer was the brother of Clem, according to cemetery records. Curiously, according to Hilda's 1933 wedding announcement, she, like her father, worked for Western Union Telegraph Company.

This book also contains many wistful descriptions of the region. One of the more historic narratives, now unseen in the 21st century, concerns a train ride. Once again, Shoemaker describes his character mesmerized by a beautiful girl on a train. He misses an opportunity to introduce himself and then decides to search for her:

The eastbound journey seemed longer than the entire trip from New York to Sunbury had been. He chafed and fretted at the slowness in reaching the stations; he barely noticed the ball of the red setting sun poised on the very horizon and spreading its fiery effulgence over the entire broad river. Darkness, sweet, cool, summer darkness had settled down; the crickets' chorus wafted through the open car windows. The conductor, equally as self-important as the one on the westbound train had been, called out for the stop at Millersburg. There were still a goodly number of people at the station, which was illuminated by tallow candles set in glass lantern boxes; Hubert scanned their dark faces eagerly; they were not like his fair beloved. Where would he find her? Who would he ask about her? The faces he saw about him seemed to grow unsympathetic and distant, even in the candlelight.

He watched the red lights on the rear of the train as it disappeared into the darkness. A feeling of loneliness and desolation overcame him; it was the first time he had felt it in America. There was still light in the station. Through an open window, it poured out on the platform; there was the musical clicking of the telegraph keys. Inside the window sat a young man with black hair and eyes and black side whiskers; he seemed genial and approachable; whom else could he question? He addressed the operator in broken English, being answered by the youth in phrases equally unfinished.

A coincidence that he approaches the telegraph operator? Does he ever meet the girl? You will have to read on to find out!

Lawrence Knorr
Boiling Springs, Pa., 2023

EXPLANATORY PREFACE

THE WRITER of these lines has always felt the thrill of the words *Black Forest*. As a small boy, he used to gaze at the bold outlines of the Allegheny Mountains, on the opposite side of the broad valley from the old-fashioned home where he spent most of his time, which formed the southern boundary of the vast regions of hemlock, spruce, and pine. All kinds of fancies flashed through his mind, dreams of strange races of people, of Indians, of outlaws, of witches, ghosts, lumbermen, wild beasts, and birds that must inhabit this wilderness. And for more definite information, he inquired of the old people and strangers how the Black Forest really looked, how big it was, and who lived there. The general replies were that it was a vast domain of enormous trees, mostly evergreens, that it was sixty miles from east to west, and forty miles from north to south, that hunters, lumbermen and some farmers lived in it, also many bears and deer, a few panthers, and that until a few years previously there had been wolves, elks and countless flocks of wild pigeons.

As a result of this information, a great longing arose in him to visit the Black Forest, to see it with actual vision rather than with the eye of faith. Every account of lumbering or hunting that had its location there, which appeared in the county newspapers, was eagerly read and enlarged in the imagination; every person who might have views of any kind concerning it was questioned.

But life, with its strange deprivations, withheld this joy until the summer of 1898 when the writer was a young college student. But it was not too late; much of the Black Forest remained, in range after range of hemlock-clad mountains, even though the big lumber companies had commenced their cruel inroads. Many of the old pioneers and hunters, as well as a few of the Indians, still lived and were ready to impart their stories of the past to any respectful listener. And those days and nights in the original forest, amid strange scenes and stranger imageries, will never be forgotten. In 1899, 1900, 1901, and 1902 other pilgrimages through the forest were made, on foot, horseback, or carriages. The impression made in 1898 was further cemented into the soul by a host of fresh experiences and dreams. Then life withheld the Black Forest until 1907, although the famous German Schwartzwald had been visited and admired and reverenced in the meantime.

But what a change those five years had made. Where was the Black Forest? Miles of slashings, fire-swept wastes, emptiness, desolation, ruin met the eye on every side; the lumbermen had done their work. Hoping against hope, the writer rode on, but only dreariness was his portion. Gone were the hemlocks, beeches, maples, and pines; gone were the sweet singing birds, the balmy breezes; gone even were the lumbermen with their red or blue shirts, the lumber camps, the stemwinder log railways; gone was everything but ruin. Other trips were taken into the "forest" in 1908, 1909, and 1910. These visits only accentuated the sense of sadness for the arboreal paradise that was no more, which on the wholesale plan, lumbering had swept away. The hand of man had changed the face of nature from green to brown. During these latter visits, the writer thought more of the ancient legends, which were so easy to hear in 1898 but so difficult to obtain in 1910. What were listened to with seeming indifference then were listened to breathlessly toward the last. As a result, the contents of this volume were obtained, and many more, and written out in the form of notes. So that their origin can be traced, the names of the persons who told the narratives are set down in the table of contents; some of these informants still live, while others, unfortunately, have passed to their reward.

During the past month or so, eighteen of the legends have been transferred from notes into enlarged form. They are exactly as told by the old people and others, except here and there, names of persons and places, and a few dates have been changed to avoid giving offense. But sometimes, the "offense" is on the other side. A letter was received after the publication last winter of another collection of legends, *In the Seven Mountains*, in which a gentleman, born and raised in the region described, stated that the stories were correct, only they were "badly dislocated." This had been purposely done in some cases, but in others, it was unintentionally due to the lack of exactness of the various informants in recounting incidents that happened years before. One newspaper commented that the characters used such good English in their dialogues; it seemed strange that backwoodsmen could be such rhetoricians. But there was no need for dialect in these stories; they were preserved as folklore and not as samples of backwoods talk. The quaintness of the tales themselves and not how they were told warranted their preservation.

Dialect stories are galore; there is hardly room for more, even though the Pennsylvania mountains are still without their Charles Egbert Craddock, John Fox, Jr., or Amelie Rives. There seems to be a valid reason for writing out these legends. They treat a phase of life that is no more, in a region that has been laid waste, that can never be restored. They are a chapter added to American folklore, especially relating to the Indians. It is interesting to observe that some of them undoubtedly have a common origin with legends across the sea. This summer, while the writer was on a driving trip in the Blue Mountains of Eastern Pennsylvania, in Berks, Lehigh, Schuylkill, and Lebanon Counties, he found legends similar to ones collected in the Black Forest. If the writer had been born in time to make his first trip through this matchless forest in 1878 or even in 1888 instead of when he did, he is certain that he could have collected many more and far more quaint old tales. Think of the pioneers and Indians who went to their graves with their stories unrecorded! The modest graves in highland cemeteries in 1898 and many thereafter, whose occupants the writer was not fortunate enough to meet, bear mute testimony to this.

Doubtless, someone could have done this work more thoroughly or better, it deserved more time, but the truth remains that no one else has tried. But the writer can say that he has written with sympathy, for he loved the people whose curious lives he sought to portray; he loved the grand forest, which was the background, and the crowning influence in their existence. He has sought to show what was beautiful and best, although if the result may have been painted in somber tones, they were the tones of truth. He believes in the reliability of his sources of information; he has verified wherever possible, though verification, where there is no documentary evidence, is fraught with difficulties. He believes that in years to come, the folklore and traditions of inland Pennsylvania, as set forth in his several volumes, will rank with the old tales of Scotland, Ireland, France, Germany, and Russia, which have been so systematically collected and preserved. This historical byproduct has a right to live on, for there is value to it, just as was the case with gasoline, so long wasted by oil manufacturers. It will come to its own, and Central and Northern Pennsylvania as a land of romance will rank with other regions immortal in song and story. To those who admire these beautiful regions, which surely God loved best, the bizarre happenings of the sturdy pioneers and the doomed Indians must always awaken a pang of interest.

And this is the writer's explanation or apology if any is needed. But before he closes, he wishes to thank the press and public for their continued and exceptional kindness toward his former volumes. He wishes to express his gratitude to the old men and women who took the time to tell him the legends. They have all made him realize how many very kind people there are in the world, especially in Pennsylvania.

HENRY W. SHOEMAKER
Riverside, Connecticut, June 8, 1914

JOHN DECKER'S ELK

(A Black Forest Souvenir)

I T WAS springtime on Portage Branch. The elk wood was in bloom. In the recesses of a deep swamp, along the edges of which Great Blue Herons nested in the stag-topped crests of the tall white pines, three Wapitis or Pennsylvania Stags were resting themselves. Their leader was an enormous bull, long-bodied, drab-colored, strong of antlers to which the velvet still hung in clusters like the maple-bud rosettes, whose deep, full brown eyes betokened unusual intelligence and patience. By his side stood a well-formed, drab-colored cow with eyes like those of her lord and master but infinitely deeper and kinder. Hidden behind her was a very robust-looking bull-calf, unusually large and vigorous for his age. At frequent intervals, he shook his little head and bristled his tiny mane, for he was restless and anxious to see more of the beautiful forest world into which he had been so recently born.

The Springtime soon ushered in the summer, and even the young calf relished the cool retirement of the swamp, so silent save for the occasional croak of the nesting herons and the frogs. Then the nights became colder, and on the summits of the nearby but unseen mountains, wolves barked. The cricket and katydid songs suddenly diminished from full choruses to occasional wandering minstrels.

The first snow came, and the elk sought the valleys, browsed and huddled together while the fierce winds rattled the dead tops of the pines. Sometimes through the openings in the branches above, their coats were dappled by cold starlight. Then came heavy rains, warm days, and the disappearance of the snow. The skunk cabbage quickly appeared along the edges of the swamp; there were bird songs that recalled the previous year. The elk family wandered back to higher lands, finding themselves again in the inaccessible swamp on Portage Branch.

One morning the stalwart bull-calf awoke to find a newcomer in the family circle. The slimmer neck, narrower head, and wilder, more appealing eyes betokened that it was a sister who had come to swell their numbers.

With the blooming of the elk wood, the bull-calf felt a tickling sensation on the crown of his head. He began to rub his skull against the brown bark of the original pines but could find no surcease. Soon little growths, like swellings, appeared. They dripped blood at the slightest contact with other substances. As the season advanced and the little sister waxed slimmer, lither, and more beautiful, the bumps on the bull-calf's head became more like miniature horns. The bull-calf was very proud of his embryo antlers and tossed his head and sometimes tried to roar like his sire, but his voice cracked in an adolescent squeak. All through the summer, the elk family was quiescent. The bull-calf wondered why no effort was made to venture far from the deep insect-teeming swamp. The nights became colder. The herons flew away. The katydid and cricket choruses lessened, bird songs were no more, and even the wild pigeons had ceased their cooing. Only a solitary *hylode* piped. Wolves barked on the unseen heights. Once a panther's scream, its love song, long, weird, and terrible, reverberated the entire nocturnal atmosphere. On grey afternoons, the "dum, dum, dum" drumming of the ruffed grouse was heard.

One morning, when the sun was climbing over the mountain tops, and the maple leaves were particularly golden, a strange series of sounds came to the ears of the elk family. It was *bang, bang, bang,* and to the minds of all of them, some instinct said that it was the report of the weapons of their most inexorable and incomprehensible foe, mankind. All that day and that night, the elk family huddled more closely together in the depths of the dismal swamp. The bull-calf needed no one to tell him now why his elders were so cautious. While he had never seen a man, he had been born with a fear of an arch and horrible enemy, beside which panther, wolf, or rattlesnake paled into insignificance. But the instinct of the race grew stronger every night. The voice first a tremolo, then cracked and unmusical, grew into something loud and sonorous. One night he poured forth his soul to the wilderness, and in tones of which he was not ashamed. But the only answer was the echo from the unseen mountains. Other nights produced no other results. Again, the instinct which always made for self-preservation told him that there never would be an answer, that if he must continue his race, his mate must be his little sister. This dulled a little the keenness of his joy of masculinity. But he showed it in no other way than that he stopped his night song. His eyes assumed a softer expression, and he became more solicitous for the comfort of his mate-to-be, edging her to where the browse was choicest.

The winter came on again. With bumps on his skull now fashioned into erect broad prongs and with throat full and mane shaggy, he was almost a match for his majestic sire. Snow fell, and the elk family migrated southward to another hidden swamp in the lowlands. There they were in comfort for a while. One morning they were roused from their rumi-nations by a savage yelping, a sound that lacked all the noble melody of wolfish or catlike cries. Man's henchmen, dogs, were somewhere in the forest. It was too late to fly; the elk family must wait; perhaps the enemies would pass them by. But it was not to be. There came an awful crackling of brush and twigs, and soon two spotted, hideous-looking hounds with flapping ears bounded into the center of the swamp.

Quick as a flash, the old bull went at them with lowered antlers and tossed them torn and bleeding among the hazels. Barely had they been dispatched when a *man,* thickset, bearded, red-capped, clad in furs, bearing something long and glistening, appeared at the verge of the swale. He was Jim Jacobs, a full-blooded Seneca hunter, the terror of the wapitis of Northern Pennsylvania.

The thought flashed through the bull-calf's mind, "How can this little thing hurt us, wipe out our race, level the forest covers, change the very aspect of the world? How dare he!"

Quick as he could think, the diminutive Indian had the long, glistening thing—his rifle, to his shoulder, and aiming, fired, and down fell the mother elk, choicest of the quartette from a pot hunter's point of view. Blood, bright red, gushed from a hole in her neck as she toppled over on her side into the snow. The old bull-elk gave a snort of alarm and command and trotted away, followed by his two offspring who trusted him implicitly. There was no second shot.

Evidently, Jacobs was satisfied with the cow elk, for when far to the north, the elk trio paused for breath, there came no further apprehensions of danger. The episode produced a profound impression on the survivors. They wintered in a northern swamp, enduring great hardships. On some nights, they were almost buried in avalanches of snow. There was browse enough if they could but reach it. The elk family became very lean and listless as the long winter waned. The bull-elk hung his head; he acted like some old, discouraged man. The younger elks longed for the chance to move and wander, but their sire's will was strong enough to hold them close to the confines of the swamp. Before the snow was all gone, even before the mayflower budded, the ominous barking of the wolves on the unseen mountains disturbed the peaceful slumbers of the elks. The night winds rattled the dead tops of the ancient white pines, banshee-like in their warnings.

One grey morning, while the elk family stood motionless, a strange patter of feet was heard. It could not be man's ally, the dogs; there was no yelping or barking. The enemies, whatever they were, were approaching silently save for their footfalls on the rattling leaves and snow patches. Like a sudden storm, they were upon the elks, running about them in circles, great, gaunt, grey creatures, all jaws—wolves. At a snarling order from the leader, the ugly mob singled out the old bull elk for their fury. Reaching with the wide jaws for his gambrel joints, they bit him fiercely,

IN OLE BULL'S VALLEY

and he was quickly rendered crippled and helpless. As he fell to his knees, the leader of the wolves, with one snap, tore his throat open.

Meanwhile, the two younger wapitis had a chance to escape, and they made good use of it. They traveled steadily until nightfall. Self-preservation dulled their grief for their sire. When they stopped, the rustle of leaves frightened them, sounding like wolfish footfalls.

They traveled all night aimlessly, but their direction was southerly. They rested a while in a secluded swamp at dawn, but soon their instinct moved them on. At noon they came to a broad stream of water, the Sinnemahoning; they were making ready to plunge into it, and to cross, when they noticed a log cabin, with creatures, *human beings,* moving about it, on the opposite shore. The elks slunk back into the tangle wood and remained motionless until all was dark. Then for the first time in their lives, they *swam* and were soon on the other side, landing about a quarter of a mile below the log cabin. A high mountain reared its precipitous cliffs close to the water's edge. The refugees did not attempt to scale it or to reconnoiter until the next morning when their mutual decision was to find sanctuary among its pinnacles. They wandered in an easterly direction along its base, through a tangle of wild grapes, water-birches, and elders, until they came to a little draft, where now a mountain torrent gushed out from under a hemlock canopy. Lowering their heads, they wended their way up the mountain, their feet displacing and rolling down the smooth stones in the stream bed. They stopped many times to catch their breaths or to pick a twig off some deciduous tree, but they were on the bare, bleak, open summit in time to greet the afternoon sun before it reached the level of the Knobs, the highest of the western peaks. In the clear afternoon light, they had an admirable opportunity to look about them. There were mountain peaks, mostly bare, cold, and grey on every side, but in the sides of all of them were furrows or hollows heavily timbered, mostly with hemlocks running almost to the summits. These looked like avenues of escape. Doubtless, one of these would lead into some sequestered valley or plateau where they might follow their destiny for a while.

The young elks made a handsome pair. The young bull was unusually large for his age; he had a proud head and eye; there was an almost Roman curve to brow and nostrils. His winter coat was almost olive or drab. The young cow had a fine expression; the eyes were larger than ever through that perception that only suffering gives. Her lines were symmetrical; she was short coupled, almost like a western elk. Her color was somewhat lighter than her mate's. The two hunted beasts gazed at the limitless expanse for a while and then, at a common impulse, started down one of the worn watercourses with moss-covered banks that seemed like a path, and which led into the big timber below.

At nightfall, they found themselves in a soggy upland bog caused by many windfalls damming up the brook, which flowed down through the draft. It was probably a thousand feet above the valley, which was a little wider than the Moshannon and the West Branch of the Susquehanna, which had their confluence in it. It was a good place to tarry because it was so hard to get to; few outside foes would ever invade its solitude. Stretching from it were flats or "benches," where a little grass was apt to grow, and beeches, birches, and maples were abundant. But the prevailing forest was hemlock. Here the young elks spent many happy days. Gradually a sense of security returned. The weather became warm, and though it was but springtime, the flow of the mountain torrent diminished. There was plenty to eat and still enough dampness left to sink into up to the fetlocks, so the elks were contented to remain into the summer. Fresh antlers were coming on the head of the young stag. This time two points appeared on each horn, and the circumference of the horns was greater; they gave their wearer a bolder appearance. And he carried himself as befitted his added dignity.

Through July and August, the weather became intolerably hot. The elks climbed to the topmost peaks at night to get the breezes, which were always there. They were alarmed at times to notice great clouds, like mist, rising from the drafts; these had a peculiar smell, for they were smoke. There were, too, red tongues of light, the color of the sunset—*forest fires*. One night, especially hot, was spent on a rocky point, where their rest was marred by smoke rising from a hollow behind them. They remained as long as they could and then started downwards toward their hidden vale. They had only gone a few hundred yards when fresh smoke began coming toward them. They looked back; it was also trailing after them.

In front, it was not so dense, so they plowed ahead. Several hundred yards more, the atmosphere became thick with smoke on all sides. They looked back; a tongue of flame running among the ferns was coming on after them. They struck a trot; they surely would escape it if they ambled *faster, faster.* Their speed only brought them to a point where they encountered a long garland of flame, like an incoming tide on a beach, advancing to meet them. The smoke was terrific. But they plunged into it. There was nothing else to do. The smoke became thicker and blacker. Neither one could see the other. But it could not always be like this. The young bull plunged ahead. He heard a crackling. Was it his mate or the flames? He strained his big, prominent eyes to see. A great gulf of yellow fire blazed up out of the forest depths, revealing the tottering and confused form of his beautiful mate. He could not succor her. He was half stupefied himself. He saw her fall—*into the flames*—he loped forward; he kept going somehow; he did not know what he was doing—he found himself at the riverbank. It was cool there—there was no fire on the opposite shore.

Dazed, he stood in the water for many hours, then resumed his trot—to *somewhere.* He must have traveled for several days and rested very little at night. Sometimes he came dangerously near cleared lands; he heard dogs barking and sounds like men's voices. His equipoise was returning. He browsed, he drank, and he slept calmly. He was resting quietly one afternoon when he felt a blow at his side; he wheeled about; a deer, a buck, had struck him with his antlers, on which hung traces of the velvet. Striking at him with his short but stout horns, the elk tore a gash in his foe's shoulder. Then the deer took to heels with the excited elk after him.

They raced over mountains, through lumbermen's slashings, past a logging camp, where a woman sat on a bench, peeling potatoes for supper, into the virgin forest again, out into a vast open field—at the far edge of which was a log-cabin with blue smoke curling out of the big stone chimney. It was a dangerous place to pursue animosity, but both animals plunged on. They were too excited to hear a woman's voice shouting, *"Look at the deer, John, look at the deer;"* too wilted to see a sturdily built backwoodsman with a black chin beard leave his woodpile and run to the cabin for his gun. The deer with the angry wapiti at his

IN THE FOREST

heels had almost reached the timberline on the southern border of the big clearing when a loud report rang out on the calm September air. The deer disappeared into the dogwood thicket and escaped, but the elk turned a complete somersault and fell over into the stubble *stone dead. The last of his race in Pennsylvania.* Now the story must sound like every other hunting narrative.

"That's no deer," said John Decker, the intrepid hunter of Decker Valley, as he stood beside the bleeding, steaming carcass. "Yet it's just twenty years since the last elk hereabouts was killed across the mountains in Treaster Valley." Then he began skinning the dead animal. "It must have been chased in here by those big forest fires in Clearfield County and the Black Forest. There are no other places in the state where the 'Pennsylvania stag' hangs on."

At sundown, the hide was nailed on the barndoor to cure, the carcass had been cut up and was in the cellar, the skull and horns hung on the woodhouse, among diverse other heads of *deer.* And night closed in, and a lonely cricket started to chirp somewhere near the garden gate. A red light gleamed from the cabin window. A wolf on the knob to the south saw it, and his keen scent told him of the recent carnage; becoming envious of the cozy glow and the feed, he set up a melancholy howl. The hunter's dog "Rover," part wolf himself, answered, and it was almost midnight when their duet ceased. Then commenced a tap, tap, tap, the night wind blowing the skull of the dead wapiti against the woodshed or was it the tramp, tramp, tramp of the soul of the last elk bound for that borne where all is life, and there is no chase.

Seven and thirty years have passed since that clear September afternoon when John Decker nailed the elk's skull to his woodshed in the remote little valley bearing his name. Terrible winters have come and gone, and the blackened bones and faded horns have been decked out with snow, ice, and frost. Spring, summer, and autumn have shed their radiance on the melancholy relics, but the black sockets of the eyes bespeak not even a question. But at night, winter or summer, there comes a mysterious night wind to the place, and a soft tap, tap, tap sways the moldering skull nailed there against the shed. Is it the soul of the last elk still traveling to the unknown country, where he will find his race unsullied, his beautiful mate to greet him? Or is it the spirit of the wilderness, blotted out by man never to return, while our race lives, whispering of better and freer days, of vast distances and open places, of beauty, justice, and truth, which were banished with that last elk? Only those who lived in Pennsylvania in such days can answer, and their ranks are growing thin—they are following the last elk to the land of light—where there is no chase.

And old John Decker, his chin beard now snow white, looking proudly at his crumbling trophy, in the afternoon light says, "It was just about this time of day when I saw him in the stubble field over yonder. It seems only yesterday. I brought him down with one shot."

And as we drive away, we almost feel as if we were living in those grand days, and in our mind's eye, we can see the actors in the pageant of the times, Indians, elks, panthers, wolves, settlers, all going over the unseen mountains.

II

WHY THE SENECAS WOULD NOT EAT TROUT

(A Story of the Coudersport Pike)

THE INDIANS had finished setting potatoes on the Fenstermaker place and had gathered at the old farmhouse for supper. It was a cold, bleak day, although past the middle part of May. Very few blossoms were out, as the season on the mountaintop was said to be two weeks behind that in the valleys. The farm occupied a bare space hewed out of the ancient forest on a high plateau, with the higher mountains of the Black Forest surrounding it on all sides. Several trout fishermen from Williamsport were spending the night at the farmhouse, and the good wife had kindly consented to cook a "mess" of their fish for supper. They were small, puny trout, to be sure, but the city fishermen could not have been prouder of them had they all been over a foot in length.

"It looks like harvest time," remarked old Daddy Fenstermaker as he stared at the dozen faces assembled at the long table when he had finished saying "Grace."

The six Indians were a stolid, unimaginative-looking crew, dregs of the proud race of the Senecas, once the rulers of Northern Pennsylvania. They presented an unkempt contrast to the short-haired sportsmen with their cropped mustaches, spectacles, and tweed suits, and even to old man Fenstermaker himself. For the sake of politeness, the fishermen passed the big dish containing the trout to the Indians, but they declined the fish, one after another. The fishermen thought at first that it was because the Indians feared to deprive them of some of the results of their outing and urged them to take some, and one went so far as to remark jokingly that Indians doubtless preferred bigger trout.

The situation required some explanation, so Daddy Fenstermaker spoke up and said that members of the Seneca tribe never ate trout. "I don't know why it is," he continued, "but no Indian who ever worked for me would touch a trout; perhaps someone here can tell the gentlemen the reason?"

There was a moment's silence, and then Billy Shongo, the most charismatic of the Indians, ventured to say that his people were a queer lot, that if he was doing the right thing, he could not be even engaged in farm work. "One of our wise men, advising us to keep out of farming, put it this way, 'You ask me to plow the ground! Shall I take a knife and tear my mother's bosom? Then when I die, she will not take me to her bosom to rest. You ask me to grub out stones! Shall I dig under her skin for bones? Then when I die, I cannot enter her body to be born again. You ask me to cut grass and make hay and sell it and be rich like white men! But how dare I cut off my mother's hair?'"

"That reminds me of Chief Red Jacket's indignant reply to the request that he sell land, 'Why not sell the sea, the air, and the sky,'" said one of the fishermen.

"We have violated all this and more, but very few of us have eaten any trout," Shongo continued impressively.

All of us, including the fishermen, urged the Seneca to tell us why his tribe would not eat trout. To us, they seemed to be the sweetest and cleanest of all fish.

"All right, I'll tell you, but please excuse me if I detain you too long."

"Go on, go on," said almost everybody, so Shongo commenced his story.

"It was long, long ago, when this world was new, and the Senecas were the chosen people of the Great Spirit. In those days, the Indians lived along the banks of big rivers such as the Allegheny, the Genesee, and the Susquehanna. There were broad flats on both sides of the banks where they raised corn, sweet potatoes, and muskmelons and where their orchards were located. Some Indians owned orchards that covered over a thousand acres, all planted with the best apple, peach, and plum trees. In those days, the Indians gave all their attention to farming and gave little time to hunting. They sometimes shot water birds, which flew along the rivers or sieved with their bark nets, the fine shad, salmon, and other river fish. They never visited the mountain streams, which were said to be alive with serpents, allies of the Evil One.

"But farming brought them into evil ways. The democracy of the hunting camps could not exist among them. Some became very rich and powerful, and the sons and daughters of these were proud, arrogant, and cruel. As they rose on the social scale, they forced their less fortunate fellow beings who did the real work into a state bordering on slavery. The wealthy ones thought only of pleasure. They desired no offspring. They invented queer dances, copied from the antics of the beasts and birds of the woods, and at these, they indulged themselves all night long and slept by day. All kinds of vice and crime thrived among these idlers. The only religious rites they cared about were those where human sacrifices were made, and they gloated, laughed, and sang lewd songs while the victims were being tortured horribly. They would not speak to the Indians of the coarser sort and boasted loudly about 'divine right,' a 'ruling class,' and the like.

"Among themselves, they were not one whit less mean. They robbed and plundered one another when they could; they were jealous and envious to the last degree. But their immoralities were the worst part of them. First of all, whenever they saw a beautiful young girl in the home of one of their slaves, they stole her away, toyed with her for a while, and when they saw a prettier or fresher one, they had the predecessor put to death by slow torture. Some wicked Indians of the lower classes sold their daughters as playthings for the rich. Then they got to stealing one another's wives. In some of their orgies, when steeped with a corn liquor that they distilled, they exchanged wives. Love was reduced to commercialism and lust, and all the higher, finer impulses, such as the Great Spirit willed the Senecas to possess, were dead.

"All this was about two thousand years ago or more. I am glad it was so long ago that we can almost imagine that it was a myth. We say to our young people that such doings were exaggerated, but in our hearts, we know that it was all only too true. From his home among the clouds, above the tallest mountains, the Great Spirit viewed the state of affairs with growing concern. He loved the Senecas above all his other creations, and it grieved him to see their degeneracy. He breathed his soul deeply into some wise men and sent them among the rich as teachers. But when they had been laughed to scorn, the Master Mind realized that he must adopt more drastic measures.

"The rich people were so imbued with their importance that they must be shocked into a sense of right. He sent horrible new diseases among them, cutting down the powerful, the young, and the beautiful. The dancing groves became burial places. There were so many dead to lay away. But with the nearness of death, the Indians resolved to 'have a good time while life lasted' and plunged deeper into foul lasciviousness. They did not mind death if they could extract the last ounce of pleasure from life while it lasted. The Great Spirit delayed his vengeance. His divine pressure produced such slight results that he began to doubt his omnipotence. But as matters were steadily growing worse, he launched his final thunderbolt. The idle rich had planned a great outdoor dance carnival. Like beasts, they were to dance all the new steps scantily clad and then feast and drink until they fell to the earth from the excess of pleasure.

"A level plain, shaded by tall, hardwood trees, was selected as the place for the orgy. Once, it had been a pasture ground for buffaloes and elks, but the animals had moved into other localities, and it had become overgrown with trees and brush. The undergrowth was cut away, so the vast area presented a park-like appearance. On the edges of this park, where the old forest was dense, hearths and pits were constructed to roast the whole carcasses of animals, such as moose, elks, and buffaloes. Many new dance steps were invented for the occasion, and the entertainment began with human sacrifices. Fifty beautiful young girls of the poorer class were tortured to death to arouse the jaded instincts of the pleasure-seekers.

"Then the dancing began; it was to last until hunger overcame the revelers, then they were to gorge themselves into insensibility with the elaborate repast provided. The Great Spirit viewed these arrangements with disgust and made ready for his retribution. The ungrateful beings had perverted his lofty purpose in placing them in the world; they had made his image a silly mockery. The sun was shining brightly when the exercises commenced, and the groans of the dying girls drowned out a breeze that had sprung up among the feathery tops of the tall hardwoods.

"Just as the Indian players struck up the first weird notes of the dance music, the clouds darkened, and there were several deafening peals of thunder. Some few of the more delicately nurtured were for dropping out of the dances and running to the more sheltered woods or caves, but the leaders of the entertainment who believed in pleasure at any cost shouted, 'on with the dance, it will be a new sensation to dance with the water dripping down our backs.' So, the dance proceeded, many reasoning that the thunder and lightning only portended a passing shower. But when the rain fell, the Heavens literally opened, and soon the level plain was indented with water courses. The amazed dancers strove to keep their feet, but the heavy downpour literally laid them low. They sprawled all over the muddy earth, and some tried to roll to places of safety. Many fell into the water courses and were swept away in the brown, grimy torrents.

"Those who rolled over the ground experienced a peculiar sensation. They felt slimy like fish, their hands and feet congealed to the shape of fins, and great gaping gills appeared in the corners of their throats. They felt themselves diminishing in size. As they struck the water, they felt the horrible obsession that they were fish. Struggle they could not. Was it all a dream produced by superabundant pleasure, or had they been seized with another new disease? If so, their lofty position in the world's social scale would soon lessen it for them; they believed they never suffered as acutely as the plainer sort. But on this occasion, they ceased to be the petted darlings of infinity; they were fish, and for all time. The rain, or whatever it was, continued until the last member of the wealthy class had been washed into the new-formed streams and transformed into fish.

"Then the sky suddenly became light, and the muddy water-courses transparent mountain brooks. In these brooks swam myriads of handsome speckled fish. The spots, we were told, corresponded with the number of sins committed by the creatures while in human form. We were ordered never to eat a spotted fish, as it would mean accepting another's sins. The spotted fish soon accustomed themselves to their new environment and began recognizing old friends. Life might have been quite pleasant in the cool, shaded brooks; only they found that water ran into their throats enough to choke them when they attempted to speak. Those who uttered a single word perished miserably, came to the surface,

GOLDEN HOUR AT A LUMBER CAMP

and floated with white stomachs upwards. They polluted the habitations of the survivors, so few attempted to open their mouths except to breathe and take in nourishment.

"No sooner had they begun adjusting to this situation when a fresh peril appeared. From under logs and stobs which lay in the streams issued an army of hideous, brown serpents, water snakes. They emerged so suddenly that the frightened trout had no time to turn around. Great numbers were partially swallowed, horribly bitten, and disgorged by the slimy monsters. Others were completely eaten, distending the sides of their devourers. The fish became panic-stricken and swam hither and thither, some even throwing themselves on the banks, where they could not get their breath, dying there and becoming food for small animals, flies, and bugs.

"The most sagacious fish managed to exist somehow. But they knew no peace, by day or night. They were ever on the alert to escape the rapacious water snakes. Even their spawn or young were devoured by the millions. A fresh enemy, though on a smaller scale, green frogs, assailed them in quarters where the snakes seldom visited. These creatures were particularly destructive of the fry or small fish, as well as of the spawn. Despite their lowly position, the erstwhile pleasure-seekers now felt the desire to carry on their race; their normal instincts returned with their metamorphosis. Formerly they had evolved too high for their own good; a check was needed. Perhaps their punishment was only temporary, but as time wore on, there was no sign that there would be a change. And worst of all, not a single trout died a natural death. As they grew older and weaker, they were devoured by the water snakes or even frogs, lizards, or eels, passing away mutilated and miserably.

"But they found that they had a guardian angel, the Great Blue Heron. This bird was the sworn enemy of the water snakes and frogs. It hunted them with the same avidity as the snakes pursued the fish. And many a six-foot snake slid down the long throats of the herons. And as new generations of fish were born, they regarded the herons as their divinities. But all the same, the old, weak fish were regularly eaten by the serpents, as there were never enough herons to diminish the number of snakes appreciably. It was a horrible destiny, but it was warranted by the hideous lives that the spotted fish had lived while in human form. But a still more horrible fate was in store.

"A few Indians had escaped from the dreadful flood. They were mostly of the baser sort, who had shunned agriculture, and lived by the chase, and on berries and roots, in the deep forests. These were joined by a few survivors of the dance orgy, who were near the edges of the big timber when the storm broke and rushed pell-mell into the forest depths, escaping being swept into the streams. These had a chance to note what had happened and informed the other Indians they later met, who dwelt in the innermost recesses of the forests. And that was why when they assembled at the banks of the streams, which were swimming full of speckled trout, they refrained from catching or eating them. Their wise men told them they would become responsible for the sins of the fishes' ancestors if they touched them. And they accepted it as fact.

"For centuries, the Senecas never tasted trout, and the streams in Northern Pennsylvania fairly teemed with them. They were polluted, tainted food, while the spots or sins showed out on them. But the natives loved the clean, pure river fish and were experts in netting and snaring them. Also, they kept their hands off farming; it had been the cause of the terrible downfall of the others. But all was different when the settlers came. They did not stop to inquire if the Indians ate trout or not. They started to catch the 'speckled beauties' with their hands, then with hooks and nets, and when they could not get them fast enough these ways, they placed dynamite in the creeks. The fish, who knew the story of their unhappy origin, it was somehow handed down to each new generation, shrank with horror from being hooked and seined by these beings, in form though not in color, as they had been. And they even had to gaze upon the destruction of their divinities, the herons.

"The misguided fishermen attacked the heronries, calling the poor birds 'enemies of the fish,' and slaughtered them without quarter. The water snakes increased in numbers, and likewise, the frogs; it became harder for the trout to exist. Lumber mills, which dumped unwholesome sawdust into the streams, sprang up on all sides, and later on, tanneries and acid factories poured rank poisons into every water course. It seemed as if the final fate of the cursed trout was to be their worst. The poisons produced loathsome sores and corruptions on their spotted sides; they actually rotted to death.

"But the fish laws made still more suffering for them. When trout less than six inches in length were caught, the law compelled the sportsmen to throw them back into the water. But the touch of human fingers was an added curse. It produced on every small fish, thus given his freedom, cancers and foul sores worse than the poisons had created. The fish sloughed away, dying hideously, or being easily captured by the snakes in their weakened condition. Man's final blight was more than they had ever dreamed could come to them. Now, you know why the Senecas will never eat trout."

It was pitchy dark in the little dining room when Billy Shongo finished his narrative. The supper things remained on the table in front of us, and several full cups of coffee were untasted. The good wife and the hired girl sat open-mouthed on chairs, too much interested to clear off the table or to bring in the lamp. The fire in the little wood stove between the windows had burned down to grey ash. The room had become uncomfortably cold. But we had heard a tragic story and were well recompensed.

"How strange it is," said one of the prosperous looking fishermen, "that we are out here as agents to wreak a further punishment on those fish; why I must have thrown back fifty trout this morning for being undersize. I feel like swearing off trout fishing."

His companions laughed, and then everybody got up and went into the roomy kitchen adjoining, where it was warmer. The Indians went out on the porch and leaned against the wooden uprights; their instinct seemed to always take them into the open. We could hear a sheep-bell tinkling in the nearby barnyard. Down in the swamp, the "peepers" were chorusing shrilly. We listened to them for a while.

Then Billy Shongo spoke again. "Even those little creatures eat lots of young trout at certain seasons of the year. I don't see how the fish can survive with so many enemies. Man, instead of protecting them, is making it harder for them to exist every year. But I'm thankful that the herons are to be protected again. It is silly to kill them and let water snakes live. But then, we can never understand the white man's ways."

III

YOUNG WOMAN'S CREEK

(The Story of a Mountain Stream)

HISTORY DIFFERS as to the origin of the name of Young Woman's Creek, which rises in the Black Forest, emptying into the West Branch of the Susquehanna, several miles below Renovo. The historical versions are contradictory and not well authenticated, whereas there is a legendary story that has every mark of truth.

It was related by an aged Swedenborgian named Billy Patterson, who was one of the pioneers of a strange colony of that sect which established itself over forty years ago on the mountain summits near the headwaters of Young Woman's Creek. Most of the colony has been dispersed by death or dearth of occupation, but to this day, a few linger on, faithful to the lofty motives which drew them to the remote spot. Old Thomas Simcox, a pioneer riverman and hunter, accompanied the writer on several visits to this colony some years ago. He had done some prospecting for fire clay near there a season or two previously, boarding with one of the Swedenborgian families.

On the night of our first visit, we found that the main house was full of people, but we were invited to stay at a shack or log cabin, the family's original home, which stood in the corner of the lot. Billy Patterson, the oldest member of the colony, was lodging there. We found him sitting outside the door, reading a New Church book in the waning light of the evening. He was an intelligent looking old man, past seventy, with fine features, a clear, light blue eye, and a white beard worn very full, which hung below his waist. We spoke about the stream whose course we had followed to the settlement and its peculiar name.

"Did you ever hear how it got that name?" said the old man, with a twinkle in his keen eyes.

We recited briefly to him the well-known versions, but he shook his head at each and said that they were not correct, that an old Indian named Jack Berry had told him the story the first year that he had moved on the mountain, which was about 1868. Berry was so old at the time that he could remember a number of historical characters very well, including Mary Jemison, the White Woman of the Genesee; in fact, she had mentioned him in her very remarkable "Narrative." Berry had said his father was Hi-Berry, a chief for whom Berry's Mountain in Dauphin County was named. His story of Young Woman's Creek dated back to 1780 when the history of the upper reaches of the West Branch was wrapped in a haze. The Indians were still numerous and belligerent, and the few settlers had to maintain eternal vigilance.

One of the hardiest pioneers was Mordecai Wolford, of Quaker parentage, originally from Buffalo Valley, who located on some arable land near the headwaters of Beech Creek. With his family in 1776, he had traveled overland from his old home in what is now Union County, following the West Branch to the present site of Lock Haven, and from thence along the Bald Eagle Creek to the "Nest" of the celebrated chieftain Bald Eagle, which was on the right bank of the stream near the present town of Milesburg.

That part of the country was populous until the "Great Runaway" of 1778. Already large farms were pre-empted, and the powerful land-grabbers from Philadelphia had laid claim to what was left. Wolford was of an independent turn of mind; he would buy land from immigrants. He would purchase or conquer it from the rightful owners, the Indians, or not at all. Consequently, he had to go to the tableland where Beech Creek heads before he could settle unmolested. He found an Indian clearing with a few choice apple trees and a good spring and, aided by his growing sons, was not long in putting up a serviceable log cabin. When completed, the structure resembled more a fort than a dwelling, but that was natural as he had modeled it after Samuel Horn's farm on Curts' Run, in what is now Clinton County, which he had seen as he trekked up the Susquehanna Valley. He had reason to believe that the Indians were friendly to him, although his beautiful daughter, Mary, had the misfortune to have once aroused the affections of the mighty Bald Eagle, and her indifference had angered the chieftain.

In his heart Mordecai Wolford had no love for the natives, so he could not conscientiously chide his daughter for her attitude. But he trusted that the larger events in life would make the warrior forget his heart sore. But Quaker-like, he miscalculated; affairs of the heart are the largest things in life. There is nothing more important or unforgettable. The Wolfords located on their farm early in 1778, and in July of that year, James Q. Brady, son of Captain John Brady, a young man who had been attentive to Mary and of whom Bald Eagle had been insanely jealous, was killed by Indians near Muncy Town. The slayers were led presumably by the jealous chief himself. The news of the killing did not reach the remote clearing on Beech Creek until exactly two years later when a band of tribesmen conveyed it in a rather unpleasant manner.

In a year, the Wolford family had worked wonders with their plantation. It actually looked as well as many farms "down country" with its neat "Indian fences"—surely a good living would be made off it. In addition to putting out rye and barley, there were other crops and a thriving lot of livestock. Hunting and trapping were good, and in the two winters, the Wolford family captured twenty panthers, two hundred wolves, fifty black bears, two brown bears, and an almost countless number of smaller animals, otters, beavers, wild cats, and such, all attracted to the neighborhood by the livestock or crops. Most of these hides were taken in prime condition and were sold to a trader from Berks County, who journeyed through Bald Eagle Valley every year.

Thus, it could be seen that the outlook for the future seemed very favorable. The news of the pioneer's prosperity was sent in some mysterious way to the Indian, Captain David, who had been the farm's original owner. He had gone off to the wars, abandoning the place, and had opportunities without number to settle in better localities if he had so chosen. But he preferred a wandering and predatory life until he heard that a squatter was profiting by his early industry. Accompanied by three Indian comrades, he started on an expedition from the headwaters of the Allegheny to recover his property. On the way, they met the mother of Jack Berry, who was then a boy of about twelve years of age and induced the good squaw to let the lad go with them on their warlike jaunt. There is a strong suspicion, from the presence of Whistle-Town with the party, that the real motive was not the recovery of Captain David's farm.

Whistle-Town was known never to leave Bald Eagle's side; he was his shadow, in fact, unless he went on some punitive expedition for his chief. He did the "dirty work," being willing to stain his hands with murders, which would have blackened the character of Bald Eagle had he been the actual perpetrator of them. The party traveled quickly, being well-armed and provisioned. Within a week after starting, they reached Mordecai Wolford's farm, finding the industrious frontiersman in his hay field, taking in a goodly crop. In an adjoining field were two mares with colts, three cows with calves, and twenty-five sheep, all animals which generally would have aroused the cupidity of Indians. The four Indians emerged from the forest, saluting the pioneer and his sons in a friendly manner.

After a preliminary talk, in which the death of the "Young Captain" James Brady was mentioned, Captain David, who was an Indian of venerable appearance and a veteran of Braddock's campaign, asked Wolford if he was aware whose farm he was occupying. The pioneer replied that he had found the place deserted and fast growing up with brush and felt he was the lawful owner because of the improvements he had made. The old Indian then asked if he knew the party who had originally cleared the land.

"I have been told," said Wolford, "that Captain David cleared it."

"Right you are," said the Indian, "and I am Captain David. Furthermore, I have decided to return here and live."

Wolford looked around him; neither he nor his boys were armed; with a false sense of security, they had left their rifles in the cabin. It was four armed men against one unarmed man and two unarmed boys. A little business talk would be better than a fight. But he did not like the looks of his visitors. The penetrating sunlight showed him that one of them, who kept in the background, wore a wig and false beard.

"What will you take for your farm," said the pioneer without further parley.

"What will you give?" answered Captain David.

"Twenty pounds, all the money I have got," said Wolford.

"That's not nearly enough," replied the Indian, with a sneer in his voice; he was fast losing his politeness.

THE FALLEN MONARCH (Portage Creek)

"Twenty pounds and those horses and cattle," said Wolford, "that's giving you good measure."

"Give me one hundred pounds, all your stock, guns, ammunition, furniture, clothing, everything, then you get the place, and for not a farthing less," said the Indian.

"I'm afraid I can't meet your terms; I couldn't make that in my life," answered Wolford.

"Then off the place you go, now," said the Indian, edging up to the white man.

Just then, a rifle shot rang out on the calm summer air. The Indian with the wig and false beard fell against a haystack, badly wounded. In a moment of hot-headedness, Mary Wolford, the pioneer's beautiful daughter, had fired from the kitchen door, using her father's weapon. This was the signal for the Indians' attack. The question of who was to fire first had been settled just as they wanted it. Three shots quickly fired laid Wolford and his two sons low, and they were scalped in the "twinkling of an eye." The Indians then ran to the cabin, but Mary Wolford, her mother, and her sister were nowhere to be found. The wily warriors separated and continued the chase. A quarter of a mile down the creek, Loon Bird found Wolford's wife and little girl, cut their throats, and scalped them.

It was not until sundown that Mary Wolford was apprehended in a peculiar way. When she fancied that her pursuers were far from the cabin, she doubled on her tracks and returned. She hoped that her mother and sister had escaped as she had heard no more shots, and if she met them, she might assist them in their flight. She found no traces of them and made bold to visit the bodies of her father and brothers.

The masquerading Indian, whom she had shot, noticed her approach and decided to play 'possum, a favorite Indian trick. He stretched out stiff against the haystack, closed his eyes, and opened his mouth, feigning death. The bullet which had gone through his neck had somehow severed no artery and was not mortal. He knew that he had been wounded worse in other battles and recovered. Mary bit her thin, white lips when she viewed the mutilated corpses of her loved ones, but her clear, limestone-colored eyes betrayed no traces of tears. Her alabaster skin grew whiter than of yore, and she clutched her gunstock nervously. It was the most horrible sight she had ever witnessed or dreamed of witnessing. Death and blood seemed so out of place that calm summer evening, with the smell of the newly cut grass everywhere, the even-songs of robins still afield. Then she walked back to where her supposed victim lay. She looked at him, fancying that she had made a kill that single shot. As she leaned over the prostrate form, strangely overcome by the hideous countenance, the crafty warrior girded himself together and sprang to his feet, seizing the girl by her light brown hair. But Mary was a tall, wiry girl, able to care for herself. She was nearly six feet tall and grappled with the Indian in such a way that, for a moment, it looked as if she might be the captor and he the captive. She had to let go of her rifle in the scuffle, but she also knocked off the Indian's wig and false beard.

"Oh, ho, it's you, Whistle-Town, you scoundrel, I know you; I can see that your chief, Bald Eagle, is back of all this," she shouted as she wound her long arms about the ugly wretch.

The warrior was resourceful and uttered a piercing war-whoop, which echoed among the pine-covered hills. Then the girl feared all was lost. Within a minute, Captain David, Loon Bird, Black Richard, and little Jack Berry appeared in the field. They had not been far away, as they reasoned that the girl would return to the cabin. They laid heavy hands on her and bound her arms behind her back with stout cords. Then they put a wooden gag in her mouth and ordered her to march on ahead of them.

It was now that she began to feel physical and nervous exhaustion, but it looked as if she would have to march all night, as Indians never liked to linger close to a crime scene. They feared ghosts, they always said. Her only chance for rest would be if Whistle-Town's wound became painful or started to bleed again. Evidently, the savages were prepared for such an emergency, for they smeared the wound with wolf fat from a pouch that Captain David carried and wrapped it tightly with a piece of dead Mordecai Wolford's shirt. The wounded Indian liked to show his prowess, for he stepped out even livelier than the rest. The only laggard was the little Indian boy, Jack Berry, who could hardly stand the long tramp, and frequently the older Indians spoke to him sharply and threatened him with death unless he traveled more briskly.

There was no moon; hence progress was slow, though the Indians knew the forest trails, and the starlight helped considerably. But the following day at noon, the party had reached the shores of the Susquehanna, coming out at the mouth of Baker's Run. There, many signs of an Indian encampment were to be seen. There were tent poles, racks for hanging up game, the ashes of recent fires, bones and skulls of animals. By the water's edge, a pirogue was moored. A halt for dinner, the first meal Mary had taken since the day before at the same time, was made. Loon Bird, who seemed to be at home at the old camp, went to the run and lifted out of a deep hole several haunches of venison, which he had evidently sunk there several days before. He lit a fire, a surprisingly small one for the size of the pieces of meat to be cooked, and soon began roasting the venison, which gave out a savory odor to the starving captive. When the meal had been prepared, Loon Bird, who seemed to be the gentlest of the warriors, removed the gag from the girl's mouth and led her to a cool spring, where he washed her face and gave her a gourd full of water to drink. The girl felt much refreshed and was able to enjoy the feast. In fact, she ate more than the Indians, who had become strangely glum and taciturn. Doubtless, they had begun to realize the enormity of their wholesale murdering of the day previous and how if the settlers learned of it, they would be given up to the authorities while the powerful instigator went free.

After the dinner, Loon Bird was put on as sentry while the other Indians slept on the grass. Just at dark, the guard awakened them, and they all went to the riverbank and got into the pirogue. Evidently, they did not want to be seen crossing the river. They landed safely on the opposite shore, tied the boat to the projecting root of a red birch, and commenced another march.

Mary had slept a little during the afternoon, but it had been difficult with the crude gag in her mouth. Every time she shut her jaws hard in sleep, she woke with a violent start. But in the main, she was feeling rested and moved along the trail with ease. They traveled all night through dark forests and, in the early morning, arrived at the mouth of a large stream, which was to go down to history closely associated with the fair captive, Mary Wolford. By this time, Whistle-Town felt much improved, though his neck was still closely bandaged. After another nap, he started up the river in a canoe, accompanied by Jack Berry. Mary suspected that he would inform Bald Eagle of the captive's approach or tell him where she was held so that he might visit her. At any rate, she was left in charge of Captain David, Black Richard, and Loon Bird, but the last was named as her special keeper.

The day after Whistle-Town had departed, the three Indians decided to go on a buffalo calf hunt, but they disliked the idea of bundling the girl along with them. Mary could overhear them talking about it. All kinds of plans were devised, but they finally decided to tie her to a tree until they returned.

"She can stand it for a day or two," insisted Captain David.

Loon Bird nodded his cheery acquiescence, which made Mary feel bad as she had begun to suspect that Indian of more than commonly humane impulses. Black Richard was the last to give in to the idea.

"It's death for us all if anything should happen to her while we are away. I don't feel like leaving her," he kept repeating to his comrades.

But Captain David pointed out that Whistle-Town would probably not be back for a week, and it would be very tiresome doing nothing waiting for his return.

Bright and early in the morning, the three nimrods were ready to start. Their destination, as near as Mary could make out, was Nittany Valley, where many buffalo calves were pasturing. When Loon Bird was tying her to a large gum tree, he made a sign to her as if he was not fastening tightly that she could make her escape if she would. She made no motion to him that she understood, lest he was trying to trap her.

She waited patiently until evening and then twisted the ropes, finding them loose and easily managed. By this time, the three Indians must have been ten miles away, she thought. Just as she was wrenching herself free, something caused her to look around. To her horror and surprise, Black Richard was not twenty feet from her. It appeared that after the Indians had gone about five miles, this Indian had become suspicious of Loon Bird's attitude and taxed him with having tied Mary so she might free herself. Loon Bird denied the charge indignantly, but he was seized by his two friends and thrown to the ground and bound hand and foot.

Captain David watched him while Black Richard retraced his way to ascertain the truth or falsity of the suspicion.

The charge was only too true, but he had arrived at the very nick of time. When he saw the girl freeing herself, he dropped his rifle; he did not want to shoot but must capture her alive at any cost. Though her legs were free, she could not untwist the ropes that bound her pretty, white hands behind her back. Perhaps nervousness prevented a dexterous handling of the situation. She started on a run while struggling to unbind her wrists, with the warrior in hot pursuit. She was running in the direction of the big creek, there was no bridge or ford, and the water near the confluence with the river was quite deep.

There had been heavy rains the week before. As she neared the brink, she would have screamed woman-like, only the cruel gag was still in her mouth. There was no time to lose. Better risk the watery depths than again fall into the hands of the captors. She might be able to wade across, and once on the other shore, she knew that she was a swifter runner than her foe. Bravely she plunged in and was in mid-stream before the Indian's feet were wet. He saw that he would lose his prize and had dropped his rifle back in the brush when he had first come upon her. Picking up a big rock, he hurled it at her, striking her between the shoulder blades. She was up to her hips in the swift water, but the force of the impact made her lose her footing on the slippery rock bottom, and she fell over into the current.

The Indian realizing what he had done, sprang after her, but she was swept away in the gathering dusk before he could get to her. He spent the entire night about the mouth of the stream, but the slim, fair body had been carried on into the river. With a gag in her mouth, the poor girl quickly choked with water, and she could not attempt to swim with her arms pinioned.

The next morning, Captain David, having become suspicious owing to his friend's non-appearance, visited the spot where the girl had been left. She was gone, and he soon located Black Richard pottering about at the mouth of the creek. The two Indians were horrified when they realized Loon Bird's duplicity and hurried back to Rattlesnake Run, where they had left him, and cut him to bits with their tomahawks. Then they went up the run and traveled until they were out of Bald Eagle's jurisdiction in New York State.

Great was Whistle-Town's horror when he returned to "Young Woman's Creek" to find girl and Indians missing. It is said that Bald Eagle had the faithful Whistle-Town executed and set a price on the heads of the other Indians, so great was his chagrin at losing his coveted prize, Mary Wolford. But as for her, fair girl, she floated, a corpse with many vicissitudes down the river, drifted, nibbled at by fish and eels, unseen, until at length she was washed ashore at the foot of a grass-grown hill near Shamokin Town, now Sunbury. On that hill were many more or less erect brownstone slabs, erected in memory of the dead, for it was the pioneers' graveyard. One of these stones, fresher and stronger than the rest, was visited weekly by a very tiny woman with sandy hair, freckles, and bright blue eyes. It was Mary Q. Brady who went there to place summer flowers on the last resting place of her beloved son, James, slain in 1778 by the jealous fury of Chief Bald Eagle. One morning, she noticed something long and brown, like an old log, half submerged in the water close to shore. She climbed down the grassy hill and waded out to where the object lay. She saw something like a very white hand; she seized it and drew a dead body up on dry land. She laid it on the bank, sat beside it, and studied the face. All at once, the little woman cried, "My God, it's Mary Wolford's corpse—is she gone too? Well, well, she has come in death to be united to the boy she loved."

That afternoon the body was buried close to that of the "Young Captain of the Susquehanna," whom in life she had loved so well. And as for Bald Eagle, after all his plots and murders, where was now his victory!

IV

CONQUERING FATE
(A Story of the Panther Caves)

W E HAD decided to stop awhile at the Panther Caves near the mouth of Treaster Valley. It was partly because there was a beautiful greensward along the banks of Treaster Brook, where we could cook dinner and feed the horses, but our principal reason was to look at and photograph the remarkable cliffs, which resembled the homes of the Arizona cave dwellers. As far as is known, no human beings ever resided in these rocky caverns, but in the past three-quarters of a century, more than a score of Pennsylvania lions had been slain in and about them.

We were gazing at their serrated facades when two gaunt mountaineers walked slowly up the muddy road, their hands wedged in the narrow change pockets in their overalls. Red-haired, sandy-mustached, and unshaven, they presented a unique appearance. When they drew near, we spoke to them pleasantly, and they replied in their peculiar drawl, and we soon found them intelligent and companionable men. They noted our interest in the cave and gave us much interesting information on the subject. They led us across the mucky lowland where the brook had receded after the spring rains and showed us the great, circular tracks of a panther, which headed in the direction of one of the caverns.

"That critter lives in there now," said one of the mountaineers. "He's got a lot of nerve with lumber wagons and fishermen passing by every day. Surprisingly, the panthers hang on in this valley; there always is one here. They have followed me several times, and none have been killed since Clem Herlacher went in the caves and carried off a nest of cubs about twenty years ago."

But we were principally concerned about an Indian legend that had reached its dramatic climax at the main opening of the caverns, from which a stream issues in the spring of the year and after particularly heavy rains. This water empties into Treaster Brook. Some years before, in the Black Forest, we had been shown the remains of an Indian clearing in the center of a virgin hemlock forest, not far from the headwaters of the main branch of Slate Run.

Old "Pappy" Gast, who spent much time wandering among the hills and dales of the Black Forest, had called our attention to it and related the legend which accompanied every spot where Indians had been. The old Indian couple who had lived there up to about the middle of the 19th century were "Southerners," that is, they had moved there from some of the more southerly Pennsylvania counties; in this case, they were from Treaster Valley, in Mifflin County. Yet the native stock of Indians had mostly vanished from that region before they were born, so tradition had it there that they came from the north. It was almost necessary to visit both sections to obtain the entire story so that when we halted our team by the Panther Caves and noted the "lay of the land" as it were, the entire narrative pieced itself together very naturally.

In the days before the lumbermen had penetrated the Black Forest, but after the native Indians had been collected at the reservation in the vicinity of Cornplant's Island on the Allegheny, an aged pair of Indians appeared mysteriously on Slate Run and started to build a shanty. The ownership of this land was in the same chaotic state that enabled the visionary John F. Cowan to sell tracts he did not own to the celebrated Ole Bull, so there was no one to order the newcomers away. They selected a spot off all the known paths and seemed particularly anxious not to meet any of their own people.

At that time, numbers of "reservation" Indians ranged over the Black Forest, hunting and trapping, and a few of them worked at lumbering and rafting along Pine Creek and the Susquehanna. Among them were Tallchief and his son, the Jimmersons, the Shongos, Half-Town, Little Beard, Jack Berry, Old Nicholas, and many others. Most of these belonged to the Seneca tribe or to the tribes which had constituted the "Smooct" or Six Nations. *Smooct* was a familiar abbreviation of Seneca,

Mohawk, Oneida, Onondaga, Cayuga, and Tuscarora, who constituted this once-powerful Indian confederation.

The aged Indian couple from the south went by the names of Honest George and Old Susie—very serviceable names in any locality where their exact characteristics were unknown. They said they were of the Shawnee tribe, having been born at Shawnee Cabins, a noted Indian settlement not far from the present town of Schellsburg in Bedford County and that after marrying, they had migrated to Treaster Valley. But they were silent as to why they had moved into the colder and more isolated Black Forest at their advanced time of lives. Their difference in tribal affiliations easily explained their desire to be away from the local Indians. But with George Gast, afterward called affectionately "Pappy," they were on greater terms of intimacy. They confided their true history to him, with the injunction that he never revealed it to a soul until after they were dead. It seems that most humans must have a *confidante* for secrets, and Indians were no exception.

In the old days, when the Senecas were supreme, they indulged in many beautiful and impressive religious exercises or canticos; in fact, their religion has been called the most highly colored in the world. No wonder Red Jacket called Christianity dull. Among their religious fetes was an annual sacrifice to the Water Spirit, which took place in the early autumn at the historic Falls of the Genesee. The most beautiful maiden was selected, and though death was the price paid, there was continual scheming and wire-pulling to secure the coveted honor. The wise men made the selection, and all kinds of pressure was brought to bear on them. But usually, the most beautiful maiden was chosen, to the great lamentations of the rejected, their friends, and relatives. The chosen sacrifice was sent over the falls in an exquisitely fashioned white birch canoe decked with autumn leaves, fruits, and flowers.

It was said that on many occasions, lovers of the victims begged to be allowed to accompany them on the death errand, and when their wish was refused, hurled themselves over the precipice, and the two bodies would be washed ashore miles below simultaneously. A lover dying for this lofty principle was considered greatly blessed.

In those remote days, Honest George was none other than Wischalow, or The Frightener, a noted Seneca brave, while Old Susie's name was

A BLACK FOREST TRAPPER   (E. N. Woodcock)

Ehelilda, or Flowing Spring, one of the fairest of Indian maids. She was the daughter of a powerful warrior named Curvencheck, or Pine Wood, famed for his physical strength and sagacity. From the time she was a small child, by common consent, it was allowed that when she reached the age of sixteen, she would be chosen for the supreme honor of giving up her life to the Water Spirit. She admitted to her relatives and friends that she was destined for this great privilege, and as a result, she led a retired and sheltered life filled with prayers of thanksgiving to the Great Spirit, who had given her the gift of grace and beauty worthy of the selection.

But even in the Indian days, there were some few jealous persons, girls who declared that they were just as fair as Ehelilda, that the wise men should not be prejudiced by all this talk about one being so pre-eminently fitted for the honor. But such talk came to naught when folks saw Ehelilda. Women were highly regarded by the Senecas; in this, they were much like the old Greeks.

As time went by, the opposition grew less, and as the fair maiden's sixteenth birthday approached, no word was heard except favorable to her beauty and fitness. Her birthday was properly celebrated, her illustrious father giving a garden party for her, which was attended by all the noble youths and maidens who resided the entire length of the Genesee River.

Among those present was young Wischalow, two years older than Ehelilda; his home was near the source of the Genesee, and it was a case of love at first sight with both. During the lovely moonlit evening, while the Indian musicians played weird tunes with drums, flageolets, and whistles, interpolating these with old tribal songs, in short, melodic phrases, the handsome young couple strolled to the riverbank. They seated themselves on a great, fallen elm and watched the moonlight playing on the eddying, rippling water, which was gaining in velocity for its leap over the falls but a hundred yards further on. Wischalow did not delay long in declaring his love, to which the maiden gave her assent by clasping his sinewy hand. Then she pointed to the cataract, over which she had elected to sacrifice herself ever since she was a small child.

"Truly do I love you," she said, her voice filled with emotion, "but my destiny is to go over the falls in honor of the Water Spirit, the source of our continued life and prosperity."

"I grant that you will go over the falls," said the young warrior. Then he let his voice die to a whisper, and to himself, he repeated *at* the foot of the cataract I will meet you, and we will be together for life.

The sadness in Wischalow's voice was all gone; a plan had come to him to permit Ehelilda to fulfill her mission and yet become his wife. Just before they returned to join the merrymakers, the young brave clasped the slender form to his breast, whispering in her pretty ear: "We will meet after you have accepted your destiny."

"That will be in Paradise," answered Ehelilda.

Wischalow gave these words a different interpretation than the girl had intended and was well content. The week after the birthday festival, the wise men met and, on the first ballot, unanimously chose Ehelilda for the honor of going over the falls. In previous years other candidates received a complimentary vote, and on a few occasions, many ballots had to be taken before the solons could arrive at a choice. This year it was easy as Ehelilda was so transcendentally lovely.

The time for the sacrifice was always in the first week of what the civilized world calls September. It was during the period of droughts when the Water Spirit had shown his spleen in withholding his blessing. There were many beautiful autumn flowers at that time, deep purples and yellows, asters, Joe Pye weed, ironweed, vervain, fireweed, golden-rod and tansy, and a few maple and hickory leaves were highly tinged with yellow. There was much early fruit on the trees. The red clusters of the crab apples were particularly noticeable. It was one of nature's many periods of lavish beauty. The ceremony was called for the late afternoon, just before the sun set behind the western hills. The banks and rock promontories were thronged with Indians of all stations and ages.

The lovely sacrifice attended by her proud father met the wise men in the council house an hour before the exercises began. There she was ushered into an inner chamber where her garments were removed and burnt by twelve maidens of high degree who clothed her in a flowing gown woven from the hair of snow-white fawns. A garland of meadow sweet was placed on her broad brow. When all was completed, the maidens escorted the fair victim back to the council of wise men, where in their presence, she bade a smiling farewell to her father. Then the native musicians who waited outside began beating their drums and shaking their rattles. Heading the procession of wise men and maidens, Ehelilda emerged from the council house. When they saw her, the vast throng of Indians gave out their shout of joy and approval—"Hoh, hoh, hoh!" repeated many times like a college yell.

The procession headed for the riverbank, where the graceful canoe made from "paper" birch was anchored. It was garlanded with flowers, corn tassels, and heads of wheat, while its interior contained a couch made from different kinds of fruit. Old Curvencheck, the father, helped her into the craft and tied her fast with coils of otter hide. Then it was launched by the handmaidens. As the foaming current caught it, the Indian multitude again gave vent to their call of triumph, and "Hoh, hoh, hoh, hoh, hoh!" resounded above the roar of the waterfall. All was over in an instant; the canoe, with its smiling, happy victim, was over the falls before the throng could realize it. Then they silently dispersed. Many regretted seeing the fair girl disappear, never to return.

At some distance from the foot of the waterfall, another canoe manned by a stalwart young brave was waiting under the overhanging branches. Back of these overhanging branches was a "lost" or "hidden" river of a kind well known by the Indians—that is, a river that has an underground channel. While some of the Senecas knew of the existence of this particular sink, they had never explored it, imagining that it led to the underworld or land of evil spirits.

Wisehalow had, from earliest boyhood, listened to the old soothsayers and witches, beings without the pale of the Seneca religion but not wanting in exact knowledge of the phenomena of nature. From several of these, he had learned the story of the sinking river, how it wound like a labyrinth for six hundred miles through caverns lit by crevices that penetrated to the outer world and hung with marvelous, transparent stalactites. At the end of the six hundred miles, the stream issued out of a chasm in the rocky face of a mountain into a beautiful valley where the paw paws and persimmons grew and where the redbud bloomed in purple profusion in mid-May. Wisehalow, a wonderful swimmer, had full confidence in his powers. From his hidden point of vantage, he could see the white canoe with its precious freight come over the falls and disappear in the froth and foam below. He calculated the number of moments it would take for it to reach the headwater and come to the surface again. He reasoned that Ehelilda could not be dead unless she should die of fright or collide with a submerged rock.

When the right amount of time had elapsed, he dived from the bow of his canoe and swam underwater to the spot where he calculated the sacrificial canoe must be. And he judged wisely, for, on one of his outward strokes, his fingers touched the side of the precious craft. Under the water, as he was, he almost shouted for joy. He reached out further, seized the canoe, and drew it back to his hidden retreat under the overhanging birches. Then he got his first look at Ehelilda since her terrible ordeal. Her pink face was deadly white; her long lashes closed over her sleeping eyes. He quickly felt her hand; it was as cold as the mountain water she had just been through. But Wischalow could not believe life was extinct. He cut the cords which bound her and lifted her tenderly into his boat. Then he fastened the white canoe behind his own by the same cords. The luscious fruit would be useful on the long journey which faced them, although he had provisioned his craft before beginning his vigil. With a few deft strokes of the paddle, he was in the hidden river, traveling under crystal arches with his unconscious companion.

When he had caught the proper current, he allowed the canoes to drift and began rubbing the fair girl's hands and blowing his breath into her mouth. By the mysterious light from the crevices above, he could see the color coming back to her lips and cheeks; her hands were growing less clammy. All night long, they drifted, with the young warrior breathing back life into his beloved. When the rays of daylight again filtered through the rocky roof, he was overjoyed to see her opening her eyes. When she saw who was bending over, she said faintly but distinctly, "How sweet it is to wake in Paradise."

Then Wischalow kissed her, and when she was strong enough, he assured her that she was not dead, that instead, she was in an earthly Paradise, where love would last as long as life. Ehelilda soon understood it all and was overjoyed at how her lover had conquered fate.

The underground journey proved happy in the extreme; it was so ecstatic that they did not attempt to count the time. One clear afternoon they saw bright sunlight ahead, and shortly afterward, the canoe floated out into a pond of clear water with tall, red lilies along its banks, with beaver dams at one end of it, at the foot of a great, castellated cliff. By the pool was a greensward, shaded by huge hemlock trees, through whose interspaces could be seen rolling hills, lavender in the light of coming evening.

Wischalow let the canoes drift to shore, then he leaped out, shouting, "Hoh, hoh, hoh," he was so happy! A nice fire was built, and dried meat soon cooked over it. A lean-to for the night was pitched, and work on a lodge house began the next morning. The few native Indians received them kindly; only the panthers who lived in the cliff disputed their possession. And there, the Indian couple lived happily for over sixty years.

Meanwhile, the native Indians had died out or moved away, and settlers encroached to within a few miles of the cozy camp at the foot of the great cliffs. The panthers became more elusive and less apt to question their rights, the elk were killed off, and the deer and beavers became very scarce. Then, the Indian couple began thinking of the land of their youth, far to the north in the Genesee country. They could not return against the swift current in the hidden river, but they decided to walk to the north until they found a secluded spot and there erect another home. When death overtook them, they would be near childhood scenes. It is a strange desire for men and animals to want to die near the youthful home, but it is not so strange when we realize that the youthful scenes are usually places where we loved and first learned happiness.

The pilgrimage was made in the beautiful summertime. The aged couple supported themselves by selling a goodly store of baskets, cups, beads, and trinkets and were well treated in the different counties traversed. At length, they entered the majestic Black Forest, where Wischalow had hunted the elk, the black bear, and the panther in his youth, and which as yet was unvisited by the rapacious and wasteful Pennsylvania lumbermen. This would be the ideal region for another home. A site was selected with good water and a commanding view; a lean-to was thrown up the first night, and work on a lodge house of logs commenced the next morning. It was taken as a good sign that a panther screamed about the lean-to that first night, just as one had done at the Panther Caves in Treaster Valley sixty years before.

The final days of the old couple were very happy. They made several secret visits to the Genesee country but did not see a single face who could have betrayed them.

"We will see them all in Paradise," said Wischalow, "they will be surprised that you are getting there so long after their arrival."

"I am in no hurry to meet them," replied Ehelilda. "I have found Paradise in this old world with you."

And Wischalow, while he mused over the strange events of his long life, concluded that it was worthwhile to have tried to conquer fate.

"Everything is possible to mankind," he often said, "if we would but try. I am one of those who have tried and seen my gain."

Then he would point to his wife, working at her household duties outside the cabin door.

When death finally visited, Wischalow and Ehelilda were estimated to be over ninety years of age. They died two weeks apart, and after they were both laid to rest, side by side, near the Coudersport Pike, Senecas came to their graves and sprinkled them with forget-me-nots. Perhaps these tribesmen guessed their story but were too good to interfere.

V

IN THE RAFTERS

(A Tale of the Mountaineers' Conscience)

ABOUT THIRTY years ago, lumbering operations at Leary's Summit commenced in earnest. The railroad, which completely bisected the Black Forest, was completed, opening up a vast territory covered with virgin timber. At the juncture of the main line and the road which ran through the forest, an enormous sawmill was erected, which ran night and day. A new population was brought into the town, representing humanity's best and worst elements. There were the owners and superintendents of the sawmills, stave mills, planing mills, lath mills, veneer works, acid factories, and such, with their families; the operators, the shopkeepers, the serving class, and the saloonkeepers, which last named gentry catered to a long-suppressed instinct of the woods-people.

With a street lined with liquor stores, there was temptation a-plenty for the mountaineers who were drawn to the town by its bright lights and brisk development. The facility of obtaining work and the high wages sowed a disinclination to labor in many, while the abundance of liquor seemed the only goal worth striving for. Many men who had lived by sporadic logging and trapping, and saw little real money, now worked for a week or two in the big bark-peeling camps or sawmills and then went on long sprees with their rolls of easily earned "greenbacks." A spirit of recklessness was engendered, and the general moral tone of the mountaineers lowered decidedly after a year or two of prosperity.

Out on Powder Hill, about three miles back of the lumber town, lived Abel Sweek and his wife. Early in life, this man had shown promise of being an industrious worker, but he grew to spend most of his time in the saloons and neglected his chances for legitimate employment. Instead

THE "STONY LICK" COUNTRY

of trying to raise him, his wife sunk to his level and often imbibed too freely. The couple had one child, a pretty, curly-haired boy of four years, to whom they were apparently devoted. It was a lonely place for a child to be brought up, out on the bleak hill, in the shack of hemlock boards, unplaned, unpainted, and lopsided. The yard and garden fences were built of slabs from the mill. Huge hemlock stumps were everywhere, even in the garden three or four, on which the morning glories twined, reared their blackened heads.

Formerly, this had been a great hunting country, but with the removal of the timber, a person could travel for hours and scarcely see a chipmunk. Despite this apparent state of affairs, Sweek always liked to regale the saloon idlers with stories of animals he claimed he was seeing or hearing around his home. One day he would come into town and tell about a wildcat that was carrying off his chickens; another time, it was a bear that scared his wife while she was coming from the spring; another time, he had heard a panther scream on the top of the hill, in the rear of the house. Besides these, he was always tracking deer and seeing many grouse or "pheasants." Though no one else saw or heard anything, few doubted the stories, as Sweek's record for untruthfulness had not been established. In most communities, a man is believed until he is proven a falsifier. In this case, untruthful though he might be, the yarns proved an agreeable break in the monotonous existence of the dwellers in the lumber town.

One night, just before Christmas, the Sweek shanty was burned to the ground. The chimney had become overheated and ignited the wall, and in a quarter of an hour, not even the foundations remained. The family escaped with their clothing. The next morning Sweek went to Leary's Summit to secure sympathy. A subscription paper was passed about in the barrooms, but the beneficiary drank up and treated away most of the fund before he started homeward along the crossties. It was a cold evening when he reached the ruins, and naturally, his wife and little boy had departed. When he started for town, they wended their way across the hills to the home of the woman's mother. This old lady, Mrs. Maria Ehrenwhoof, lived in a cozy little cottage at the edge of the original forest. The timber had been cut away on the opposite side of the road; there was not a green tree in that direction as far as the eye could reach. But back of the cottage, the smooth, grey boles of the white hemlocks rose in level rows sixty feet to the lowest branches. The canopy of foliage was so dense that the sun could not penetrate. The patch where the cottage stood had been cleared thirty-five years before; consequently, the hemlocks along the edge of the forest had become accustomed to the light, and the frail trees had died and been cut away years before. In that way, the fringe of brown, dead timber, so conspicuous along the boundaries of a hemlock forest, was missing. The little yard and garden were filled with fruit trees, while a Virginia creeper and a grapevine spread over the entire front side of the neat log cabin, the chinks in which were carefully plastered. Old "Mammy" Ehrenwhoof lived there with her unmarried son, Henwood, and the pair naturally welcomed the Sweek family into their midst after the unhappy holocaust.

Everything might have run smoothly had Sweek not continued his drinking and repeatedly quarreled with his brother-in-law. Henwood Ehrenwhoof was a sober, industrious fellow, a trackwalker on the Black Forest Railway. After one particularly bitter row, he gathered together his belongings and moved into a deserted hunter's shanty, which stood about a mile further in the forest. Sweek then proceeded to make his mother-in-law's life miserable. The old lady was over seventy and not very strong, and her son-in-law's insolence and her daughter's shiftlessness told heavily about her health. She took her bed about the first of February and passed away late in March.

Before the funeral, Henwood blamed the Sweeks for the old lady's death, saying they had worried her into her grave. In reply, the son was told that he should have taken his mother with him when he moved away. But the old woman would never have gone; she loved her little home where she had lived most of her married life too much. There was another quarrel over the funeral expenses, and Sweek went on a terrible spree due to his inability to pay his share. He lay in bed for over a week, finally broken in health and nerves. He was now unable to work, even if he were willing to do so; he owed a store bill, a doctor's bill, and a part of his mother-in-law's funeral expenses. It was enough to worry anyone, let alone an inebriated, half-crazy backwoodsman. As time progressed, he began to fancy that everybody was neglecting him, and that the public should help him in his indigent condition.

Springtime came along, and the peach and plum trees bloomed in the tiny yard and garden. The little home was a bower of loveliness if only the inmates could appreciate it. But they pursued their sullen, ungrateful way, always complaining at the world, which they considered owed them a living in idleness.

Then, all at once, the town of Leary's Summit was startled by the report that the couple's little son, Sammy, had been lost or kidnapped. The parents had gone to effect a reconciliation with Henwood Ehrenwhoof, finding him not at home. When they returned, the little boy they had left playing in the yard was nowhere to be found. The couple was frantic with grief. While the husband hurried to town for financial aid and liquor to steady his nerves, the wife rolled about on the floor, surrounded by sympathizing mountain women.

"Their hearts are in the right place after all," was the general verdict of the public, "else they would not take on so over the loss of their child."

The big sawmill granted a half-holiday for its employees to scour the woods. The managers and superintendents of the different plants subscribed liberally for the comfort of the sorrowing parents. Letters were written to the newspapers at Smethport, Coudersport, and Renovo; some public-spirited lumbermen offered a cash reward for the child's body, dead or alive. All kinds of solutions for the mystery were offered. Gypsies had been seen traveling along the Portage Road; perhaps they had fled with the child to New York State—the haven of every escaping scalawag. The little one might have wandered off into the woods, fallen into a brook, and drowned. Perhaps one of those fierce panthers or bears Sweek saw so often had devoured the boy. Suspicion even fell on Henwood Ehrenwhoof; he might have kidnapped the child for revenge.

The Sweeks became the center of interest and, in one way or another, kept it up for nearly a month. These were very profitable days; it was like finding money, Mrs. Sweek would say. But despite all the donations and loans and sympathy and counsel, the couple looked like a pair of hunted beasts. They lost flesh; they could not eat, and their bloodshot eyes popped from their heads.

"They are dying of grief; we must find their boy," echoed from one mountaineer to another.

The rich and prosperous made the long journey out to the lonely cabin, nearly everyone dropping a five-dollar bill into the woman's hands before taking leave. There were also curiosity seekers who paid for the privilege of offering condolences.

But the strangest part of all was that the county authorities took no official cognizance of the child's disappearance. Of course, thirty years ago, police departments in mountainous county seats were not in a high degree of efficiency, and news and exact information traveled slowly. The general feeling was that the little boy would "turn up;" hence, the wheels of officialdom were slow of motion. There was surprisingly little space devoted to the affair in the county newspapers. Grover Cleveland and Blaine were of more news interest than a vanished mountain boy.

But in the home of the Sweeks, there was sensation enough to atone for the seeming indifference of the world. Their nights were rendered intolerable by the patter of childish feet on the attic floor above where they slept. There was a constant cracking and creaking of the attic rafters. At times, the entire house seemed to sway and rock. The wind whistled with an almost human wail. Doors of closets opened and shut noisily; furniture overturned itself, lights were blown out, sleep became out of the question, and the approach of night was terrifying.

Many persons would gladly have slept in the cabin with them and eased their nightly misery had they dared to confide the awful story to them. But instead, they had to remain silent and endure it as long as they could. For up in the garret, in a soapbox resting across two of the narrow rafters, lay the body of their little boy.

The child had always seemed in the way; it required money to keep him, which might have been spent for his parents' pleasures. He required care when his parents were not physically able to look after him when overcome by insobriety. One night, when the couple was lying fully dressed on their bed, well under the influence of cheap whiskey, the horrible idea came to them of putting the child out of the way. Sweek suggested it, and the wife readily assented.

They reasoned that if they caused the little boy to disappear mysteriously, it would arouse the sympathies of the wealthy people at Leary's Summit, they would be given lots of money, and when the donations ceased, they would be the better off because there would only be the two of them. The people in the town had about reached the limit of their generosity as matters stood; this new episode would arouse them afresh. There was no telling to what ends their liberality might reach. The story could be given out that the child had vanished from the yard while they were away seeking reconciliation with Henwood Ehrenwhoof; after a while, they could place the body in the forest, and it would look as if the child had become lost and perished from starvation.

Meanwhile, all plausible causes for its absence could be spread abroad. Chuckling over their evil intentions, the couple staggered to their feet and went over to the crude wooden trestle which served as the child's bed. The little fellow was sound asleep, and the father, with his huge, bony fingers, strangled him to death where he lay. Then the mother dressed the child and doubled the body into a soap box which had served as a receptacle for stove-wood. The woman laid some boards loosely over the top. Then the couple started up the rickety stairs to the attic; Sweek went ahead carrying a small kerosene lamp. At the next to the top step, he slipped, dropping the lamp. Luckily, as it fell, it went out, preventing an explosion that might have incinerated the murderers, victim, house, and all. Mrs. Sweek dropped the box containing the little corpse, and it rolled out in a heap on the floor at the foot of the stairs.

Sweek swore long and loudly, ordering his wife to go down and get another lamp. She protested that she had broken the other lamp the day before; in reality, she was afraid. Sweek was just as scared as she, so he compromised by lighting numerous matches in his trousers' pockets. By this uncertain light, the woman could pick up the child's body and put it in the box, and the trip to the lonely garret was resumed.

Then the dog outside set up a piteous howling. In some way, he had become aware that something was amiss. Sweek cursed the dog, vowing to "settle it" if it did not quiet down by the time, he finished hiding away his child's body. The dog did not grow quiet, and to the tune of this awful uproar, the box was placed in a remote corner of the rafters, just where they joined the eaves. Other boxes were moved over against it.

"When the first excitement is over," said Sweek, wiping the sweat from his brow with his elbow, "we'll take the body out into the woods; over by the old wolf caves would be a good place."

Then he went downstairs, followed by his wife, to attend to the barking dog. Picking up a heavy cane that his late mother-in-law had used in her latter days, he opened the kitchen door. The infuriated dog sprang at him, but he beat it off. Angered beyond measure, he pursued the brute to its kennel, where it cowered with fright. He ran back to the house, finding his wife drinking whiskey by the light of one feeble tallow candle. He took his revolver out of the cupboard and returned to the doghouse, firing without aim, in the darkness, into where the dog lay. There were some hideous howls of pain then all was still,

Sweek went indoors and, with his wife, drank whiskey until daylight when the supply was exhausted. By that time, the two plotters had patched their story together so that it had no weak point. Sweek went out and buried the dead dog in the garden. Then he shaved with an unsteady hand, tidied his clothes as best he could, and went for a walk into the forest accompanied by his wife. This was to give actual color to their story that the child had disappeared while they were seeking reconciliation with Henwood Ehrenwhoof. On their stroll, they passed Henwood's cabin, but they knew he was not at home, as he generally slept in the tool-house by day, near the section which he patrolled after the evening "combination" train pulled in.

That night Sweek visited Leary's Summit. The effect of his story of the missing child was all that he anticipated and more. He was the hero of the hour; people of prosaic life must have excitement. A lost child story was more blood-curdling than a panther or bear story.

When he reached home at daybreak, he was accompanied by a dozen volunteer hunters for the child, among them Henwood Ehrenwhoof. He noticed that his wife was looking bad, caused either by a lack of alcohol or the excitement of the last twenty-four hours. When she could speak to him alone, she whispered that she had heard the child running about the attic all night.

"You are drunk or crazy," said the husband with an ugly leer.

"Wait and hear for yourself, Abel," was all the woman would say in reply.

Night fell, and what a terrible night it was. All manner of horrid noises, and most hideous of all, the child's footsteps pattering about on the badly swung attic floor. Many times, the guilty souls were convinced that the child was not dead or had come to life again. This thought was pleasing to them; it soothed them temporarily. But neither dared to go to the garret and see for themselves.

They were burned and stung and torn by conscience, something they never dreamed they possessed. The next night was worse, and the night following was still more terrible. In fact, every night added to the torture. Finally, Sweek suggested to his wife that the time had come to take the body into the forest, but neither dared to. They quarreled and almost came to blows over this. Then it was decided that they move away. But where and when? They dared not attract suspicion, but how could they remain longer under the roof where such sounds made the night so damnably horrible?

One night while they were eating supper, with the inevitable quart bottle of whiskey on the table, they heard the cover of the dough-tray fall to the floor. Looking around, they were certain they saw the bent form of the old, dead woman. Mammy Ehrenwhoof, carrying the corpse of the murdered child in her arms. Sweek and his wife uttered a series of piercing yells and fell off their chairs in a maudlin, fainting condition. When they recovered themselves, both were animated by a different spirit. They stared at one another and dragged themselves to their feet.

"I'm going to the county jail and give myself up," drawled Sweek.

"I'll go with you; there's just as much guilt on me," said the wife.

The stars were out; the road over the hill toward the county seat twenty miles away was broad and well known to them. So, they put on their hats and coats; the night air in May was sometimes frosty in the Alleghanies. And through the Black Forest, they toiled along, reaching the county town at dawn on a misty morning. They knew the county jail well, with its iron grated windows and brownstone jail yard wall.

They seated themselves, a frowsy pair, on the front steps of the Sheriff's house next door to the jail building, back of the prim old court-house. The blinds were down, and the worthy official evidently was a late sleeper. As the sun drove away the melancholy mists, Sweek and his wife appeared to be smiling to themselves.

The woman noticed the improved expression on her husband's face and said, "Abe, you look ten years younger."

THE LAST SKIDWAY ON KETTLE CREEK

"So do you, Maggie," replied the man. "It's an awful load off our minds now that we are giving ourselves up."

"Yes," said the woman, "and in our suffering, we have been punished for that hellish deed that whiskey done in us. But say, does it seem right that after our consciences have ripped us to pieces, that law has to step in and punish us all over again?"

"If you feel that way, woman, there's time to leave here; no one's seen us yet."

"I don't care," answered the woman, "let the law take its course; I'm done."

Just at that minute, the heavy, walnut door of the sheriff's home was unbolted from within, and a big, blond, round-faced man, collarless and in carpet slippers, stepped out on the porch.

VI

THE WINTER OF THE WOLVES

(A Story of Windfall Run)

URING INDIAN days wolves were never over-prevalent in the Black Forest. The natives were a safety valve that kept their numbers within bounds. They hunted the animals persistently for their hides but, at the same time, would never have thought of exterminating them; they had an eye for the future and a sense of responsibility for future generations. There must be sport and fur for these.

It was in the brief period after the Indians had withdrawn from the Black Forest and the settlers had not arrived in great numbers that the wolves threatened to become a menace. Unmolested, they increased rapidly, driving the elks and deer into more settled regions, west and south, where they fell easy victims to the rifles of the pioneers. When the settlers began making clearings in the forest, they found the wolves ready to devour their sheep, and they cried loudly for a county and then a state bounty to encourage their destruction.

The legislators at Harrisburg, always eager to vote away the taxpayers' money, fixed the bounty rate so high that it became more profitable to hunt wolves than to raise sheep. Many respectable settlers abandoned farming and stock-raising altogether and became professional wolfers. The effect was demoralizing to the proper opening of a new country, and agriculture was given a backset from which it took half a century to recover. In some sections, it never recovered. Everyone enjoyed hunting; it was easy money; even after the wolves, panthers, catamounts, and other proscribed animals disappeared, the professional bounty-chasers were loath to return to the plow and grubbing hoe.

Shortly after the departure of most of the native Indians of the Black Forest, it was in the first quarter of the nineteenth century that fur traders were attracted to the region by tales of the plentitude of wolves and fur-bearing animals in general. Among these was a Polish refugee named John Wallize, who had settled in Philadelphia as a shopkeeper, but who was glad to go back to his early calling of wolf-hunter when he learned that similar animals abounded in parts of northern Pennsylvania. Pennsylvania wolf hides shown him were remarkably like wolf hides from Poland and Russia. He sold his notion shop and devoted the proceeds to fitting out an expedition to be gone an entire winter to get the hides in prime condition.

He boated his supplies from Harrisburg to Jersey Shore, where he engaged packhorses to take him into the big forests to the north. In Jersey Shore, he also found several Indians who offered their services as wolfers, who knew the country well. He was recommended to hire Tallchief, then a youth of eighteen or twenty, and a fine, six-foot warrior he was. Little Canoe, a short Indian but well versed in woodcraft, and Jack Berry, an excellent cook and general handyman on the trap line or in the shanty.

These Indians said that from all reports, wolves would be unusually prevalent—that it would be a regular winter of the wolves.

Wallize explained to them that he wished to secure at least five hundred prime wolf hides, one hundred black bear skins, one hundred black fox skins, and other hides, or else it would not pay him to start on such a costly expedition. The Indians assured him that a catch of that size would be possible and offered their services free if a smaller number of hides were secured.

This seemed like a good guarantee for results, so preparations were completed. Although the youngest of the party, Tallchief seemed to be the most experienced wolfer, so he was appealed to for the selection of the campsite or headquarters. He said that he had once spent a winter on Windfall Run, in what is now Potter County, that wolves bred in the rocks all along the creek, and that they gathered in the mountains there by the hundreds.

It was before the days of the Coudersport Pike, so the pack horses had to follow a narrow trail through the forest. The beasts were owned by Zack Banghart, who carried on a profitable packing business through the unsettled mountainous regions. It was arranged that he would come for the campers again on or about April first if the snow was gone sufficiently by that time; the start was made the first week in December. The weather was unusually cold for that time of the year, but that was rather pleasing to Wallize; it meant finer furs, he said. At least, it was that way in the old country.

It was a journey of several days over range after range of black forested mountains and across scores of swift streams until the Windfall Run region was reached. This creek is a tributary of the Cross Fork of Kettle Creek and flows through a narrow, rocky valley. Here, centuries before, panthers and wolves had fought for the undisputed possession of the caverns, the wolves coming out victorious. The Indians trapped and shot many wolves in this vicinity, but not enough to make the animals abandon the region. It was an ideal breeding and feeding ground; it would take a general crusade to drive them out.

Wallize was delighted with the appearance of the valley. Already covered with snow, wolf tracks were everywhere. Windfalls had thrown the giant hemlocks, which grew in abundance against the face of the cliffs and concealed the wolf dens from view. One could not guess the proximity or number of wolves in the valley unless seeing their tracks after a snowfall. As they had not learned the habit from imitating dogs, the primitive wolves of Windfall Run seldom barked. All their time was spent foraging; they had no time for barking antics. Wallize purposely brought no dogs along, as these animals only excited the wolves and kept them constantly moving. Wolf-hunting with dogs worked very well on the steppes or plains in the old country but not in hilly regions. He wished to trap quietly, in the old-fashioned Indian style, and the wolves would be scarcely aware of his efforts to capture them, so stealthily would he pursue his purpose. He brought many iron traps modeled after the kind used so successfully in Europe at the time, but he also planned to use pitfalls and snares, which Indian trappers assured him worked very well. He would first try three or four methods, one after another, then devote his whole time to the best method.

The camp was pitched on the small clearing that Tallchief and his brothers had used when wolfing in the valley three winters before. A waterfall ran out of the rocks close at hand, which flowed into a pebbly bowl, admirable for washing or drinking purposes. A log cabin was quickly constructed, its rear wall abutting against the steep mountain-side and close to where the cascade poured out of the rocks. It seemed ideal, and Wallize could not help but loudly express his gratification. The Indians laid out the traps along the wolves' favorite paths; the European method was to be tried first. An especial effort was made to set out bear traps, as these animals were soon due to den up for the winter.

The result of the first twenty-four hours' trapping was startlingly successful. Twenty-five wolves and four black bears were brought into camp, all captured within a radius of one mile of the headquarters. Wallize was overjoyed. He examined the wolf hides carefully, remarking that they compared favorably with any taken in the coldest parts of Russia. *They* were grey wolves, and some weighed close to a hundred pounds in life. The first week of trapping by the European method brought in one hundred and ten wolves and eight black bears. These numbers were greater than the Pole had anticipated, so he made this his standard method during the winter. There were more snowfalls, yet the trapping continued good. On the first day, traps were set within one mile of camp; gradually, this radius was widened to four miles by the eighth day. A ten-mile radius was the greatest territory to be "set" unless luck would materially change for the worse.

The wolves seemed very tame and easily fooled into involving themselves with the traps. The bear traps did not do so well, but the Indians said that the heavy snow had hurried the sluggish creatures into winter quarters. But if they did not get the expected number of bear hides, it looked as if they would obtain at least a thousand wolves, and there were prospects that a big number of otters would be speared through the ice in various nearby streams.

Wallize made no complaint; it was much better than he had anticipated. During the second week in camp, there was a snowstorm every day. The gradual accretion was becoming considerable as there were no thaws. It banked about the cabin clear to the bottom of the windows; on the level ground, it measured four and a half feet on Christmas Eve. During these daily blizzards, trapping came to a temporary standstill. The traps were buried in the drifts, and the wolves and other animals remained in their fastnesses. In the second week, only twenty-four wolves and one black bear were brought into camp. But Wallize did not complain; he knew he was in a country rich in fur-bearing animals; wholesale trapping would resume when the snow went off.

On Christmas Eve, a mammoth panther, a rare animal in the valley, visited the cabin. It was evidently hunger-crazed, for it leaped from the mountainside on the shanty roof. It tore at the bark roof so savagely that Little Canoe, fearing it would rip a hole and fall in on the trappers, seized his rifle and shot in the direction from whence the sounds came. The shot was a good one, for the brute uttered a howl of pain and sprang into space, landing in the snow twenty feet in front of the shack. The trappers went out and found it had been shot through the heart. It was very old, as it was practically toothless; even its claws were worn almost down to the quick. Wallize measured it according to his expert methods. Before skinning, the monster was ten feet five inches from tip to tip, or the length of the largest African lion on record. After skinning, it stretched ten feet ten and one-half inches. Many sporting writers and naturalists state that Pennsylvania panthers could not have been so big as the old hunters claimed, but there are several authentic instances showing that the animals were much larger than modern hunters, used only to measuring woodchucks and foxes, believed them to be.

On Christmas morning, the snow began in earnest. It looked like the veritable "down mattress" was being dumped from the heavens. Little Canoe and Jack Berry spent the morning preparing a grand mid-day feast, with panther steak and wolf fore-quarters, the *pièces de résistance*. The cooking meat in the great, open fireplace gave out a savory odor and turned the minds of the trappers from the dreary aspect outside. When the dinner began, the snow banked halfway to the tops of the windows and still was coming down.

"It ought to quit by night," said Tallchief, who, young as he was, had been looked to as the weather prophet of the party. When night closed in, the snow was level with the tops of the windows. It had been so dark for hours before that the only way time could be figured was by Wallize's silver watch. It was one of the first the Indians had seen, and they were fascinated by its mechanism and neatness. When the watch told the trappers that morning had arrived, they found that the snow was packed so solidly about the cabin that they could not get out. They estimated that the drifts were as high as the roof. They would have smothered to death had it not been for the tall stone chimney, which proved to be an admirable ventilator. Judging from the snow that fell down the chimney, the storm was still in progress. It had now gone on without a break for over thirty-six hours, and there seemed to be no signs of it letting up. During the day, the snow diminished, but a wind of high velocity arose. Even in the sheltered valley, it howled and whistled around the rocks, trees, and gullies.

There was nothing for the trappers to do but to be patient, and as they thought they were well-provisioned, they viewed the situation with nonchalance. For the next week, there were more snowstorms and several more terrific windstorms. By the awful noises outside, many big trees were being blown over. The supply of fresh meat, mostly bear steaks, on which they had feasted at first, ran out, and they found that the rest of their provisions were of a kind unfitted to sustain four strong, healthy men in long captivity. The air in the shanty was becoming close and unwholesome from constant breathing, to say nothing of the proximity of so many animal hides. The chimney was all right enough for a few days, but the volume of impure air proved too great for its capacity in time. The men made a desperate effort to get out. They lifted the door from its hinges, finding a wall of snow higher than the shanty. They attacked with picks and shovels but found they were getting nowhere. While they worked, the snow was falling, and the wind drifted it wherever they made slight headway in clearing a path.

When night set in, no actual progress had been made. At about nine o'clock in the evening, the wind attained a greater velocity than ever before. If the cabin had not been hedged in by immense snowdrifts, it would have been blown to pieces. Several stones were blown off the chimney, reducing its height to the level of the drifts. There was a constant boom, bang, and crash of falling trees and of rocks, rolling from the sides of the steep mountains.

"If a big rock from above us should fall on our roof it would be an end to us," said Jack Berry.

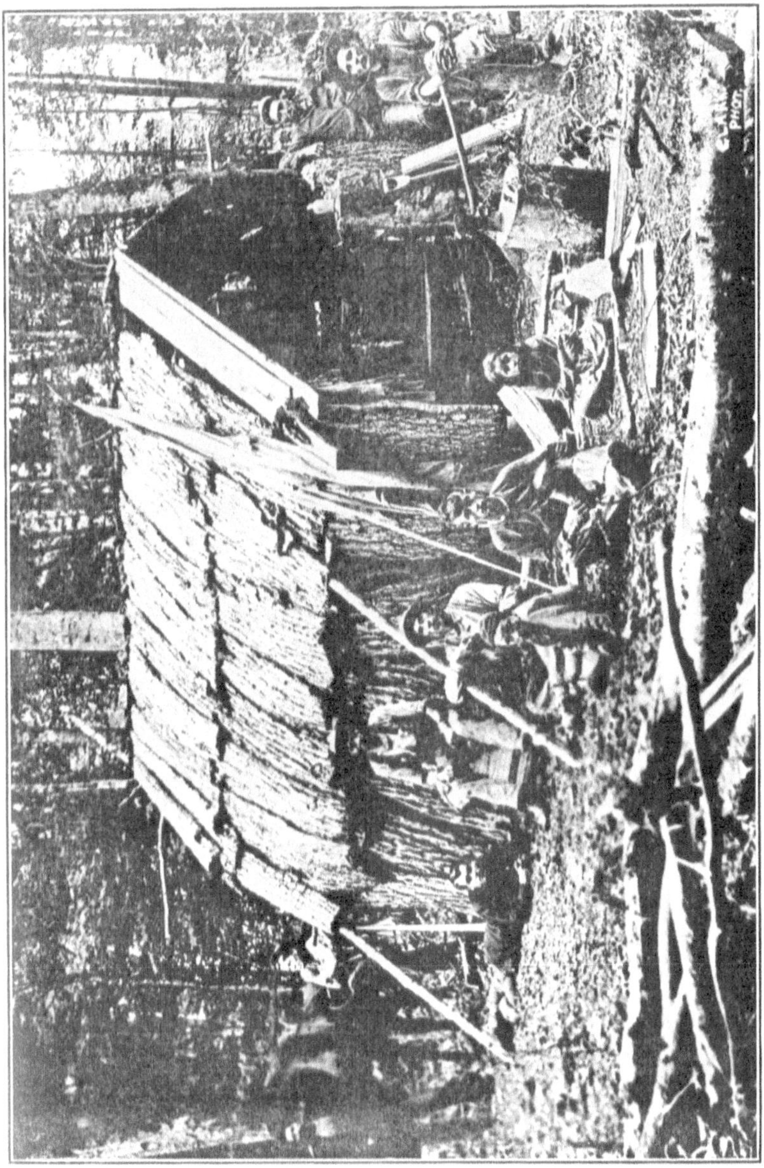

A BARK CABIN (Corbett, Pa.)

The rest of the party accepted his views in silence. They knew what he said was only too true.

About midnight they heard a terrific rumbling and ripping far up on the mountain above the cabin. The wind swept in dreadful gales, so cold that it penetrated the sheltered hut. Since the upper stones of the chimney had been knocked off, the fire would not draw well, and the men who became half frozen, as well as overcome by the impure air, huddled under the piles of wolf hides, which now were most useful as coverings.

It was not long until the wind shook loose a group of giant hemlocks which grew on the face of the mountain, a quarter of a mile straight up from the cabin. With their roots gripping heavy rocks, earth, and ice, they started downward with a roar like the end of the world. It was the most terrible sound ever heard by the trappers. They thought that their hour had come.

Down the mountain, the avalanche came, carrying everything with it. As it neared the shanty, it sent its immense volume over the roof, completely burying it under tons of debris. The fact that the mass of matter swept *over* the cabin, and did not fall straight *on* it, prevented its complete annihilation. As it was, it was little short of a miracle that cabin, and inmates escaped. But their situation was one of grave danger. Even if the snowstorms ceased, the captives would take days of work to dig themselves out. The provisions, such as they had, were sure to run out; without fresh meat, they would quickly finish the goods on hand.

There seemed to be some opening that let in ventilation through the chimney, but not much. The captives surveyed the situation and resolved to dig out at any cost. The giant trees loosened by the tornado had slid down the mountain butts foremost. The huge roots, in which were matted rocks, earth, ice, and snow, had lodged directly in front of the cabin, where the doors and two small windows were located. This cut off that direction as an avenue of escape. The only way to get out would be to knock a hole in the house on one of the other sides. The side opposite the entrance abutted against the mountain; on one other side, the chimney was almost the width of the structure.

There was one way to escape, and the trappers commenced pulling off the log walls on that side. When they had made an opening sufficiently large, they began their attack on the snow. To their intense disappointment, they found that part of the landslide had also engulfed that side of the cabin, and the spring had frozen the entire debris into a solid mass. They now began to calculate that the hut was entirely buried beneath the avalanche.

The wolf-hunters were as securely trapped as any of the furbearers had been. But they determined to continue their efforts for escape, although the faint ventilation received was barely enough to keep them alive. They threw themselves down on the piles of furs, distressed in body and spirit. But sometimes hope appears at the darkest moment.

Wallize, resting on the side of the cabin nearest the big chimney, fancied he heard a scraping noise outside. At first, he put his hand to his fevered brow, imagining that it was some hallucination of a disordered intellect. As time wore on, he felt sure that the sound was outside and not from within his head. He listened intently; it was not as close to the structure as he thought. It sounded like dogs digging at a woodchuck's hole, only much louder. The three Indians became deathly ill from lack of air and rolled about on the furs as if seasick, oblivious to everything.

The sound of something moving outside had a reviving effect on Wallize. Some living force was coming to the rescue of the unfortunate trappers. Yet it could not be human aid, not possibly. Yet what could it be? He feared to tell the others lest it subside and cause a greater depression of spirits among the Indians than before. He had read and been told of the stolidity of the Indians, but in this instance, he, the pale face, was facing death with more equanimity than the native stoics. He kept listening; the scraping grew louder and louder. All day, it continued; how much longer it had been at work, he knew not.

At nightfall, a snapping and snarling like savage dogs was added to the scraping sound. This the Indians heard; pale as corpses and tottering, they were on their feet instantly.

"The wolves are outside, the wolves are outside," shouted Little Canoe in delirious ecstasy.

"Take your axes, boys, and cut away that wall," shouted Wallize.

The noise was too loud to be far off now. The weakened savages began slashing at the logs beside the chimney, great chips flying all over the disordered room. Working all at once and crazed with excitement, their ax bits often struck together with sonorous music. Soon the wall was demolished, and but two feet of snow remained between the trappers and the pack of wolves.

The beasts were crazed with hunger and were working as fast as the trappers. The snow was brushed away, and the faces of a pack of lean, hideous-looking beasts peered in on the human captives. The smell of living beings and food inflamed the starving creatures, and they pressed one another forward into the breach. The Indians allowed the first dozen to get into the room; then, they began splitting their skulls with the axes. The impact of those behind forced the others forward, and they kept appearing at the opening, where the subtle trappers met them.

With the wolves came a gust of fresh air, which added to the ardor of the home defenders. The battle with the wolves must have kept up for hours. Every wolf in Windfall Valley seemed to be a participant. But if so, not a single one escaped with his life.

The "grandfather" wolf, a veritable giant which usually led the pack, was the last to appear and the hardest to brain. He insisted on forcing himself into the room, though his skull had been cleaved at the door. With remarkable vitality, he leaped about the room, snapping furiously. He buried his fangs in Little Canoe's hip before he was chopped to death.

With a free opening to outdoors, the released captives made for the open through the tunnel dug by the wolves. They did not wait to count the dead wolves. Once outside in the snowdrifts, with the clear moonlight shining down on them, they offered up a prayer of thanksgiving. Wallize, a renegade Roman Catholic and hardened free-thinker, experienced genuine repentance. The Indians danced hysterically, singing bits of hymns and rhapsodies they had learned from the celebrated missionary, Jemima Wilkinson.

Then they became hungry and persuaded Wallize to re-enter the cabin and help them drag the cooking utensils outside, to prepare for a feast. By the moonlight, it could be seen that the cabin had been completely engulfed by hundreds of tons of earth and timber, and had it not been for the wolves, the men would have been slowly starved and smothered to death.

"What a shame it was to kill those wolves, our deliverers," said Wallize as he was helping Little Canoe skin a young wolf—apparently the fattest of a very lean pack.

"It was wrong, especially as we Indians belong to the clan whose patron saint is the wolf," replied the limping little Indian, "but what were we to do? The wolves dug us out, not because they wanted to save us, but because they wanted to eat us."

Meanwhile, Tallchief emerged from the tunnel, clapping his hands. "Mister Wallize," he said, "I have happy news for you; there are nearly three hundred dead wolves in there; those with the hides we had before bring the number almost to five hundred, the amount you wanted. The wolves saved our lives and made us keep our promise to you. They have surely blessed us."

Wallize smiled and said, "That is good news, but I would have been satisfied with less wolves this winter; it was hard to kill our saviors."

By this time, the hindquarters of the young wolf had been roasted to a turn, and an enjoyable feast began. All agreed that they had never enjoyed a meal as much before in all their lives. After eating, they sang more religious songs. Then they all set to skinning the dead wolves, Wallize shouting for joy every time one was pulled from the pile, which was as high as the roof of the cabin, declaring them to be finer than the best Siberian pelts. After many perils, all was ending well. With the last hide peeled off, the men lay down for a much-deserved nap. They forgot to close the door to the tunnel, but if there were more wolves nigh, none bothered them.

When they awoke, perfectly refreshed, Wallize said that he was ready to set out his traps again, he would stay in camp until he got his required number of hides and until Zack Banghart, the trapper, returned in April.

The Indians had another joyous scene among themselves. "You are a real man; you are not soft; we like to work for your kind," they said in chorus.

The wolf hides on hand were then counted. They numbered four hundred and one.

"That extra one must be the old 'grandfather' that bit you so badly," said Wallize, turning to Little Canoe, who laughed loudly as he limped about the hut. The trapping went on unmarred by disagreeable incidents for the balance of the winter, and when Banghart and his horses appeared, true to agreement, the first week in April, there were nearly a thousand wolf pelts and the furs of a thousand other animals, bears, otters, beavers, all kinds of foxes, fishers, martens, and wolverines to be packed to Jersey Shore. These Wallize sold to good advantage in Philadelphia.

Shortly afterward, he removed to the foot of the Blue Mountains in Schuylkill County, where he opened a general store. He had shown pluck in fighting down all obstacles in the Black Forest, but he did not desire to trap again. Providence had seen him through; he would not risk it more. He was well over eighty when he died, leaving many descendants, all of whom he delighted on cold evenings before a blazing fire to describe his remarkable story of the winter of the wolves.

VII

THE THREE RIVERS

(A Legend of Potter County)

O UT ON the Bell farm near Newfield, in Potter County, three beautiful, crystalline springs rise not half a mile apart. Their store of limpid water never grows less, even in protracted dry spells—their temperature is the same at all seasons of the year. So pure and lovely are they that it would seem as if they came straight and unsullied from the heart of Mother Earth. For centuries they have quenched the thirst of natives, of settlers, of wild and domestic beasts and birds, and flowing through woods and pastures been a blessing to the world. As they progress from their sources, they appear to grow in strength as well as volume; they attract other springs, rivulets, and cascades, and swelling into maternity, become majestic and useful rivers. One grows to become the Genesee, which empties into Lake Ontario, thence into the St. Lawrence River and Gulf of St. Lawrence, into the North Atlantic; another develops into the Alleghany, which runs into the Ohio, which in turn is merged in the Red River, a tributary of the Mississippi, which 'empties into the Gulf of Mexico, while the third is known by the name of Tiadaghton, and empties into the West Branch of the Susquehanna, which flows into Chesapeake Bay and the Atlantic Ocean, three very remarkable, yet dissimilar destinies, though they are lives filled with good deeds and honors.

The geographers and the historians never bring out their books without a paragraph or two devoted to the three springs on the Bell farm and how they became three great rivers. Old and young have heard of them but pass over the subject as quickly as the scientific writers and history-makers do.

Underneath the scientific facts and historical basis runs a quaint legend, which only the Indians repeated because only the Indians cared. A beautiful spot always conveyed more to these children of the forests than mere physical beauty—they sought the soul underneath. They admired a mountain not for its bigness but for the spiritual element it represented. When they saw a person they admired, they were taught to refrain from saying, "What a beautiful person," but instead would inquire, "What is that person's story? What has he done in his life that is of interest?" And when they saw a beautiful spot, they at once asked what history was connected with it, what legends of the unseen or supernatural worlds clustered about it—they delved for its inmost meaning, which lasts longest.

It is a mistake to feel that romantic or even supernatural things do not happen now. They surely do, only we do not look for that side of things these days. At least most of us don't. From earliest childhood, we have been taught to doubt and disbelieve. What is within and unseen is called impossible. Even religion has been questioned, but only because everything else has been. Doubt has crept into every nook and corner—the faithful have had to hide themselves. They are ashamed of every underground stream in their spirits. They are worse off than the earliest professors of Christianity. But as the legend of the three springs, which grow into the three great rivers, concerns something which we see and benefits us all, it may have some excuse in this practical generation for being repeated in these pages.

Many, many years ago, when the Indian world was new and mankind in closer touch with the Gitchi-Manitto or the Great Spirit than at present, there dwelt on one of the highest mountains in the Seneca country, a shaman named Nahimen, or Sailor-Down-the-Stream. He was strangely gifted with the power of second sight in an age of soothsayers and wise men. He saw so acutely into the future that it caused him much pain. Only when he could interest himself in the affairs of everyday life, in commonplaces, would his soul give him any rest. But that was not often, as his intellect had trained itself to introspection.

Loving the world and its people, he could see the wretched end of everyone, and it tinged his thoughts and speech with sadness. The mystery of why the Omnipotent permitted so much suffering among the creatures of his world bowed him with constant striving to unravel the unknowable. He was sure it was all for the best; he accepted the will of the Great Spirit but with an unforgettable sadness.

Early in life, he met and loved the most beautiful maid in the entire mountain country, the delectable Pechamawayo or Wild Red Plum. The love was reciprocated, and the young couple joined in bonds of happy matrimony. The union was ideal, not a cloud to mar its harmony, and three little daughters were born to cement the bonds tighter.

Then the fair Pechamawayo fell sick and died so quickly that nothing could be done to save her. She vanished from the world like the lovely blossom of the wild red plum in May. Nahimen was heartbroken, but he tried to bear his sorrow bravely. He had the three little girls, which was more than was left in many stricken homes he knew. He resolved to cherish his wife's memory by bringing up the children as carefully as possible to make them worthy of the best in life. And the forces of nature, or perhaps the Great Spirit, seeing this, granted Nahimen the power to converse with the soul of his departed wife.

While this seemed like a marvelous benefice, it was not without its element of melancholy. Pechamawayo, beyond the veil, knew the past, present, and future, but only passively. She could not help in any way, though she knew the certitude of evil destinies for her late friends and those she loved. She could tell her knowledge to her husband, but even he knew no way to check inexorable fate. Maybe it was better to have everything come unexpectedly as the Great Spirit has arranged it for most of us.

But human nature wants to know what is beyond—generally living in a happy or unhappy tomorrow, generally the former state. Nahimen, with all his wisdom, delighted in learning what was ahead, even though it came through his dead wife's departed spirit and might not describe a comfortable future for his loved ones. Had he not been of superior intellect, he could not have obtained the boon of being in tune with the infinite. While he enjoyed his intellectual pride, more truly fortunate were the simple souls who could not tell one day ahead. In that way, the Great Spirit is eminently fair in dividing his favors. There is no Class of the spiritually elect. Nahimen discussed the futures of most of his friends and relatives with the shade of his deceased wife. Everyone was destined to a miserable end; some would meet it within a few hours or days of the revelations.

There was one subject he longed to touch, yet he feared to do so, and that was the future of the three little girls he cared for so tenderly. In his heart of hearts, he knew their fates could not be better than the rest of humanity, yet unknowing, he rejoiced in the superficial opinion that calmness and joy awaited them, that their lives would be prolonged into dim, distant, uncountable years—that when they came to die it would be sought, and like some gentle sleep. This was a blissful vision, only his heart told him it wouldn't come true, and all the while, the soul of Pechamawayo knew and could tell him if he asked her. She never volunteered any information—he had to ask her everything, but with cosmic sense, she never failed to give the exact answer. Someday he would sum up courage and ask her how the three little girls were to fare. If well, then his hopes were confirmed; if illy, then he would be prepared, and he was bold enough to think that perhaps in some way he might circumvent the catastrophe, he could not grasp the full meaning of the word *inevitable*.

All the while, Pechamawayo knew that this was on his mind, and she strove to influence him as spirits do, to refrain from mentioning the subject. Yet she knew when she answered him that a part of his soul would refuse to believe—if it was unfavorable to the daughters' welfare. The question of what would happen to the three girls, Allie-gay-nay, Gay-nay-sayo, and Tya-dagh-tune, preyed on the wise man's mind. It is said that every wise man is a fool somewhere, and the future of the three daughters certainly was Nahimen's most unphilosophic aspect.

At length, he made bold to ask the spirit of Pechamawayo what was to become of the beloved girls. There was sadness in the phantom's voice when she answered him. His disembodied will was not as strong as his incarnate will; she would have to divulge it all.

So, she told him that all would go well with the fair creatures until they were almost out of their teens, when they would fall in with evil associates, becoming corrupted, polluted, and wretched. Their suffering would cause untold grief to their parents, who would be powerless to help them. At the time of their downfall, Pechamawayo declared that

BARK PEELERS AT WORK

Nahimen would be a resident of the spirit world. This looked as if he would soon die. All this was more than the truth-seeker could stand. Strong man that he was, he fainted dead away.

When he was unconscious, the spirit of his father, who had been dead for many years, appeared to him. In his trance, he asked the venerable ancestor what, if anything, could be done to save the three girls from the horrible fate their mother's soul predicted. The shade pointed a way, and when Nahimen came to his senses, there was a smile on his face. The shock of so much bad news, followed by the solution received in a trance, made Nahimen very ill. He lay in his lodge house for many weeks suffering from a consuming fever. Despite this, he was not irrational. He had a single fixed purpose—to get well and save his daughters from dishonor and loathsome misery. He was so anxious to get well that it retarded his recovery. It took all his force as a man of science and intellect to get him back on his feet again.

When he could again summon his wife's spirit before him, he asked her how he could save the young girls from their awful predestination. Pechamawayo's shade replied that there was only one way, to have them changed into other and less corruptible forms, a tree, a rhododendron bush, a rock, a river.

Nahimen liked the river idea best, a stream flowing practically forever, watering and fertilizing a broad land and causing prosperity and comfort to untold numbers of beings. And three daughters, might they not become three rivers?

Pechamawayo replied that it could easily be done. Nahimen's bosom swelled with pride. It would be hard to lose the companionship and intellectual sympathy of the young girls, but now they would become immortals, saints of bounty and goodness.

Then his wife's shadowy reflection explained carefully how the change could be made. It would be quick and painless, first of all. That was good news. She went on to say that there was an aged sorceress named Alliakquot, or Land Rain, who, in early spring and late fall, crossed over the high mountain where Nahimen lived. In some way, she was allied with the Spirit of Spring Showers and the Spirit of the Equinox; her kinship with these great forces was very close. It was too late to see her that year, but she would be back in the spring after the first warm day following the melting of the snow. He would know by her bent body, dripping hair, and the fact that she had a bunch of mayflower or arbutus tied to her long staff.

Nahimen was comforted. He settled down to make the most of his last winter with his daughters. They grew wonderfully in every way; their spiritual natures were developed far beyond those of girls of their ages. But into this blissful state came the question of whether he should inform the girls what would be done with them when spring came. Should the news be broken or wait until old Alliaquot appeared? What if the girls objected to the procedure of being changed into rivers? Was it right to keep the facts from them? They might kill themselves or run away if they heard it. If they committed self-destruction, they lost their souls; if they ran off and drifted into evil ways, their souls would be destroyed. Their souls must be saved.

Yet before keeping up the deception longer, he decided to consult with the shade of Pechamawayo. His wife's spirit at once told him that he must tell the girls without delay. She knew they would be pleased; they had beautiful souls, and the idea would appeal to them. They had not the selfish, earthly idea of preserving the individual consciousness at any cost; they were living for the general good of the world and would gladly merge their souls into some grand cosmic purpose like a river.

This high estimate of the young women was gratifying to Nahimen, and he questioned no more. The next morning, before breakfast, he called his daughters about him and told them what their mother's spirit had prophesied but that they could escape all the horror and degradation by being changed into some less personal force. He mentioned trees, rocks, and streams, adding that he preferred the idea of streams because they did so much good for the world.

The daughters accepted all this talk with equanimity. They were very sensible beings and knew their mother's spirit spoke from a land where the future was an open book. But it was distressing to leave this beautiful world, cast away their consciousness, which enabled them to appreciate the wonders about them, and become instead existing but unthinking forms. But as rivers, they would forever help life and the world; it would be a noble destiny, and it was a privilege to embrace it. But Tya-dagh-tune, the most spirited of the trio, was the least pleased.

"Father," she said, "I appreciate that your talks with our mother's wraith have revealed our complete destinies—what you have heard is very terrible—it seems unbelievable to girls of our simple, exemplary lives—but from the Infinite we know there can be no mistake—all there is an actuality. However, if we are to become degraded and polluted, will we not become so as rivers, just as we would be continuing in our present shapes? Ponder over that."

Nahimen listened attentively and then made reply, "Your words show great sagacity, Tya-dagh-tune, but I cannot believe that a river can become degraded or polluted. Think of the fair land it must flow through, the forests, fields, orchards, vineyards, the lowlands grown to the water's edge with blue flags and reeds, the pastoral people, the hunters, the wild game, the water birds, the graceful canoes, and the silver-coated fish that will float like jewels on your bosom. It is unthinkable to me. Besides, your mother said that an evil fate could be prevented by such a change."

Then he was silent. The fair girls bowed their heads in acquiescence. They kissed their father, and no more was said. They cheerfully waited for the coming of old Alliaquot, who would change them into three beautiful, beneficent rivers.

The winter was severe, yet it passed quickly for Nahimen and his daughters. It passed too quickly to suit the father, as he knew this would be the last winter he would ever pass with them in their present forms. He hoped the snow would not melt and the cold weather might continue indefinitely. But the inevitable thaws came, the days gradually growing warmer. At length came a day as close and humid as midsummer. The sun was partially obscured by haze. About noon, just after the girls had prepared dinner, he noticed an aged woman coming up the path. She was bent and shriveled and helped herself along by leaning on a high staff, on the top of which was tied a rich spray of pink arbutus. Nahimen was overcome by conflicting emotions. The woman who would save his daughters from degradation was coming, but she would also make him lose their fair, fresh faces forever. The girls called him to dinner, but he sat transfixed, watching the old hag draw near. When she came opposite him, he got up, and she stepped forward to greet him.

"Nahimen, you are, I believe," said the old woman, shaking her wet head and holding out her bony hand.

"How did you know my name?" queried the Indian, considerably surprised.

"I was told by some friends in the unseen to stop that you had a task for me to perform."

"Yes, it is true," said Nahimen. "But won't you first have some meat with us?"

"No, I thank you," replied the witch, "I cannot work my spells on a full stomach."

Then she wiped her wet brow and sat down on the bench, apparently very tired. "And, please, good Nahimen, tell your girls not to eat; I cannot work my spell on them if their stomachs are full."

The Indian went around the house to where the girls bent over a fire cooking cornbread and told them they must not eat.

"Then Alliaquot is here," they said together.

"She has come," answered the father, his voice full of emotion.

He beckoned the girls to follow him, so they went to the front of the cabin where the old woman was seated. She smiled grimly when she saw them; it was the smile of an executioner.

"What beautiful girls you are," she said, addressing them with her coarse, gurgling voice.

Then she turned to Nahimen, "I have come a long way," she said, "I have a long distance to go tonight; let us be through with what I have to do here."

"Now—not right away?" inquired Nahimen.

"The present moment is the best time. Where would you have the three springs which will form the three rivers," she said.

"It is sad that this must be, but it is for the best," answered Nahimen. "Right near my lodge-house, where I have lived these many years, which would be the best place."

The old woman rose to her feet and made a pass in the air with her staff. The clear sky became dark. Drops of water, tears of the clouds, began to fall. Nahimen took the fair Allie-gay-nay by the hand and led her to a sequestered nook, old Alliaquot following. When they reached the spot, the witch placed her hand on the girl's head. The raindrops began to fall more heavily, and the outlines of the fair girl began to liquefy. She became transparent like a ghost or water sprite. Nahimen stood motionless, watching her fade away. Soon she lost all semblance to human form, becoming like a small fountain or bethesda. She speedily became smaller and smaller and spread out until she was a sweet spring, purling out from the rocks beneath a giant hemlock tree.

Then the old woman turned and led the dazed parent back to the lodge house. Arriving there, she took Gay-nay-sayo by the hand and, with Nahimen following, wandered to another fair spot. There she turned the maiden into a spring, or source, as she had done with Allie-gay-nay. The sight of his second daughter lost to him was a hard blow for Nahimen to bear. But it was harder when he saw the third and last one, Tya-dagh-tune, gone from him forever. Yet, in a sense, he had triumphed over a great element like Destiny; he had saved his daughters from becoming the prey of scheming and wicked men.

When the task was completed, the rain fell in a perfect torrent. Nahimen asked the old witch to spend the night in his now desolated home, but she thanked him and said she must be on her way. She had to cross the mountain that night.

After a night, which was one of mingled sadness and triumph, Nahimen hurried in the early morning light to the three springs. He found them sweet and pure. When he bent over each, he saw the faces of his daughters reflected in their limpid depths. They were not gone after all. It was lovely to see them as rivulets bubbling over the rocks and running into brooks, which gradually swelled in volume into dancing, sparkling torrents. Fascinated, he followed them, one by one, as they bounded over their new-made beds, increasing in volume and force as they rushed along. The three girls were now the three rivers, later called the Alleghany, the Genesee, and the Tiadaghton. Nahimen lived at his lonely lodge house for many years. He felt the companionship of his daughters-of-water as at night he lay on his couch of buffalo hides, listening to them singing their joyous lays over their mossy beds. They seemed so happy and contented

that he rejoiced at his foresight in saving them from pollution and consequent misery. When he died at the age of one hundred and ten years, his
sorrowing relatives buried him on the highest point of the mountain on
the "backbone" of the range, near where the three springs rose.

Years passed, possibly several thousand years, and the three rivers
amply fulfilled their destiny of cheer and helpfulness. Free from pollution,
they were a benison to every redskin's heart. They brought prosperity,
comfort, and freedom from care to all who lived near their strand. But
then the pioneers came, spreading like some cutaneous disease over the
fair face of mother earth. They leveled and burned the fragrant forests of
pine, beech, and hemlock; they killed the Indians or herded them in narrow spaces called reservations; they slaughtered the wild beasts and birds
without mercy; they blew the fish to atoms with their dynamite; they
trampled the wildflowers; they seemed bent on making the Black Forest a
scene of untold gloom and desolation. They erected huge, hideous buildings called sawmills, tanneries, dynamite works, acid factories, and pulp
mills, all along the three beautiful rivers, the Alleghany, the Genesee,
and the Tiadaghton, the three rivers which were once the daughters of
the sage Nahimen. And from the tops of these unsightly piles of lumber
and iron poured forth foul smoke and vapor, which blackened the atmosphere, and from their foundations gushed red, green, blue, and yellow
poisons, called waste, a stench to the air, which polluted and befouled
the streams, making black sediment on their bottoms, killing fish, and
making the water unfit for use.

And the three fair rivers shrunk with wounded pride, for they realized that, after all, the will of the Great Spirit could not be thwarted, even
after thousands of years. They realized that the efforts of their good father
Nahimen, or the Sailor-Down-the-Stream, were in vain—their destiny
was to be polluted in some form or other, and their happy songs ceased at
night. Those who hear them now say that their singing resembles a dirge
as they turn dirty water wheels of foul bubbling fluid, and the burden
of their song is "Great is the will of Gitchi-Manitto, the Omnipotent,
who takes from us our high estate, but we submit, we are resigned to
pollution and degradation, as it proves to us His might, great is the will
of the Maker of All Things."

The few Indians who remain alone care and are sad. Often, they drop a tear into the turgid waters of the now shrunken, odoriferous rivers, which sing them their story. From them, they realize how little is life, how futile is hope, how everything is nothing compared to the inexorable—where ten thousand years are as a drop of water on the sands of time and three rivers but as a dream.

VIII

A STORY OF REGINA

(Another Fragment of the Popular Legend)

I T WAS on one of those delightful trips with the late Thomas Simcox, of beloved memory, that the writer was introduced to an old gentleman who was able to furnish another word on the subject of Regina Hartman, thus adding to a legend that is to Pennsylvania folklore what Ticonderoga is to the Scotch, the Headless Horseman to the Germans. On this occasion, we were tramping to Leetonia, over the mountains, on a warm, sunshiny day in early September. The distance seemed further than anticipated. We always expected to see the little lumber town lying at the foot of the next high ridge to be crossed, but it was always one ridge further on. As the afternoon drew to a close, the sky became paler but more faultlessly blue, and the trees on the summits and in the deep hollows where the sun had ceased to shine, became darker and more distinct in outline. The odor of the pine was more noticeable, and also that damp mossy smell, which exudes from brooks that flow in heavy shade. The tinkle of the distant cowbells was the only audible sound from nature's late siesta. On the very top of a high ridge, which rose from the opposite side of the ravine, separating us from it, we could make out a small clearing, apparently planted with buckwheat. Upon a second glance, we noticed a tiny log cabin well concealed by trees.

"That's where the old prospector, 'Daddy' Portzline, lives," said our companion.

The writer ventured that though it was an inspiring place to reside, he wondered if water would not be difficult to obtain on the comb of such a bold mountaintop. The old mountain man smiled and said that it was as the Indians used to put it, "If you cut your head, blood will flow just as quickly as if you cut your foot." Thus, it comes that water can be drawn on a mountain top. Our road led across the ridge near the old prospector's home, and as we toiled toward it, perspiring even in the cool air of the late afternoon, it seemed like a pleasing place to tarry a while when the summit was gained before climbing down the mountain to Leetonia. With this beacon ahead, the climb did not seem so hard or so long. Our companion had prospected with old man Portzline and seemed anxious to meet him again and renew the acquaintance. The old fellow had only moved to the mountaintop a year or two before, having gotten too old to dig for the hidden treasures of the Alleghanies, which were principally fireclay, coal, bluestone, and marble. Previous to that, he had boarded with different families, but now when past sixty, he was to have a home of his own. An old-time wolf hunter and pigeon trapper had made the clearing over half a century before, and after he had moved further west, it had been occupied by diverse hunters, fishermen, and bark-peelers, so that the young growth of trees had not been given a chance to overrun it. Several of the old prospector's friends had helped him put it in order so that the work was not greater than the result. Our companion recounted all this as we toiled up the steep path, which had once been a trail road for logs and bark teams. The higher we climbed, the cooler became the atmosphere, so we had every promise of a refreshing rest when we gained the top. And our companion kept repeating that there was a very cold well by the house, which was most gratifying after the tepid water carried in our army canteen.

When we emerged into the clearing, we found the old prospector sitting on a dry-goods box beside his cabin door, smoking his corncob pipe. He seemed to be musing and half-dreaming over the expansive view that stretched out before him. He must have been on the highest knob, as all the other mountains lay below him in the vast panorama. It was enough to make anyone feel content that the rest of the world was petty and very far away! A guinea fowl gave the first notice of our approach, but the alarm was soon taken up by a small, shaggy black dog. Old Portzline looked up quickly and, seeing us, smiled brightly through his rusty spectacles, which half hid his keen blue eyes. The greeting between the two old men was of a most cordial nature. Portzline seemed overcome to

THE PANTHER CLIFFS

think that his fellow prospector of other days would seek him out in his eyrie and bring a friend along.

"No, you must not go to Leetonia this evening; you've got to spend at least one night with me here. I'd tell you there was smallpox down there rather than let you go."

This was certainly a pressing invitation to remain, but our companion waited to see if we cared to do so before definitely accepting. When we signified our intention to remain, there was much gratification expressed by both elderly men.

Soon from the little back kitchen came the savory odor of frying ham, eggs, and potatoes and the sound of the coffee grinder. The two prospectors conversed in the kitchen while we sat on the dry-goods box to enjoy the commanding view. Every knob and ridge was clearly out-lined in the fading golden light, and some of the more distant ranges were already assuming the lavender tint that comes just before dusk. The Bald Eagle Mountains, from whence we had come, showed up well in the array of mountain chains. We need not be ashamed of the "dark and somber hills" which threw up their proud battlements so close to our home. What was left of the Black Forest stretched like a black-green carpet over the mountains to the west and north, its limits clearly defined by the light green or brown slashings on the ridges nearer to us. Off to the west, Mount Pipsisseway was not lost and still held the honor of being the last to bid goodnight to the setting sun.

As the sun sunk lower to the confiding mountain, where it would at length hide its face, a dry chilliness seemed to rise from every draft and ravine. The jingle of the cow and sheep bells grew louder; we could hear a cow bawling somewhere, and the faint echo of a dog's bark—like an excited dog does when chasing cattle homeward. But these sounds were very small and faint compared with the vast expanses of country, where all was steeped in evening's tranquility. We heard a single birdsong, a wood robin's spray of bell-like notes, near the shady well. A lonely grasshopper set up chirping in the weeds near our feet.

Old Portzline came to the door to interrupt our meditations with the news that supper was ready. And what a good supper it was! Memory carries recollections of few meals through the years, but this was one of those that is unforgotten after fifteen years. Oh, joyous days when we never knew what worry was. With more developed intellect, we are happier now, but dull care, an uncongenial companion, is here to remain until the end.

During the meal, our companion took pains to explain that his friend was much interested in the history of central Pennsylvania and especially in the old, unwritten legends. This seemed to please Daddy Portzline, like most aged people we met in those days. Let it be said that the older generation in the Pennsylvania mountains dearly loved and were anxious to have preserved their fast-vanishing folklore. Thus it was that they clung to and pasted into scrapbooks, Bibles, or even the blank leaves of cookbooks, the few legends which at that time had found their way into print—the stories relating to Ole Bull and his castle, the last elk, Cornplanter's Ring, the Bald Eagle silver mines, and the like, which industrious writers in the *Grit*, the *Utica Globe*, and other widely-read papers turned into such really popular stuff, that it was republished so many times as to be overdone. The writer of this story was criticized by one country newspaper when his first little volume of legends appeared eleven years ago because he attempted to retell some of these popular but too well-known tales.

The old prospector went on to say that he had always been interested in history, especially that of the Indians. He had been born in a little log cabin near the site of Pomfret Castle in Snyder County, where in the ancient days, one Hugh Mitcheltree had been carried off screaming and yelling by six Indians in the presence of a well-armed but badly scared garrison. His parents were natives of Schuylkill County, in the Blue Mountains, and his mother was a niece of the celebrated Regina Hartman, "the German Captive."

This was wonderful information. The story of Regina had thrilled our youthful hearts in school days, and although noted historians like Dr. S. P. Heilman and Rev. A. Stapleton have pretty well exploded the old-time version by this time, we will give Daddy Portzline's account, firmly believing that it can be nothing else but the truth. We showed considerable interest in what the old man was saying, especially when we told him that this "captive girl" was our favorite heroine in all the romances of Pennsylvania history. This pleased him mightily, and he arose from the table and went to an old cupboard that looked as if it had first done duty in some Snyder County farmhouse.

Opening the glass doors, he fumbled about in the growing darkness until he found a brown, wrinkled, pasteboard-covered book, in size, probably four by three inches. Opening it at the flyleaf, he beckoned us to come to the door where the light was stronger. We quickly followed, and he held the book so we could see written on the inside of the front cover, in faded, trembling English characters, yellow with age, *"Regina Hartmann, from Anders Boon, 1769."*

"This book," he said, holding it out proudly after we had read the inscription, "was given to my great-aunt by her lover, Lieutenant Boon, who was killed at the awful massacre at Fort Freeland in 1779. It is in the Swedish language. It is a Catechism of Archbishop Suebilius, and though it has no date, it was published in Stockholm for the Swedes in Pennsylvania, probably during the early part of the eighteenth century. It does not seem likely that Aunt Regina spoke Swedish or that Captain Boon could very much either, but he came of the Swedish stock that settled in eastern Berks County at a very early day, and the little book was more of a love token than a brief of religious instruction.

"In our family, we always had it that Daniel Boone was of the Swedish race. He was tall and fair like the Norsemen; he could speak Swedish and German like a native. His father's real name was Sven Boon; English historians called him 'Squire Boon'—but I know differently because I came from the old stock. Indians kidnaped Regina Hartman in 1755; her father, brother, and one sister were killed at the time. One sister, Mary, was kidnapped with her. This girl, the Indians killed for some unaccountable reason. The mother and sisters, Barbara and Margaret, one of who was my grandmother, escaped. They were absent from home at the time.

"The kidnapping occurred at Hartman's Spring, near the present town of Orwigsburg in Schuylkill County. That story of Regina's being rescued out of a line of captives at Carlisle by her mother at the instance of Colonel Henry Bouquet by singing a German song refers to some other Regina. My great-aunt escaped from the Indians even before they saw that they were beaten and were escorted home by a friendly Indian named Galasko. She was eighteen when she came home, having been born in 1746. She was blue-eyed, blonde, and very beautiful. The Indian who escorted her was the nephew of the old squaw Talala, or White Cedar, who had been her foster mother during her captivity.

"When peace was declared, he was on friendly terms with the Provincial forces and was trusted with his fair companion, at least from Harris' Ferry to Orwigsburg. It is interesting to learn how he first became concerned with Regina. Old Talala treated her cruelly, treated her own children cruelly, for that matter; she seemed to take a pleasure in hearing them screaming. She beat the poor white girl repeatedly when she failed to bring a sufficient quantity of berries, nuts, or medicinal herbs and roots into the village. On one occasion, the squaw was maltreating the beautiful girl in a particularly brutal manner. This was too much for the chivalrous Galasko, who appeared on the scene at that moment. He seized the ironwood staff from the old woman's hand and broke it across his thigh. In the excitement, the squaw claimed that the young warrior had knocked her down. This he stoutly denied, but he became unpopular in the camp and withdrew to the woods, becoming a wandering hunter. But he always kept his eye on Regina and, at rare intervals, met her clandestinely in the depths of the forest; Talala suspected this and made her own daughters spy on the girl.

"When she had the proper evidence, she confronted the girl, who was the very soul of truthfulness, and she confessed. For this, she was horribly beaten and kept in semi-captivity until released. Galasko learned the story from a renegade Indian, who was about the camp at the time, and though he dared not put in an appearance, he kept within an easy radius of the place where his sweetheart was confined. At last, he could stand the suspense no longer, so one dark night he broke into the village, murdering several Indians but ultimately making off with Regina. He placed her in a waiting canoe on the North Branch near Nanticoke.

"Two months later, peace was declared, and he at once journeyed down the river with his prize and handed her over to the authorities. He was well-known as an expert shot and a thorough guide in the wilderness; consequently, his appearance was greeted with friendly acclaim. Previously, in Colonel Conrad Weiser's lifetime, he had been praised for his honesty and skill in woodcraft; consequently, he was no stranger to those in charge of the colonial headquarters. He was instructed to escort Regina to her mother's home, and they traveled there on foot along the summits of the Blue Mountains.

"On the way, the young Indian, who had always been most reserved and decorous in his attitude toward the lovely girl, declared his love. She told him that she had loved him, if not from the first time she saw him, which was probable, at least from the day when he had first interfered on her behalf when she was roughly treated by old Talala. She would marry him gladly if her mother gave her consent. She had good reason to believe that her parent still lived and said she wanted to atone for her long absence through some years of devotion. However, she had found a love of a different kind, but to be fair to both sides, her mother's consent would have to be granted. She knew that if she married him, she would have to go away with him.

"From German people with whom she conversed, she had learned that Indians were still very unpopular along the 'Blauen Bergen;' an Indian married to a white girl would be subjected to all kinds of annoyances and ostracism. Irish boys had murdered several Indians with white wives. Galasko might be the next. The erstwhile warrior wanted to lead a peaceful existence; besides, the Blue Mountain country was too thickly settled to suit him as a permanent abode. He would risk obtaining her mother's sanction, and if obtained, he would take her into the wild Sinnemahoning or 'Stony Lick' country, where few pioneers had ever penetrated. On their way, they spent a night with the celebrated Dolly Hope, widow of Dietrich Snyder, who still lived in the old fort, which was situated at the very summit of the Blue Mountain above the present town of Schubert. It was a commanding position, giving a view of the Swatara, Snyder, and Panther, as well as the Tulpehocken and Schuylkill Valleys.

"Dolly Snyder was surprised to find that the long-absent Regina had grown to be such an attractive young woman. She praised her for her beauty and charm, telling her that she should be a great lady like her name, which was that of a queen and not a simple backwoods maid. She told how old 'Mammy' Hartman hated the Indians, how she had grieved for her during her absence, and that when peace was declared, the good old soul had ridden on horseback to Harris's Ferry, Reading, Maxatawney and Heidelberg, asking questions and scanning the faces of returned prisoners. Regina thought it strange that no one at Harris's Ferry had mentioned that her mother had been there; perhaps there was some mistake in identity marked against her on the records.

"Dolly Snyder was shrewd enough to guess that the Indian escort loved the girl. There was fervor in her voice when she wished the young people Godspeed on their departure in the morning. Dolly Snyder lived to the advanced age of one hundred and fifteen years, and her grave is not far from Regina's in the ancient Lutheran Cemetery in Stouchsburg, Berks County. When Regina and Galasko reached the Schuylkill, they had a practical example of the lingering hostility against the Indians. It was necessary to cross the river, which was much too deep for wading. An aged German who lived on the bank had a neat canoe moored in front of his cabin.

"The girl and her swarthy companion knocked on the door, which was opened by the churl, and she asked him politely in German if he would ferry them across.

"The German, with his eyes blazing in anger and hate, exclaimed, 'I would gladly carry you anywhere, my fair girl, but no *damned* Indian shall ever ride in my boat.'

"Then he slammed the door in their faces. But the wily Galasko was undaunted. He told Regina to seat herself on the strand while he went to look for some other means of transportation. Several hundred yards from where she sat, he found a pine log, which had been washed down the stream, and was held by some projecting roots into which it had drifted. This he dragged to where the girl was seated and told her to stand erect on it. Then he pushed the butt off from shore and waded out after it until the water became too deep when he clambered on board. He used a long pole to guide it, and almost before they knew they were safe and sound on the opposite bank.

"Then they climbed the high mountain on the far side of which lay the fair valley where the former Hartman home had been located. Dolly Snyder had told Regina that her mother had rebuilt on the site of the old house so that it would not be hard to find. It had stood in an open clearing that could be seen from the mountains, but the chief landmark was an enormous white pine tree, or as the Germans called it a *bind Baum*, which shaded the cabin and spring, and where the sweet-cooing and love-making wild pigeons had loved to roost. When the Indians burned the cabin, the tree had been badly scorched, but its vitality was such that it sent out fresh green needles and apparently was as much alive as ever.

"When they reached the broad summit, the familiar view brought tears to Regina's eyes. There were few changes in the past nine years, except that there was more cleared ground in the valley and more settlers' houses. The picturesque 'Red Church,' which the Indians had burned before Regina had been carried off, was replaced by a new and larger edifice. The giant old pine rose in his accustomed place; in the shadow of his sheltering branches, could be noticed a trim log house, with the chinks white plastered, presumably Mother Hartman's new home. Regina could only exclaim, 'Washock, washock,' the Indian word for the green tree. She had learned to think in the Indian language.

"Many conflicting emotions stirred in Regina's breast as she gazed at the scenes of her youth. They were not all pleasurable, and she held her companion's hand tightly. It was a benighted existence she was returning to, little better than she had left in the Indian village on the North Branch, except that her mother was a kind, Christian woman. But the girl's sense of duty soon asserted itself, and she realized how her mother had suffered. Even if returning home meant sending her lover, Galasko, adrift, she would have the reward of a satisfied conscience. This conscience made her long to see her loved ones again and not drift into comparative savagery like another Indian captive, Mary Jemison, the famous 'white woman of the Genesee,' whose bronze statue adorns Letchworth Park in New York State.

"A cool breeze stirred the red leaves of the gum and maple trees on the summit where she stood; it was like a signal to commence the last stage of her journey. At the foot of the mountain, she passed through a large field of Indian corn, dry and ready to be cut. In the center of this field stood an ancient white oak.

BLACK FOREST CAMP LIFE

"Regina suggested that the Indian remain there until she had seen and interviewed her mother. It might be disconcerting after Dolly Snyder's warning for her to enter the house after her long absence accompanied by one of those hated warriors. She would break the news gently that she wanted to marry an Indian, and if all was well, she would return to the field and escort the prospective son-in-law to the Hartman cabin.

"The Indian thought this a good idea and squatted down at the foot of the old oak and drew out his long pipe. Regina kissed him goodbye. In her heart, she knew that her mother would never give her consent; it would even be hard to break the news to her with such an antipathy against Indians. But the first and only consideration was the duty she owed toward the old lady; it made everything else seem of minor consequence.

"It was late in the afternoon when she climbed the 'Indian fence,' which surrounded the Hartman clearing. A trail of blue smoke was curling up from the big chimney, indicating that supper was being prepared. The family watchdog, resting under the great pine tree, espied her, jumping up and shaking himself and barking angrily. His barking brought 'Mammy' Hartman and her daughters to the door. With a quick glance, Regina could see that her mother's hair, golden colored when she went away, was now snow white; she looked like a woman seventy years of age. At first, it shocked her, but then she realized that apart from her trials, women of the peasant class aged early in life.

"For a moment, the old woman could not identify the tall, slim, well-bred-looking girl coming toward her. Suddenly, she uttered a piercing cry in German, *Mei Lieber Gott!* Then she called to the dog to be quiet and ran forward. Regina and her mother were soon locked in a loving embrace. They were both too excited to go indoors, so they sat down on the hewed logs which served as doorsteps to the cabin. Mother Hartman, Regina, Barbara, and Margaret all wanted to talk at once.

"There was much weeping, laughing, and embracing. The dog, noting that something unusual was in progress, apologized for his rudeness by crouching at Regina's feet and licking her skirts.

"When the first flush of the excitement was over, the mother held the girl at arm's length, exclaiming, 'How beautiful you are, how beautiful you are, you resemble, oh so much, the wonderful Countess of Falcken-steyn and Bruck, whom my mother admired so much as a little girl. Her picture, a very little one, was the only plaything I dared bring with me from the old country, and now you have grown to be like her, my ideal of loveliness.'

"The old woman's taste was correct, for Regina was a paragon of girl-ish beauty. Her large full eyes, which were her finest feature, were grey in color, the lashes and brows black, and she always kept the lids half closed. Her nose was slender, aquiline in contour; her lips were full and red, her complexion clear, her hair ashen blonde, her slim, erect figure easy and graceful. Peasant girl that she was, suffering and high thinking had made her every inch a noble woman; physically, she was one of the few beings who lived up to her soul.

"Supper was almost forgotten, but at length, Regina said she was hungry, and it was hurriedly gotten ready and placed on the slab table. During the meal, Mother Hartman asked Regina if she had found a lover in all these years, for early marriage was the rule with the working classes. The beautiful girl flushed a guilty red. She looked her mother full in the eyes for a moment as if to ascertain how she would receive the news that she was about to break.

"'Yes, I have a lover, a splendid young man. He is waiting even at this minute under a tree in the cornfield until I have asked your permission that I can become his bride. He is an Indian.'

"At the word 'Indian,' the old woman clutched at the edge of the table, missed her hold, and fell against the water bench in a swoon. Regina and Margaret picked her up and laid her on her couch. They fanned her and threw water on her face until she recovered.

"When she opened her eyes, she looked at Regina saying, 'Is this what you have come home for, my darling, to tell me that you would marry a member of that horrible race, who killed your father, your little brother, your little sister, burned our home and stole our belongings?'

"Regina's worst fears were realized. Sobbing, she sank on the floor by the old woman and threw her arms about her. 'No, no, no, I would not give you more unhappiness. Much as I love my brave and hand-some Galasko, I love you more. You have suffered for many years; now, I intend to make you happy. I will send my lover away.' She rose to her feet and gazed out of the cabin door. It was almost dark. 'Mother,' she said, 'I must go to the wood and send him away.'

"Before the old woman could restrain her, she was gone. Galasko was still smoking when she returned. He took the news philosophically. It was a hard blow to him, yet knowing Regina's strength of character, he must have been, in a sense, prepared for it. But before they parted, amid tender embraces, the Indian lover arranged to meet her at the oak tree on the first night of the new moon every month. Even if they could never marry, they might continue a spiritual communion. He would reach the trysting place at noon and wait there until she could slip out unmolested, probably not until nightfall.

"The Indian did not go many miles away. He established himself on the summit of Broad Mountain, which at that time was a rendezvous for wolves, and commenced trapping them for their hides, which sold for a shilling apiece. Many traders were located at Harris' Ferry and Fort Hunter; he could support himself nicely and yet be an easy traveling distance from his beloved. If he thought that sometimes she would change her mind and leave her mother for him, he dropped no intimation.

"Meanwhile, Regina settled down to a life of worthy purpose. The only education she possessed was taught her by her mother before she had been carried off by the Indians ten years before. As intimated before, she had almost forgotten the German tongue. She tramped across the mountains to Tulpehocken and enlisted the aid of the Lutheran preacher, Reverend John Nicholas Kurtz, to educate herself. He loaned her German and English books, principally of a religious nature, and she set about to teach herself, to master both languages. She was devoted to her mother and sisters and the children and old people of the neighborhood.

"When the time rolled around for her to meet Galasko, she was on hand. She had contrived to obtain the privilege of going to the mountain every afternoon for her mother's and some neighbors' cattle. On the way, she passed the oak tree, finding the philosophic Indian lover sitting on its broad roots, smoking with characteristic stolidity. There was an affectionate greeting, and they wandered over the mountain slopes until dark, rounding up the cows. They parted at the edge of the forest, filled with protestations to meet the month following. All that winter, they met, and the following summer clear into November. It was becoming harder for both to part, and they were considering bimonthly meetings.

"In November, three young and prepossessing looking men from Exeter Township, in Berks, stopped at the Hartman cabin on their way to Bear Mountain on a hunting trip. They were named Haakon, or "Hawkins" Boon, Anders Boon, and Olle Derickson. The Boons, who were cousins, were related by marriage to young Derickson.

"Anders, tall, fair, and handsomest of the three, immediately fell in love with Regina. She was, he declared, the most beautiful woman he had ever seen. The next morning, he was loath to leave her, but his companions urged him to hold to his plans and not spoil their trip. They persuaded him to go with them, but anyone could have noticed his glumness at departing.

"Four days later came the phase of the moon, which brought the faithful Galasko to the oak tree. He arrived at the appointed time and sat down to enjoy his accustomed smoke pending his sweetheart's arrival.

"Just after Regina had left the house, Anders Boon appeared at the door. He had become so restless and unhappy that he had slipped away from his companions and returned to the scene of the awakening of his great love. Mother Hartman told him that her daughter had gone hunting the cows and pointed to the path leading to the forest, which she usually took. Bounding along like a deer, he overtook her just as she climbed the fence, which ran along the edge of the woods.

"Regina was never so disconcerted in her life; else, she might have conducted the affair with greater wisdom. She acted politely and even altered her course to pass as far from the oak tree as possible.

"But stoical though he seemed, Galasko possessed an Indian's eye and ear. He was a human eagle. Also, his acute sixth sense told him that all was not well that day. Signs had come, which meant bad luck. A bird had flown into his shack the night previously. There were too many bubbles in the spring where he drank. When he heard voices conversing in low tones, rifle in hand, he sprang to his feet, a picture of alertness and anger. He pushed his way through the crackling grape vines and hazel bushes to the clearing where he fancied the sounds emanated, coming face to face with

Regina, in company with a tall, good-looking white man with blonde curly hair. His rage was so great that he could have shot Anders Boon dead, and scalped him then and there, had not the girl, by a deft movement, twisted the weapon away from him. Then, in German, which all three understood to a certain extent, she introduced Boon to the Indian.

"Galasko controlled himself, and the fiendish blaze died out from the surface, at least of his grey eyes. He shook the white man by the hand, exchanged a few pleasantries, then, turning to Regina, said he must be going.

"'Won't you help us hunt the cows this evening?' she said to placate him.

"He replied that he had to be off, shaking hands with Boon and the girl once more. Turning on his heel, he disappeared among the pines in the gloaming, with a hanging head, a tall and melancholy figure.

"The presence of this Indian, and his strange conduct, brought young Boon's love to a 'boiling point.' On the hunt for the cows, he proclaimed his passion in words even fiercer than Galasko's declaration. Regina listened until he was finished. They stood in an open space on the mountaintop, with the cows bearing their tinkling bells clustered about them. From above, like a symbol of Galasko's love, shone the new horned moon, Astarte of the Heavens.

"It was an embarrassing position for the girl, but she told the young man that she already loved the Indian, that her mother had forbidden her to marry a member of that race who had murdered three members of their family; she had decided to obey her parent, but she would never marry anyone else. She thanked the youth for honoring her with his proposal, but her heart was another's.

"He asked her if there was any chance of changing her mind. She told him firmly that there was not. He accompanied her home and helped her milk and stable the cows. Then sadly, he said goodbye. He did not go to join his hunting companions but started for the east that same night. He would tramp until morning to starve his grief, he said.

"The next afternoon, Regina revisited the oak tree, but there were no signs of Galasko. For a week, she looked for him every day, but he did not come.

"At the end of that period, she met at the tree a strange Indian youth, who called himself Wapashah, who was lolling and smoking as Galasko had done. He told her he had been sent there to deliver a message from one who had once been her lover but was now her friend, an Indian warrior. That she would never see him again, that he had packed his belonging and was moving far into the western country. That he knew now why she would not marry him, that it was because she had another lover. That he forgave her, but all was over between them. Then Wapashah handed her a small piece of nugget gold, saying that his friend had found it in the bed of Bohundy Creek and wanted her to take it as a last remembrance.

"Regina did not propose to lose her lover through any misunderstanding. She told Wapashah that it was all a mistake, that she had only met the other man less than a week before, had only seen him twice, that he had come to her unexpectedly in the forest, that she loved the Indian warrior and no one else. She begged him to meet her at the oak tree as of yore.

"Wapashah shook his head, saying that he was afraid it would be too late to give the message, as his friend had asked him to wait until he had been gone on his journey for seven days before visiting Regina. But he would try and overtake him, nevertheless. He believed that she was telling the truth and nothing but the truth.

"Wapashah started away, leaving the girl dumbfounded, literally stunned with grief. She could only question her policy of not having married her lover in the beginning; now, she had lost him under the most distressing circumstances. But she brought home the cows that night, singing a German song and outwardly as gay as if nothing had happened.

"All that fall and winter, she worked, improving her mind, in addition to her domestic duties and her attendance on the old and poor who resided in the valley. She never missed a new moon at the oak tree, but Galasko did not return. Either Wapashah had not overtaken him, or he had chosen to disbelieve her plea of innocence.

"During the summer, she received another visit from Anders Boon. He said he had decided to swallow his pride and come again. He asked after the Indian and was told he had not returned. But Regina told him frankly that there was no hope for anyone else. He remained at the cottage for a week, reading books with her, including John Arndt's *Paradise Garden*. When he went away, he said he would be back in a year.

"In December, Regina received another unusual visitor, a young artist named Jons Gostasson, afterward known as Jack Justice, the pupil of Benjamin West. Had he lived, it was predicted he would have become a second Hesselius. The youth said he had come from Swedeland near Philadelphia. Anders Boon, he said, had sent him to paint a miniature of Regina on a smooth piece of buffalo horn. Boon had killed a monster bison on one of his hunting trips on the Karoondinha, where these beasts still lingered in considerable numbers, and wanted the fair German girl's lovely features perpetuated on it. The picture was completed in a day, and the youthful artist took it away with him, saying that the young huntsman desired it in time for Christmas as a present to himself.

"The following year, when Boon visited Regina, he showed her the picture he wore in a gold locket suspended from a chain about his neck. In a thoughtless moment, she allowed him to cut off a small curl of her golden hair, which he fastened inside the locket. His visits were made once a year, generally in mid-summer. He was always welcomed, as he was bright and congenial, and never afterward attempted to win her from her plighted troth. He always brought presents, mostly books, among them the Swedish Catechism.

"He was absent on a hunting trip on his beloved Karoondinha when the Revolutionary War broke out and hurried over to the West Branch country where his relative Hawkins Boon, who had become a landowner there, was a captain in the rangers. Men capable of taking command were badly needed, and Captain Boon dubbed him Lieutenant, pending official orders from headquarters. The similarity in names caused the two men to become confused in history, to the detriment of Anders Boon, whose name cannot be found in the military records. But he made a brave and sagacious leader, doing most of Hawkins Boon's scouting. The two Boons, Captain Samuel Dougherty, and their men were quartered at Boon's Mill, on Muddy Run, in July 1779. There seemed to be a lull in the hostilities which had been going on between the permanent settlers on one side and the Indians, renegade settlers, and English on the other.

WOODSMEN RESTING

"On the morning of the twenty-ninth of July, the garrison at Boon's Fort, numbering about thirty-three officers and men, heard firing at Fort Freeland, about seven miles away. Commanded by Captains Boon and Dougherty and Lieutenant Anders Boon, the garrison hastened to the scene of the conflict. The Indians, led by Hiokatoo, later the husband of Mary Jemison, and the ferocious Galasko, had just finished the ransacking of the surrendered fort and the tomahawking of the wounded.

"Captain Ronald MacDonald, who commanded the English, had gone down the river as escort to the women and children. The Indians had seated themselves to enjoy a sumptuous repast on the banks of the creek. In the midst of it, the party from Boon's Fort surprised them, getting within seventy-five or eighty yards of the enemy without being discovered. Each man was cautioned to take sure aim, and when all were ready, at a given signal, they fired, and at least thirty of the warriors fell dead without warning.

"As soon as they could reload, they crossed the bridge which spanned the creek and made directly for the fort, which they found manned by determined Indians. An Indian brave, Machynego, was holding the flag and was shot dead by Captain Dougherty.

"Another Indian, Galasko's friend Wapashah, took the flag and had no sooner got it erected than Dougherty dropped him as he had the first. Galasko, who was standing by, grabbed the banner from the dying Wapashah and, brandishing a rifle in his other hand, dared the frontiersmen to do their utmost. Before Dougherty could fire again, he was shot dead by Hiokatoo, who was standing close at hand, and he quickly shot Captain Hawkins Boon, who took the place of the fallen leader.

"Anders Boon, his chance to command having come, ran forward with a shout, his fair curls flying about his hatless head. The smoke had cleared for an instant, and he stood revealed to his hated rival, Galasko.

"'For God's sake, hold that flag a minute,' he called to Hiokatoo. The Indian, not knowing why, seized it; as he did so, Galasko fired his rifle. Anders Boon fell dead, shot through the heart.

"The three officers dead about them sent the surviving rangers, numbering about a dozen, into a panic, and they broke through their enemies and escaped into the thickets. Masters of the situation, the Indians set fire to the fort, which was burned to the ground.

"Then the scalping and robbing of the dead bodies commenced. Like a human eagle, Galasko was soon bending over the prostrate form of Lieutenant Anders Boon, eagle-like, tearing out his eyes before he scalped him. He ripped the clothing from his body, preparatory to cutting out the heart. Around the smooth throat hung a golden chain, a closed locket at the end. The excited Indian broke it from the dead man's neck and pried the clasp with his teeth. The calm and beautiful face of Regina Hartman looked up at him; fastened across the picture was a lock of her pale, gold hair.

"'By all the gods,' shrieked Galasko, 'she was false after all. It was because of him she would not marry me. That message she sent with Wapashah was all lies.' Then he proceeded to cut out the dead man's heart."

IX

THE DEATH SHOUT

(A Story of the Senecas)

IN CANFIELD'S admirable book of Indian legends, the following statement is made:

When an Indian is dying on the field of battle, he is said to utter a cry or 'Death Shout,' which is heard in Paradise and serves to let the friends he would meet there know that he has started on the long journey. In addition, it was long a custom amongst the Indians, particularly the Senecas, to frequent rivers and high wooded places or ravines with steep, precipitous sides, where reverberations could be heard for miles until they would die away in the distance. Here they would stand for hours, shouting and listening as the echoing sounds leaped from shore to shore or from hill to mountain and from mountain to valley—on and on into silence; always firmly believing that the words were called from one to another of the faithful spirits until they reached the ears of their loved ones and finally the Great Spirit himself.

It was in the breaking of a log jam, in the spring of 1864, at the mouth of Moshannon Creek, that a young Indian riverman named Billy Steele was killed. He was carried out of sight so quickly that his comrades barely missed him. He was a youth of rare promise, and none felt his untimely end more keenly than old Isaac Steele, his father, who was working not thirty feet from him when he was sucked under by the whirlpool of logs and water. The jam was caused by a sudden freshet in the Moshannon, driving out a lot of logs that had been piled on its banks into a score of timber rafts that were moored in the West Branch, a short distance below its confluence with the Moshannon.

The evening after the disaster, one of the raftsmen had occasion to go some distance up the Moshannon to a friend's cabin and was surprised to find old Isaac Steele standing on a large rock in the bed of the stream—the rock is known to this day as the "Rivermen's Torment," as more than one raft came to grief against it. The Indian, who was alone, was shouting and listening to the echoes, which at first came back to him, and then were carried into the very depths of the hemlock-covered mountains which lined the shores. With a clear, resonant voice, yet mixed with sadness, he sent echo after echo through space until the entire wilderness reverberated with the tones of anguish. The riverman knew enough of the Indians' ways to surmise that it was some religious exercise and drew back, allowing him to continue his shouting unmolested. But he was anxious to know its meaning and waited for his opportunity to inquire.

It happened that the Indian was to ride on the same raft of which this particular riverman was the pilot, and on the journey to Marietta, the chance for enlightenment presented itself. Some very warm weather set in, and when the raft was moored at night in comfortable eddies, the crew decided that it was too warm to go to the taverns, so they slept on the deck, wrapped in thin blankets. On one of these nights, when the raft was tied up at Hummers Wharf, when it was uncomfortably warm for sleeping, the pilot and the Seneca became confidential, and the reasons for the mysterious shouting were revealed.

The old native said that his son had died so unexpectedly that the poor boy did not have a chance to acquaint his friends in Paradise with his coming. It would be hard to arrive from the long and arduous journey with nobody to meet him at the crystal gates. He hoped that the shouts he had given vent to on the evening of the accident would reach the Land of Shades before his son's spirit arrived. Sometimes the journey took only a few days, but in other cases, the suddenly deceased souls lost their way, and were months to find the Promised Land.

Many strange stories clustered about the "Death Shout," some beautiful, others painfully sad. He would tell one which his old grandmother had loved to repeat when he was a little boy and lived in a hunting camp in the heart of the Black Forest. It was a story of the days when the world was new, and the Indians had not lost the personal interest of the Great Spirit by frequent acts of disobedience and indifference.

In those days, there was a certain brave young warrior and hunter—he had more human scalps and panthers' teeth on his belt than any man, old or young, in his clan. His name was Machatachten or The Coal of Fire. With his tall and graceful figure, gentle voice, and flashing grey eyes, he could have had the love of any woman he wished for. But his heart only beat for one Indian maid, the beautiful Sabeleua, or Sunlight on the Water. This great affection was fully reciprocated, and in due course of time, they were married. Sabeleua's character was as fully developed as her husband's; consequently, they could appreciate one another.

The fair bride predicted that Machatachten would rise to become the greatest Indian who had ever lived. In this, many wise men agreed. He seemed to be the favored one of the Great Spirit. Despite all the flattering words he heard, the young warrior listened mostly to the encouragement of his bride. He believed in her judgment above that of all other persons; it overjoyed him to feel that she looked upon him as a coming man. He indulged in many feats of daring to uphold her confidence, both in the chase and war. Amid all this happiness, the fair bride was seized with a swamp fever, and despite all that could be done for her, she passed away. Machatachten's grief was pitiful to witness.

Strong man that he was, he was bowed to the earth by this sudden affliction. It was like a bolt from a clear sky. The wise men who had predicted so much for him in the future came to offer their condolences. They were turned away from the warrior's lodge house, Machtachten telling them that their predictions of material triumphs were of no use; now that he had lost his love and helpmate, he had no belief in makers of false promises.

After a while, he realized that this moping in his cabin was no way for a brave man to act, it would be best to enter earnestly into warfare, to strike blow after blow at the corruption of the world, and if he fell, he would join his wife's spirit in the Paradise as a brave soul, and not as one who had grieved himself into the grave.

So, he emerged from his retirement and gathered an intrepid band of warriors about him. They traveled to distant parts of the country, putting down oppression, injustice, wrong, vice, and crime. They were always victorious, although they incurred the hatred of many chiefs who feared the existence of an aggregation of skilled warriors dedicated to such lofty purposes. It was in one of those periods in Indian history when there was much corruption and enervation; consequently, the awakening of a new Spartan spirit was viewed with disfavor by those who profited by human weakness. Yet the most appalling feature was the unbroken series of victories that the band of Spartans achieved. In a year, they had dethroned and killed fifty tyrannical or corrupt Indian kings and added vast stretches of territory to the dominions of old Magoochagook, or Copper-Head-Snake, in whose realm Machatachten and his band resided.

At first, the aged chief viewed the warfare of the intrepid young warrior with pleasurable sensations. He publicly commended him and loaded him with gifts. He raised his rank of nobility next to that of royalty. He had games and feasts given in his honor. But as time went on, he began to fear that Machatachten was becoming more popular than himself and, above all, more esteemed than his son and heir, Andhannai, or the Bull Frog. This youth was given over to luxury and viciousness and possessed more vulnerable points than many of the chieftains whom Machatachten had overthrown. The old king nursed his fears privately for a while, then he confided them to his council of wise men, who in turn suggested that the soothsayers be called in. The medicine men shook their heads sadly, saying that Magoochagook's suspicions were only too true. Machatachten, they said, was insincere, that he was only seeking notoriety, that his ultimate desire was to overthrow Magoochagook's dynasty and rule in his stead.

They advised the king to immediately order the disarmament of the young warrior and all his followers. But the soothsayers were insincere; they colored their report to suit their king, though, in their hearts, they believed in Machatachten. The king was delighted at the result of his appeal to the seers into the shadowy world. He lost no time in issuing a proclamation ordering the warrior and all his band to assemble in a deep ravine on an appointed day and give up all their arms to the royal bodyguard. This was to be carried out at the foot of the War Path, so called from this episode, on Kettle Creek, in the Black Forest. Machatachten was surprised at this order, but he was, first of all, a loyal subject and did not question. Some of his followers were almost rebellious when told to lay down their arms and fight no more, but he quieted them with his dominant will.

Marshaling them together, he marched them single file along the War Path, meeting the representatives of the king, who were drawn up along the banks of the creek in the early morning. Machatachten saluted and advanced, giving over his spears, arrows, scalping knives, and deer skinners. Then the chief representative of the king commanded the unarmed warriors to form themselves into a circle, with their leader in the center. When in this position, the royal guard quickly withdrew into the forest.

While standing thus defenseless, yet feeling perfect confidence in honor of royalty, a cruel fusillade of poisoned arrows rained down from the tops of the hemlock-covered mountains which overhung the ravine. Among the first to go down was the brave Machatachten, pierced through the jugular vein. As he fell, he had the presence of mind enough to give the Death Shout. What had been a few minutes before a sea of happy faces was now a bloody charnel house. The entire band, having been apparently slain, the executioners proceeded to scalp the victims. Machatachten's body was the first approached. It was still warm, but the heart had ceased beating; no flow of blood was apparent. The barbarous Indians tore the scalp from the head and then stamped on the prostrate form before they passed on to the next corpse.

Within an hour, two hundred scalps were collected and placed in pouches made from panther skins. The leader took the pouches and followed by his murderous crew, started for the royal pavilion on the shores of Tiadaghton Creek. All day long, the bodies of Machatachten and his mutilated followers lay in the broiling sun on the greensward by the creek side. The flow of warriors' blood pouring into the water dyed it a lurid red. Meanwhile, the Death Shout that the brave youth uttered was reverberating from ravine to ravine, from mountain to mountain, rising higher and higher, clearer and clearer, until it reached the clouds and was wafted through them to the Land of Eternal Sunshine, where the souls of the happy and the brave exist forever in unclouded bliss.

A strange shadow passed over Sabeleua's happiness there in Paradise; with cosmic intuition, her first thought was of her husband in the terrestrial world. Then came the last expiring echo of the Death Shout. Following it back through the blue ether, atmosphere, cloud masses, mountain peaks, forest-clad ravines, rocks, rivers, and streams, to its source, she found her beloved warrior lying in the growing sunlight, his life's blood ebbing away. Around him lay the bodies of his faithful followers, all dead or dying. It was a horrible sight not often seen by the calm dwellers in the bosom of the infinite. Summoning all her psychic strength, she breathed on the gaping wound in Machatachten's neck. Like magic, it closed together, becoming perfectly dry. Even as she did so, the cruel band of murderers emerged from the thickets, making the heroic leader, whose wound had ceased to flow, the first victim of their scalping lust.

This was too much for Sabeleua to bear. She sought to strike the scalpers' hands with palsy but, not being divinity, was powerless. She could aid the injured, but the well were too full of world strength to affect. So, she was compelled to witness the mutilation of her handsome Machatachten. When all the prostrate forms had been scalped and roughly used, the fiends in human form withdrew, wildly anxious to hurry the good tidings to their monarch Magoochagook. Left alone with her beloved, Sabeleua formed a heavenly shadow over him to protect him from the broiling heat of the summer day.

All day long, she brooded over him, his wound remaining closed, while she breathed her spiritual force into his dry, grey lips. When at length the sun lost its fury, and a sunset redder than warriors' blood threw its rays upon the creek, the form of Machatachten began to twitch and coil itself. Then the long, sinewy arms stretched themselves out, the fingers clenched, and flowing blood was noticeable in the blue veins. The head raised itself several times, the lips twitched and assumed a less ashen hue. Lastly, the eyes opened, staring blankly, while more depth came into them.

At length, the figure started to arise awkwardly, like a newborn colt getting on its feet for the first time. After a few efforts, equilibrium was found, and the warrior rose to his full height, which was several inches over six feet. He stretched his arms again, yawned, and re-opened his eyes; Machatachten had apparently risen from the dead. A cool evening breeze blew in his face and swept his dark, woven cloak about his legs. Consciousness seemed to come back with that zephyr, for he looked about him as if waking from a dream. Then his eyes fell on the piles of dead and mutilated corpses, and instinctively he put his hand to his head. Instead of the shock of straight, stiff hair, he was completely bald, and the top of his skull was rough and smarted at his touch. The realization came to him that he, too, had been scalped and that he had lain as dead among his henchmen an hour before. He shed tears for the brave fellows who were no more and were it not so dark, he could have searched for the remains of a few who were particularly dear to him.

He looked out on the glimmering waters of the creek, on which a solitary star was shining. It gave such a long, trailing, quavering reflection that it was almost human in its proportions. He gazed at it as if transfixed until he fancied he saw the face and form of the long-absent Sabeleua, but she was as translucent as starlight. He was so astounded to see her that his speech returned to him, and he asked if she was not the beneficent spirit who had saved his life. He had sent her the Death Shout when the poisoned arrow pierced his throat. From her presence this night, he was certain she had heard it, closed the wound, and stopped the fatal flow.

But Sabeleua's only answer was a nodding of the head, the quintessence of starlight on evening waters. Machatachten knew and understood. He asked her if she had saved him for some purpose; otherwise, it might not have been happier for them both if he had died and joined her at once in Awossagame or Heaven. Then a breeze stirred the great hemlocks which grew along the stream. They swayed, twisted, and shook their shaggy boughs until they seemed to simulate the human voice.

At length, Machatachten made out these words: "Yes, my beloved, you have a mission in this world. You cannot leave here until it is fulfilled. You must become king of all the tribes who live east of the Great Lakes and the boundless plains. Rise on Magoochagook, hurl him from power, and you will be the greatest and godliest ruler our people have ever known."

Then the rustling of the giant branches ceased, and the glimmering star, Machatachten's star of destiny, vanished from the waters; all was the overpowering stillness of the mountain night.

TELLING A PANTHER STORY

Then came a great illumination to his soul. He saw everything clearly, as in a flash of lightning. His mission was revealed to him in the dizzy glare. Looking down for an instant, he saw a scalping knife, which one of Magoochagook's retainers had left behind, lying at his feet. He stooped and picked it up, then, with rapid strides, cleared the tangled mass of bodies and started for the War Path.

Though it was a dark night, the light in his soul was such that he saw the way clearly. The steep path was part of his destiny. Just at daybreak, he encountered a handsome youth bound for the depths of the Black Forest on a hunting trip. Machatachten drew his scalping knife, quickly stabbing the youth through his jugular vein. Without a word, he sank to the earth, expiring in a pool of blood. This young hunter gave up his life as an instrument of Machatachten's fate. The inspired warrior scalped the dead man and placed the heavy shock of hair on the still sore and bleeding top of his head. Now he felt that he looked like his old self again. The wound in his throat had healed, and he was filled with more purpose and strength than ever before.

Shortly after noon, he approached Magoochagook's pavilion, near where upper Trout Run empties into Tiadaghton. The same bodyguards who had murdered the little band the day before were on duty outside the regal lodge-house. When they saw the stalwart and living form of the warrior they were sure they had killed and scalped, they fell on their knees, trembling with terror. Machatachten advanced through their lines to the door of the king's abode. The old monarch and his son sat within, smoking peacefully after their midday feast. Near them, on a carpet of panther hides, were many bloody scalps—supposedly those of Machatachten and his followers.

As the brave from the land of slain appeared, some impulse caused the royal pair to look up. Both gave agonized shrieks of terror and prostrated themselves on their faces before him, saying: "Oh, thou who art risen from the dead, take pity on us, spare us, for now, we know the Great Spirit favors you."

But Machatachten showed no pity, no quarter. Seizing both abject wretches by their long hair, he cut their throats with a single sweep of his scalping knife. Then he scalped them and pushed the bodies over in a heap. Just as he was tying the two scalps to his belt, he heard a mighty shouting behind him. Turning around, he beheld the populace, led by the late king's bodyguard, come to acclaim him as the new king. The vast throng seemed to be shouting as one man: "Hail Machatachten, Conqueror of Death, favored of the Great Spirit, King of all the tribes east of the Great Lakes and boundless plains, all hail, all reverence to him."

Machatachten smilingly accepted their greetings while an aged wise man handed him a silver crown, indicating his royal authority. The new king ruled long and well, uniting his tribes into a vast confederation, as predicted by the frail spirit of Sabeleua.

X

THE HEALING SPRING
(A Story of Quinn's Run)

LIKE THE famous springs at Bath, England, the curative properties of the famous "Healing Spring," situated near the headwaters of Quinn's Run in Clinton County, were discovered by an early pioneer noticing that cattle that had been bitten by wolves stood in it to heal their lacerated limbs.

Samuel Michael Quinn, ranger, and son of Terence Quinn, the famous Indian fighter of Dry Valley, and grandson of old Corinnus Michael, a veteran of Frederick the Great's wars, with his good friend, Peter Farley, likewise a ranger, were camped for some time at the mouth of the stream now called improperly Queen's Run, engaged in surveying work. As they contemplated a lengthy stay in the wilderness, they brought several head of cattle with them. During their spare moments, they cleared considerable ground near their shanty and set out a tolerable garden and a buckwheat patch. They kept bells on their cows, allowing them to pasture among the mountains. On account of the prevalence of panthers and wolves, the cattle rarely strayed far from the open clearing, which was guarded by hunting dogs.

During the wet periods in September, the equinoctial storms, they sometimes climbed high up on the sides of the mountains, but they could be easily apprehended by the musical tinkling of their bells. One evening they did not return, and the trained dogs scoured the adjacent knobs without locating them. The young rangers became alarmed lest the animals had been stolen by Indians or killed by wild beasts, so they determined to hunt them without further delay. Accompanied by their trusty dogs, they started out on the old Indian trail, which led along the run. Although they encountered no signs of the cattle, they continued clear to the sources of the stream, determined to cover the entire ground and return over the ridges to the camp.

When they came to the forks, Quinn and three dogs followed the westerly branch, while Farley and four dogs took the easterly. Near the heading of the west fork, Quinn's dogs caught a trail that led up on the high tableland, which lies between Quinn's Run and the waters of Lick Run. It was a region noted for its dry ground and good pasture. It was a severe climb even on a September morning, but the intrepid young frontiersman went at it with a will. At the summit, the dogs struck a straight line and went far ahead, tonguing and yelping. In those days, there was a magnificent growth of old-fashioned yellow pines on the high plateau. There was little or no underbrush, consequently an almost unobstructed view over the whole flat.

In the northwest corner of the plateau rises a bold, rocky knob, then heavily timbered with pine, hemlock, and hardwood. There, Quinn finally made out the distant barking of his dogs and the faint tinkle of cowbells. But he decided to follow the path the hounds had torn out through the grass and ferns; it might reveal some lurking bears or panthers he might slay. At last, he arrived at a spot with signs of a struggle. The ferns and indigo bushes were beaten down, and there were great splotches of blood on the leaves. The cattle had evidently made a stand against enemies here and had not been worsted as he could see where they had started away in a northerly direction toward the knob. He followed their tracks for three miles until he entered the dense forest at the foot of the eminence, all the distance seeing bloodstains on fallen logs or leaves.

In the woods, he came upon his three cows, guarded by a yearling bull and the shrewd dogs. Upon second glance, he saw that the cattle stood up to their hocks in soft, mucky clay, and not far from the swale was a spring of water dripping out of the rocks. Upon close examination, he saw that the flanks and chests of the cattle were cut and torn, and their mud-stained legs were also horribly mutilated. The young bull's head and horns were covered with hair and dried blood. Quinn took in the situation at a glance. The cattle had strayed up on the highlands and been attacked by a pack of wolves. The bull had defended them and driven the brutes away. Had the attack occurred in midwinter when the wolves had no roots or berries to eat and were famished with hunger, the result might have been different. Besides, the attacking animals were probably wolf pups, as the older animals never killed cattle in the autumn. But as it was, they had bitten the cattle cruelly, and in their extremity, the poor creatures had sought the muddy swamp to ease their wounds.

The lacerations looked remarkably healthy, considering the depth and number of the bites. Quinn resolved to investigate further and visited the spring, which was the source of the swale. The water had a peculiar look, more like oil than anything else. He bent over and drank some of it; the taste was decidedly oily. The color was unusual; evidently, a reflection from the bottom gave it the hue of freshly drawn blood. Quinn concluded that the water had some medicinal properties, which had attracted the injured cattle. He found that the animals could travel, so he started them along the plateau in the direction of the Susquehanna. He traveled by easy stages, resting where pasture was good; he did not want to crowd the wounded brutes after their unpleasant experience. It was well after dark when he got back to his cabin. Farley, who had gotten back a few minutes earlier, heard his approach by the cowbells and climbed up the hill to meet him.

As quickly as possible, Quinn told the story, to the astonishment of his companion. It must be a healing spring, to be sure, but neither of them, well versed as they were in the nooks and corners and lore of the mountains at the edge of the Black Forest, had ever heard of this spring before. The cattle soon recovered from the wounds, but the cruel scars remained.

That winter, it happened that a friendly Indian named Young James Compass, who was a well-known historical character, spent a night with the young surveyors in their cozy cabin. In the conversation before the blazing beechwood fire, the story of how the cattle had been attacked by wolves was repeated, with Quinn mentioning how the animals had retired to an oily spring on the plateau after their escape from their tormentors.

Compass was much surprised when he heard the story. "Why that's the famous 'Healing Spring,'" he said. Then he told of many cures effected by it on men and beasts. He became so interested in his story that when the coals burned low, he branched off to an ancient legend of the origin of the healing spring, which the very old people told him in his boyhood.

It was in the early days of the Indian world when there were no fixed physical laws, and anything was apt to happen to people through spiritual agencies; nothing was impossible in those days. In the Black Forest, there lived a beautiful Indian maiden named Wulissah, or the Pretty One. She was born of undistinguished parentage but always conducted herself with a charm and grace far above her station. Her kindness of heart was proverbial; she was always ready to help persons in sickness or distress. Her many good qualities, which only served to illuminate her winsome face and figure, attracted the attention of many Indians of a high degree. Yet she bore herself modestly, although among her admirers were several warriors and hunters who stood close to the king. This naturally aroused the jealousy of other Indian girls of obscure birth; they could not understand why the law of caste should be abrogated for Wulissah's benefit and not for them; for the foolish creatures believed themselves equally pretty and intelligent.

Among the heroes who courted this unusual maiden was the stalwart brave, Pegenink or Darkness. This young warrior was of swarthy complexion and powerful frame and was known far and wide as a wrestler and all-around athlete. He possessed a peculiar charm that endeared him to most women with whom he came in contact. When he smiled at a woman, she considered herself highly favored. Maidens of high and low degrees sighed for him, but he was slow in choosing a wife. When he did exhibit a preference, it was for the lovely Wulissah. The girl could hardly believe her senses when this, the most popular Indian youth, desired her company above all other women.

The old king at that time, Nendawagen, or The Torch, had an only daughter named Tiskemanis, or the Little Fisher Bird. She was an undersized girl with prominent features, protruding teeth, and snapping black eyes. Being a princess, she had her share of attention, but she was indifferent to the suitors, for she loved Pegenink. The young hero either was unaware of her passion or did not admire her, as he was utterly indifferent to her existence. This piqued her pride, but she held herself within bounds as long as she saw that the object of her adoration apparently cared for no one else.

One summer evening, she came upon Pegenink and Wulissah walking together along the shores of rippling Mahoning, now called Lick Run. She bit her lips with rage and passed on. When out of range of hearing, she asked her handmaiden, Wisohen, when the popular youth had begun his attentions to Wulissah, daughter of plain parents. The handmaiden replied that rumor had it that the affair had been going on for several moons, that they were apt to marry very shortly. Cat-like, the princess remarked that such a promising youth as Pegenink was foolish to throw himself away on such an obscure girl that surely, he could do better.

That night the slighted one lay awake in her pavilion bemoaning the fate which gave her birth and power but denied her love. Before dawn sent its faint streaks of light into her apartment, she had reasoned out a plan for revenge. She had power, and why not use it to thwart the purposes of those who had made her miserable?

Tiskemanis' handmaiden was almost as ill-favored as her royal mistress, yet she too loved Pegenink. That was why she knew all about his love story with Wulissah, when the princess first noticed the pair together. She yielded very aptly to the princess' questionings, as she saw a chance where she too might be revenged. Wulissah, she learned before long, was meeting her lover every night in a dense wood at the foot of a knob that rose from the high plateau on which the tribe's encampment had been lately removed for the summer months. This news she conveyed to her royal mistress.

The thought of the two together in blissful association, while she had to seek a lonely couch, and toss and fret for sleepless hours, was too much for the jealous princess. She waited the next evening until dark when she approached her father and asked him to summon Pegenink into his presence to discuss a war which was then in contemplation. Old King Nendawagen said he doubted if such a young man as Pegenink could give him the kind of advice he wanted. The young fellow was an athlete, a hunter, who had yet to win his laurels in the bloody conflicts of mankind. But the petted daughter insisted, and when her father yielded, she told him to send for the young man at once. Nendawagen said he was tired and did not want to discuss war that night, but the princess stamped her foot, and the poor old man reluctantly acquiesced.

PRETTY GOOD WORK (Mina, Pa.)

He sent one of his bodyguards to fetch the young brave into his presence. The guard found Pegenink none too soon, as he was already half a mile out of camp on his way to his tryst with Wulissah. While he felt honored that the king should seek his advice, he greatly disliked disappointing his sweetheart. But the royal wish always came first; common mortals could be disappointed.

While the young lover was being brought into the king's presence, the crafty Tiskemanis had dispatched a pair of hired assassins to the tryst at the knob to slay the fair Wulissah. It was difficult to obtain murderers base enough to carry such a scheme into execution, but no one cared to run the risk of refusing to do a service for a royal princess. Nevertheless, even the dregs of the tribe knew the doomed girl's unselfish and virtuous life and hated to put her out of the world. As the wretches tramped across the tableland, they heaved many deep sighs. It was the first time, in fact, that they had ever lent themselves unwillingly to a murder plot. As they neared the knob, they cursed the princess under their breaths. Back at the royal pavilion, Pegenink was brought before the king's august presence.

When the youth entered the pavilion, he found the old monarch seated on his favorite panther rug, with his daughter, Tiskemanis, beside him. Pegenink bowed profoundly to his King and the princess and then stood at attention.

The King turned to the girl and said: "You wanted me to bring this young brave here to talk about war; what shall I ask him?"

The girl flushed as she saw that her scheme had been partly unmasked. She declined to ask any questions yet acted as if she wanted the youth to remain. However, as the king was in an uncommunicative mood, the "interview" quickly terminated. Pegenink prostrated himself again and then backed out of the big lodge-house. Once outside, he broke into a trot; he might still have time to overtake Wulissah at the knob and spend a little time with her blissfully. With his athletic powers, he traveled much faster than the average man and all but overtook the two hired murderers. His pace had been accelerated because he suspected all was not right about that meeting with the king. Tiskemanis' presence seemed mysterious, yet what could be wrong? His heart beat heavily against his breast as he neared the sacred spot where he had passed so many happy hours.

At the edge of the thicket where Wulissah usually concealed herself, he could contain his feelings no longer, calling out, "My loved one, my loved one, are you there?"

No answer came to him, but he fancied that he heard a crackling 6f twigs as if caused by heavy men's feet walking through the forest cover.

He called out again, "Wulissah, loved one, my loved one, why don't you answer?"

Again, there was only silence profound and ominous.

Crazed with anxiety, he sprang into the thicket with a terrific bound, almost stumbling over the prostrate form of Wulissah. He heard her choking as if she was dying; he touched her; she was covered with blood. Though he was a man of iron nerves, he uttered a hoarse cry of horror and indignation. The girl raised her hand and pointed further into the forest depths. Seeking to apprehend the murderers, he plunged forward, but it was impossible to find any hidden objects in the darkness. He returned to his loved one and bent down over her.

"What has happened?" he gasped.

Wulissah raised her head, and after he had kissed life into her trembling lips, she told him how she had waited for his arrival, had become anxious lest harm had come to him, he was always so prompt. At length, she heard footsteps and, walking forward, came face to face with two Indians wearing masks. Before she could cry out, one of them put his heavy hand over her mouth and stabbed her again and again in the breast with his hunting knife. Weak from blood loss, she had stumbled, and the brutes, evidently hearing Pegenink's approach, had suddenly left her. A moment later, her lover had almost tripped over her body.

When she finished speaking, poor Pegenink was sobbing like a child. He could see the whole plot now. He had been summoned to an audience with the king so the murderers might have a chance to kill his sweetheart. But he could not understand the reason.

Wulissah had begun to breathe heavily again; after a few gasps and a half-articulate cry, all seemed over. All at once, she half rose and, trance-like with eyes closed, spoke again, "Pegenink, my love, I have seen it all. Tiskemanis, the king's daughter, loves you. She had you brought into her father's presence, so the murderers whom she hired could have a chance to come out here and kill me. But though you lose me now, in a brief space of time, we will be together for always in Paradise. By my death, I will carry out the good intentions which filled my heart. The Great Spirit tells me that I am to become a *healing spring*. Farewell, my love, farewell."

Wulissah then became rigid and lay dead in her lover's arms. Pegenink then buried her body where she fell and wandered off disconsolate. At dawn, he drew his hunting knife and cut his own throat, lying down to die in the bed of Lick Run. He knew living would be useless; if he refused to court Tiskemanis, she would have him accused of Wulissah's murder. And much as he hated the king's daughter before, he loathed her now for instigating a foul crime.

The murderers of Wulissah reported the next day that they had accomplished their task, but the absence of Pegenink caused the princess some uneasiness. Perhaps she had escaped after all and gone away with the man of her choice. She questioned the wretches critically but could not shake their stories. They insisted that they could show her the body to allay her doubts. Accompanied by them and her handmaiden, Wisohen, she traveled several days later to the scene of the horrid deed. To the surprise of the murderers, no traces of a corpse or any blood was to be found. Where they claimed to have stabbed her, a jet of bubbling water issued from the rocky base of the hill. It was unlike any water they had seen before, for it was thick like oil, and a deposit at its bottom gave it a red, blood-like color.

"That spring was not there when we killed the girl," they declared with emphasis.

"She is dead, but she has been turned into a spring," said one of them, awe-struck.

This man had severely scratched his hand on some brambles while escaping from Pegenink the night of the murder and reached down and bathed the sores in the soft, oily water. Immediately there was a sensation of relief.

"It's a healing spring; a miracle has occurred," exclaimed the wretch.

Tiskemanis' face darkened, and she scowled at the hired assassin, then uttered a piercing cry. "That girl won the love of the only man I ever cared for in life, now, in death, she is a healing spring, and her name will live long after mine is forgotten. Providence has slighted me with my royal blood."

Her eyes assumed a wild look of impotent hate, and she started to run up the steep hill.

Thinking she had become mad and dangerous; the murderers and the handmaiden made no effort to follow her. A month later, her mangled body was found at the bottom of a precipice on Kettle Creek, and her generation soon forgot her. But Wulissah's name lived on through her good deeds and in the healing spring.

XI

A HUNTER'S DAUGHTER

(A Story of Lewis' Run)

THE OLDER generation distinctly remembers how every spring, after the close of the hunting and trapping season, Jim Jacobs, the famous nimrod, and his little family would arrive at their camp near the source of Lewis' Run. They occupied an old hunter's shanty, which stood in the center of an Indian orchard, where a few ancient apple and plum trees still bore luscious fruit. Some gnarled old grape vines grew on one side of the house, spreading over a trellis to the woodshed. Jacobs was very fond of his garden, which he planted with characteristic Indian favorites like beans, turnips, squashes, sweet potatoes, maize, and sunflowers. He also cultivated a few stalks of tobacco and, in a shady corner, pink root and ginseng.

When his day's work was done, he would sit under his shady arbor, smoking his long pipe and enjoying the happiest hours of his life. His good wife would be nearby preparing supper while his beloved little girl, Corydalis, the only child he ever had, played at his feet. He had been married more than sixteen years before the little one was born, and when she came, he poured out on her a world of love and devotion, fully shared by his wife, Zelozella, or The Cricket.

Little Corydalis had been born when her parents were sojourning in New York State on the estate of Samuel Ogden, "the land-grabber." The shrewd Yankee had a daughter named Barbara, who interested herself in the welfare of the Indians who were being driven from their homes on an agreement drawn up while the chiefs were under the influence of liquor, and she took a fancy to Jacobs' infant, asking permission to name her Corydalis, after one of her favorite flowers.

Barbara Ogden retained her interest in the little girl even after she was taken back to Pennsylvania, frequently sending her gifts of various kinds. Among these was a string of gold beads which she always wore around her neck. These beads were the nucleus of a scheme of adornment which soon covered the person of the tiny girl. Beads of every color were secured from all possible sources and strung on her clothing, wound about in her hair; her ears were pierced, and coral pendants were hung. When she was fully decked out, and wearing a red dress, a traveling photographer named William McKeen, the first to go through that section of the country, took her picture. The result was an excellent likeness, far better than could have been made by most of the modern, high-priced "artists." One of the pictures was sent to Miss Ogden, who gave it a place of honor on her dressing table. The old Indians had many copies struck off from the negative, giving them to all persons who seemed the least bit interested.

When the photographer came through the wilderness the following year, he brought his son Rollo with him, a boy of about twelve years; Corydalis, at this time, was past ten. Another picture of the little girl was taken, also one of Jim Jacobs, holding his faithful rifle, which he called Long John. This is the celebrated photograph of the great hunter, the only one he had ever taken. It shows the keen face, the bushy locks, the stubby beard, and the quaint costume. The fact that the Jacobs family had discarded the Indian prejudice against having their pictures taken encouraged other redskins to do likewise, and all the photographer had to do was to show their likenesses to obtain fresh sitters.

Rollo McKeen was an unusually handsome lad, and even at twelve, he felt a sentimental interest in the pretty little Indian girl Corydalis. When his father moved his "studio" over to Red House, the boy remained at the cabin of the Jacobs family. He was there ostensibly to study woodcraft from the old hunter, who used to tramp the rocks and ravines every day, locating wolf dens and the haunts of other game. He also indulged in much fishing with the old hunter, who, Seneca-like, would not touch the trout in Lewis' Run, but traveled to the Allegheny to angle for the sweet river fish. His favorite fishing headquarters was near the mouth of Sugar Creek. In those days, the Allegheny was filled with such fish as the pickerel, chub, dace, suckers, shiners, and trout. Also, the old man and his boy companion frequently dug out woodchucks which added greatly to the summer larder. Little Corydalis often accompanied them on their excursions, and a few times, Jacobs' old-time hunting comrade, Johnny Hotbread, was with them. Later in the summer, they dug ginseng and golden-seal roots and shot many black squirrels.

Rollo and Corydalis, thrown constantly together and both being old for their years, became deeply enamored, and as the time drew near for the boy's father to return to his home in Chatham Valley, Tioga County, for the winter, there were many heartaches. No older lovers *felt* more keenly than these youngsters; it was a real passion of love. Both had a strain of primitive sentiment, which raised their emotion far above the commonplace. It was a clear, moonlight night in the last of September when they took their final stroll together by the path along Lewis' Run. Rollo was planning what they would do when he returned the following summer, and every summer thereafter, until they were old enough to be married, which would be when he was twenty-one, Corydalis acquiescing.

Their favorite walk was to a pigeon roost, where they would sit for hours, listening to the sweet, cooing notes of the birds, which never seemed ready to settle down for the night. On this particular evening, they found the roost deserted; it was as silent as a graveyard. There was not a murmur in the giant beech trees to tell where the amorous tenants had gone.

Corydalis said she would feel as lonely as the beechwood during the months when her lover was away. "And," she added sadly, "perhaps neither the pigeons nor you will ever return."

"Of course, I will," said the boy, with the sublime confidence of early youth.

That night they kissed many times before retiring, and in the foggy yellow light of early morning, they hid behind the woodshed for their last love and embraces.

Ever after that, Rollo hated yellow, foggy mornings—they were symbols of disappointment. He met his father at the high road, and they drove away together, the boy talking about what he would do next summer. School was already in progress at his home village, but in the distraction of his tasks, he could not forget his loving and carefree days in the old forest. He wrote the name of Corydalis many times in his geography and copy books and also cut it on his desk and the windowsill in his bedroom. He wrote to her several times, speaking of love and marriage, receiving a few scrawled words of love in return.

Shortly after the advent of the New Year, news came of the death of one of his father's uncles, who carried on a large printing business in Philadelphia. The old man was a bachelor, and to conserve his affairs, it was decided that the nephew should go there to manage the establishment. In February, the entire McKeen household removed to the City of Brotherly Love. The excitement of moving had much to do with calming Rollo's ardor for the little Indian girl in the distant wilds. The great city, new interests, and new friends, all helped to mark the mental attitude of the impressionable lad, though on the first night in his city home, he had carved his sweetheart's name on the woodwork in his room and even started a letter to her which he never finished, which began, "Dearest Corydalis, I miss you very much." It was not that he was fickle, but the latest is the greatest impression to the very young.

When summer came, no mention was made of visiting the wilds of Lewis' Run; a new life had commenced. The erstwhile photographer prospered in his new business; he was far from being the traveling mountebank that some of his relatives called him. The boy Rollo was bright in his studies and showed a decided tendency toward literary composition. He wrote verses and little hunting stories, which were commended by his teachers. Various family members predicted that he would become an editor, teacher, or lawyer. His good looks made him a prime favorite everywhere, even with his parents, brothers, and sisters. He passed through the common and high schools with distinction and was entered at the University. There he made many friends among students allied with the old Quaker families and visited their homes.

Of all these, his particular chum in his upper-class days was a lad named Victor Morris, who had a beautiful sister named Wistaria. The first time that Rollo met her, he thought how strange it was that the girls he had admired most both had the names of flowers, Corydalis and Wistaria.

Wistaria Morris was about two years his junior or approximately the same age as Corydalis Jacobs. She had pale blue eyes, much the same color as those of the flower for which she was named; her hair was dun, or pale gold color, like the leaves of the Wistaria vine in early May. Her lips, unlike those of Corydalis, were painfully thin. She seemed to like Rollo, although she had many admirers. The country-bred boy was good-looking and clever, yet he realized that there was a financial and social gulf between him and his chum's sister, which caused him to go slowly about declaring his love.

During the last months of his senior year in college, the Morris household received a visit from a maiden aunt who resided in the western part of New York State, a Miss Barbara Ogden. She met Rollo McKeen at dinner one night and seemed much interested when she learned that he had spent some of his youthful days among the Seneca Indians. She said that shortly after she had named her niece Wistaria for her favorite flower, she had given a little Indian girl the name of Corydalis after another much-loved blossom.

Rollo, for some unaccountable reason, felt his heart beat violently. He asked the lady if the little girl's last name was Jacobs; if so, he knew her and her parents well.

She replied that he was correct and, later in the evening, went to her room and brought down a tiny photograph of the little girl, decked out in her gold-bead chain and other finery. On the back of the card was stamped "William McKeen, Photographer."

Rollo admitted frankly that his father had taken it. This established the boy's social status and finally determined Wistaria, who was at heart a believer in caste, in a step she was contemplating taking.

That night Rollo lay awake thinking of his early boyhood, all of which came back to him like a dream. He was now two months past his twenty-first birthday when he had promised to come for Corydalis and make her his wife. He wondered where she was and if she remembered him after all these years; he chided himself for not having written her. But in the foreground of his heart, he saw the fair, elegant image of Wistaria, whom he planned would be his wife someday.

SHACK DWELLERS

Three days before Rollo's graduation, at which he was valedictorian, Wistaria announced her betrothal to one Horace Rambo, a young man of excellent connections, and it took all of the joy out of the exercises at which he hoped to shine to impress her with his worthiness. The marriage was not to take place until the following winter, and the disappointed boy imagined he might win her away by that time. He entered a law office and began his preparations for the bar. He saw Wistaria occasionally, but the chance never came for him to charm her or declare himself. She was married with considerable pump, the ceremony completely crushing out Rollo's interest in his law studies. He endured his lacerated feelings until summer when he felt that he must change his environment, or his heart would break.

Often, but only at night, he could see the childish image of Corydalis; would it not be interesting to enjoy an outing in the backwoods and perhaps meet the sweetheart of his youth again? Though he would not admit it, his heart had been ever true to his first love; his conscience pricked him for breaking his promise to her; it was only his pride, his hope of material advancement that was piqued by his ill-starred attachment for Wistaria. He told his parents of his projected trip; they were glad to have him go anywhere that might improve his spirits; he was suffering from overwork, in their opinion. The railroad connections to the Lewis' Run country were better than formerly; otherwise, the region was much the same as when he was last there ten years before. Lumbering was still being carried on, only sparingly, consequently most of the grand old forests were standing; game was abundant, there were even a few wolves, and the streams still teemed with fish.

He met Johnny Hotbread before he had tramped far up the creek. The old fellow was more wrinkled, his hair was snow white, but Rollo recognized him. The Indian said he was living alone in the shanty formerly occupied by Jim Jacobs.

"Where's Jim and his family?" inquired Rollo impatiently on hearing this.

The aged tribesman told him that the Jacobs family had moved away three years previously, that the intrepid old huntsman had learned of some bear caves on Freeman's Run in the very heart of the Black Forest, that he had gone there one spring with his family and never came back. He supposed that they were doing well. As for Corydalis, she was a big, fine-looking girl when she went away.

Though Rollo was a trifle disappointed at not finding his friends as easily as expected, he was not discouraged. He would enjoy the tramp to the Black Forest and invited Hotbread to accompany him as a guide. The old Indian was glad to accept, as he was always ready to make a little money. Before leaving, the sentimental youth strolled to the old pigeon roost; there were no signs of any birds, and most of the big beech trees had been cut down for firewood. It was a desolate-looking spot.

The walk over the mountains, which took nearly a week, was ideal from every point of view. The weather was warm, but they traveled along shady roads and trails almost the entire distance. The rhododendron and the laurel were in bloom, as well as other mid-summer flowers. At nightfall, they usually camped in the woods, the old guide catching a few trout for supper, which he cooked deliciously. On several occasions, their dogs' barking evoked answers wolfish from the mountaintops. When they came to the waters of Freeman's Run, they encountered a couple of timber cruisers who told them that Jim Jacobs' cabin was at the headwaters, which meant that there still were five miles between them and the shanty. The lumbermen said that the old man had been away from his cabin very little of late as he was very solicitous about his invalid daughter.

Rollo's face grew hard when he heard this, and he inquired about the cause of her illness.

"It's lung trouble," replied one of the cruisers, "the poor girl has been going downhill for the past year. It doesn't look as if she could last much longer."

Rollo knew that tuberculosis was the scourge of the Pennsylvania mountain people, especially those with Indian blood, and tears stood out in his blue eyes. He brought his talk with the cruisers to a close and hurried along the run in the direction of the cabin of the aged hunter. When he saw it, he could see that it was characteristic of the man who lived in it. In front of the door was a tiny yard planted with old-fashioned flowers. On nails on either side of the door hung many rusty bear traps to be used in the late fall when bruin's coat was in good condition. A wildcat skin hung above the door, fur inward, a huge set of elk horns was nailed above one of the windows, and a red-tailed hawk above the other.

As the door was open, Rollo and Hotbread entered, finding old Jacobs, unchanged in appearance, seated within, mending a pigeon net. He seemed delighted to see his old friends; he had no trouble remembering the boyish friend of other days, now a full-fledged man with a fine, brown mustache. Rollo asked eagerly after Mammy Jacobs and Corydalis.

At the mention of his wife's name, the old hunter smiled, saying, "she's very well," but he looked sad when Corydalis was spoken of. "I am sorry to tell you she's very poorly."

The young man asked to see her, so Jacobs led the way through the cabin, out to a covered back porch, the pillars overgrown with morning glories, where the fair girl lay on a couch. Rollo almost dropped fainting when he saw her. What a change time had wrought in *her!* Though she was barely twenty years old, her emaciated, skull-like, ashen face might have belonged to a woman of seventy. Her intensely black hair was drawn tightly back from her forehead and temples; her great, black eyes literally popped out from the ghastly sockets. Her long, emaciated hands lay limp on the crazy quilt cover, like the hands of a corpse. Under the right hand was half revealed a scrap of paper, yellow with age. Around the girl's neck was the familiar string of gold beads, given to her by the wealthy Barbara Ogden long years before. Yet something of her old charm remained, despite her changed estate.

To Rollo's surprise, the invalid recognized him instantly, uttering a half-suppressed cry of joy. Mother Jacobs, who had been in the back kitchen, heard her and came rushing in. She, too, remembered the young visitor and gave way to hysterical laughter. Then she took Rollo by the hand, exclaiming, "now Corydalis will get well."

Then she said, "the poor girl began to pine away over a year ago when you did not come to keep your promise to her."

The youth was speechless for a moment; then, he spoke out.

"I *thought* she had forgotten. I never dreamed she would remember me."

Then came a voice from the couch, "But you did not forget me, did you, Rollo?"

"No, I did not," he retorted with truth; there was never a day but what I thought of you."

"But why did you not come then or write a line," said Mother Jacobs, her excitement getting the better of discretion.

"I am very sorry," said the youth, "but many, many reasons detained me. I was getting an education; I was working hard—I meant no harm."

"I forgive you, my dear friend," said Corydalis, with her hoarse voice. "You have come, and folks say it's always better late than never."

Then she began to cough. When the paroxysm was over, she held up the piece of yellow paper. "See," she said, "that is the last letter you wrote to me—it is dated more than seven years ago. In it, you repeated your promise to come back and marry me when you were twenty-one. I never lost hope, but my loneliness made me what I am today."

Then she coughed pitifully, and her head dropped; she was exhausted. Whether her dying condition was wholly due to his failure to keep his word or came from a taint in the blood did not matter to Rollo now. He saw his duty and would perform it, regardless of the future or what his family thought.

"Dearest Corydalis," he said, stooping down and kissing her quivering lips, "I was detained by various circumstances, which I will never cease to regret, but I have come to marry you and make up for the past. I love you with all my heart."

The girl smiled faintly, and patches of hectic color rose in her drawn cheeks. "I love you, too," she said firmly.

The young man turned to Mother Jacobs, inquiring where the nearest preacher was to be found. She informed him that there was a circuit rider who came as far as the other side of the divide at Roulette and, the next day being Sunday, would find him there.

As she spoke, old Jacobs edged close to the boy, laying his hand affectionately on his shoulder. "My son," he said, "you have saved our girl's life. She was pining away for you. I admire you for your honor. No Seneca could have done more."

"Why did you not write me in all these years? That would have kept the date of my coming fresh in mind," said Rollo, whose presence of mind had returned sufficiently to want to put in a defense.

"Because," broke in Mother Jacobs, "none of us wrote very well, except Corydalis, and she kept saying that if you cared to come, you would be here without a letter to bring you."

Then Rollo said he would start across the mountain immediately and return with the preacher the next evening. After dark, the young man, accompanied by the faithful Hotbread, reached the quaint little town among the hills. They put up for the night with an old man who burned tar and whose cabin and fragrant smelting pits were located across the road from the little Disciple Church. The next afternoon, before the bearded circuit rider could dismount from his horse, Rollo had approached him and gained his consent to go to Freeman's Run and perform the ceremony. The young man attended Sunday school and "preaching," which was purposely shortened, and then the Indian, the bridegroom-to-be, and the clergyman started across the high mountain. The sunset was no more when they got to Jim Jacobs' cabin, where they found the old man waiting outside to bring the news to Corydalis the minute he saw the party approaching.

He hastened to the back porch when he espied them, and the girl's face lighted up with loving expectancy. Candles were brought in, and Rollo took his fiancée's cold hand and was united to her in marriage. That night was the happiest for many years in the poor sufferer's life; she fell asleep with a smile on her lips.

Half past one in the morning, Mother Jacobs, who slept with Corydalis, came running into the house to say that the poor girl was choking to death. Rollo, carrying a candle, was the first to reach her side. Placing the light, the flame of which the night wind threatened to extinguish, on a chair, he fell on his knees beside her. She placed her arms around his neck while she raised herself up in an effort to articulate. With a final effort, she spoke in a normal tone: "Oh, Rollo, my darling, I am so happy. I will never grieve again."

Then she sank back, breathed heavily three or four times, her hands and feet grew cold, and she expired. Rollo accompanied her body across the mountain, where it was laid to rest in the tiny churchyard in Roulette. When he gazed at her for the last time on the brink of the grave, the look of emaciation had vanished, and the smile was sweeter than ever, just like it was in the happy, carefree days on Lewis' Run. Much had been added to his human experience by the time the young man returned to Philadelphia. But for the rest of his life, which was many years, he was true to the spirit of Corydalis.

XII

THE MOMENT THE LIGHTS WERE LIT

(A Romance of the Mountains)

HUBERT LE GRAND, representing Isabella II, Queen of Spain, was on his way to the Tangascootac region to report on the value and management of the august ruler's vast properties, which included thousands of acres of timber and coal lands in the vicinity of the Susquehanna, and extending to the north into the Black Forest. It was a novel experience for this young man of twenty-four, who had been born in Madrid to French parents. Incidentally, he was riding on one of the first trains to run through from Harrisburg to Farrandsville, the Sunbury and Erie Railway having been only recently completed on to Rattlesnake, now Wetham, from its former terminus at Lock Haven.

When the train, with its wood-burner engine and bulbous smoke-stack, left the imposing depot at Harrisburg amid much puffing of black smoke, a scene of rare beauty spread out before the travelers. It is a beautiful ride today, but it was more so half a century ago before the ruthless hand of man had desolated the forests and ripped off whole sides of the majestic mountains for his stone-crushers.

It was about three o'clock, in the full glory of the afternoon, when the train emerged from the shed. In the distance loomed the dark line of the First Mountain, deeply indented at the "Narrows" as if to let the river and the railway through. As the train neared Dauphin, a mountain of majestic grandeur rose sheer up from the tracks. Tiny log cabins nestled among the pine forests on its sides. The old canal boats, drawn by drowsy horses, decked out with bells and plumes, drifted along on the side of the tracks nearest the river; the drivers cracked their blacksnake whips, and the heavy boats left a long trail of shadow in the clear water. Beyond was the on-rushing and imposing tide of the wide Susquehanna, dotted with shady islands. Over its expanses, water birds were flying.

Every few miles, it seemed that clear, sparkling brooks, Paxton, Fishing, Stony, Clark's, Powell's, and Armstrong's Creeks, ran out from the narrow valleys between the mountain ranges, inviting leisurely exploration, and all kinds of speculation as to the wild regions where they rose. The chin-bearded conductor, a pompous individual in a broad-cloth suit, a white rose in his buttonhole, and a silk hat, pulled the bell rope with his kid-gloved hand when the train drew into such quaint little settlements as Fort Hunter, Shupps, Speeceville, Green's Dam, and Fort Halifax,

The young Frenchman was so absorbed by these wild and unusual scenes that it was not until after the conductor had called out a name in his own language, "Dauphin, Dauphin, Dauphin," that he adjusted himself to his surroundings sufficiently to begin to study his fellow travelers. And a most interesting lot they were, different from any he had seen in his life. Many were lumbermen, sturdy, black-bearded fellows who had removed their coats to find relief from the August heat and sat in their red shirts, silent and impassive.

There were numerous women and children of the brunette type, except that a few of them had fine blue eyes, which set off in bolder relief the intense blackness of their hair. They represented a type evolved by hardships and frontier life, which a generation or two softened into brown and fair-haired beings with easier conditions of existence.

On the sunny side of the coach, the side nearest the river, the Frenchman noticed one person, a young girl, whose hair was comparatively light. It was noticeable partly because the other passengers were so dark, partly because the deep rays of the afternoon sun gilded the fair, naturally wavy locks into the color of molten metal. The girl wore a small "cherry-box" hat, and her heavy "waterfall" locks were kept in place by a net. She wore a lace fascinator over her black silk dress. She had lovely shoulders, and her graceful neck was ornamented by a heavy string of red coral beads.

Though she seemed "better class" than the other travelers, and her fairness was a relief after so many dark tresses, she sat in a position where the young man could barely observe her features. He gazed at her many times, but the frequent stopping of the train, and the rugged landscape outside, diverted him from a too continual scrutiny. He wondered who she might be and where she was going that glorious afternoon when the breezes stirred the leaves and corn and rippled the waters of river, canal, and creeks so wonderfully.

The sight of this fair creature made the time pass even more quickly than it would have otherwise. Millersburg was called out in stentorian tones, and the train halted at the curious little station. It appeared as if the entire population had assembled there to greet the arrival of the afternoon train just as they do today. In appearance, these villagers were much the same as Hubert's fellow travelers; they were extremely handsome, yet so different from any people he had ever seen before! Most of the occupants of the coach were getting out at this stop. They filed up the aisle to the front door of the car, smiling and chatting, their seriousness while the train was in motion having quickly vanished.

Among the first to get out was the charming light-haired girl with the cherry-box hat and the heavy red corals. Hubert looked out of the window; to his surprise and infinite pleasure, the fair creature stood before him on the platform. He saw her full face. She was the most beautiful human being he had ever looked at. He made no mental reservations, he who had seen beautiful women in half the capitals of Europe. She looked to be about nineteen or twenty years of age, an ash-blonde, of more than medium height. She was slender, with a complexion rather pale. There was a universe of love in those deep-set, drooping, almond-shaped eyes. Her lips were full, the corners of the mouth descending, and in an expression of expectancy, she showed a little of her teeth, which were white but strangely set very far apart. She had rolled back her gloves, showing hands exquisitely white, with long, tapering fingers.

She was carrying a small, black satchel; either she was going on or coming from a visit. Yet there seemed to be no one on the platform with whom she was acquainted. The young traveler was instantly deeply in love. He should have gotten off the train. But it had started amid much puffing and bellringing as their eyes met; really, he had never seen such grey eyes as hers, with such fine, black lashes and brows. But they were not open wide enough to reveal their whole story.

When the train stopped again at Liverpool, he had a strong impulse to get out. Instead, he gazed up at the unscalable height of Mahantongo Mountain, with gaunt pine trees shivering in the wind on its crest, the queer old well at its foot, the broad river, with the town on the far shore with its big brick warehouse, the massive-looking Susquehanna House, and the iron foundry looming above the other buildings and the soft, green hills beyond.

He allowed the train to start with him still on it. The same impulse seized him at Dalmatia, Herndon, Selin's Grove Junction. But he remained on board, suffering more intently. He could stand it no longer when, at sunset, the train pulled into another great terminus, Sunbury. There he left the train abruptly, fortunately finding that another train for the east was starting in a few minutes.

The eastbound journey seemed longer than the entire trip from New York to Sunbury had been. He chafed and fretted at the slowness in reaching the stations; he barely noticed the ball of the red setting sun poised on the very horizon and spreading its fiery effulgence over the entire broad river. Darkness, sweet, cool, summer darkness had settled down; the crickets' chorus wafted through the open car windows. The conductor, equally as self-important as the one on the westbound train had been, called out for the stop at Millersburg. There were still a goodly number of people at the station, which was illuminated by tallow candles set in glass lantern boxes; Hubert scanned their dark faces eagerly; they were not like his fair beloved. Where would he find her? Who would he ask about her? The faces he saw about him seemed to grow unsympathetic and distant, even in the candlelight.

He watched the red lights on the rear of the train as it disappeared into the darkness. A feeling of loneliness and desolation overcame him; it was the first time he had felt it in America. There was still light in the station. Through an open window, it poured out on the platform; there was the musical clicking of the telegraph keys. Inside the window sat a young man with black hair and eyes and black side whiskers; he seemed genial and approachable; whom else could he question? He addressed the operator in broken English, being answered by the youth in phrases equally unfinished.

The French boy inquired of the telegrapher if he spoke German, to which he replied that he could only speak the German of Pennsylvania. So, they both conversed in broken English. Hubert asked if the operator had seen a young girl, whom he described minutely, getting off the train from Harrisburg that afternoon. The railroader smiled; his sympathetic interest was aroused, but he said he had noticed no such person. Nor did he recollect any girl in the town or vicinity who answered the description.

"Come to the depot at train time for two or three days; you will find her if she lives here," was his advice.

The Frenchman could wait a day or two, and the advice sounded good. The young operator directed him to an old inn facing the public square; it was on the hill some distance back from the station. The town had a foreign look, especially the open square, much like some old city in Provence or Spain. The young lover dreamed of the fair vision all that night, but his sleep refreshed him.

Bright and early, he was at the station the next morning; he saw the incoming of all the trains that day. The customary throngs were on hand, but he saw no one remotely resembling his beloved. Between trains, he walked down to the banks of the swift-flowing Wiconisco, which rushed along so pure and rippling from its source at the head of the valley, from a line of mountains that resembled a landscape in Savoy. He daydreamed and meditated under an aged buttonwood tree by the stream until he heard the whistle of the trains, every time suffering most keenly from disappointment. He remained a second night in the old town; if she did not appear at the station by the time of the arrival of the next afternoon train from the east, he would board it and proceed on his way.

From subsequent talks with the black-whiskered agent, he concluded that the girl could not live in town. If she was visiting there, it was strange that she did not frequent the station like everybody else to see the trains come in. "Even the High Zekes," as the operator called the local aristocracy of Scotch-Irish landowners, rarely missed the arrival of the trains.

Hubert, with many feelings of sadness, boarded the afternoon train for the west the following day. He left his name and address with the operator, who promised to write him in case such a girl as he described appeared at the station later on. He traveled on up the fair valley, the scenery impressing him as much as ever but tinged with an overpowering sadness. It became somewhat dark shortly after the train left Sunbury; he could barely make out the gorgeous "meeting of the waters," where the North and West Branches of the Susquehanna unite their destinies at Northumberland. His traveling companions became stupid and sleepy; his consciousness, suffering from a heart sore, was keenly awake; how differently he felt from everyone else in the coach. He had never felt his consciousness so acute; he had never been so unhappy.

At Lock Haven, the local agent of his royal employer met him on the train. It was a fortuitous break in the single line of thought. The agent, John Sommerville by name, a big, jovial Scotchman, had much to tell about the itinerary mapped out for the young man's sojourn and began explaining away some of the unsatisfactory results of the past operations of the property. The time passed speedily until Farrandsville was reached, where the Scotchman and the French lad left the train. They would spend the night at some sleeping apartments fitted up in the offices of the estate near the railway station and, in the morning, drive to the agent's home on 'Scootac Run.

An early start was made in a handsome landau, drawn by two powerful, black horses, driven by a liveried coachman, Hartshorne Patterson, which met the party on the opposite bank of the river after they had crossed it in a rowboat. The road led through a primeval forest of white pine, hemlock, beech, birch, and maple; there were rhododendron trees forty feet high, which still retained a few late, waxy-like blossoms. They crossed and re-crossed the run, which foamed, eddied, and raced over the rocky bed. It was filled with trout and other game fish, the Scotchman said. He dilated on the plentitude of the game; there had been elks or Pennsylvania stags in the forest until a few years previous, now they had been driven further north; there were still panthers, brown bears, black bears, wild cats, perhaps a wolf or two, many foxes and countless deer. Every hundred yards or so, ruffed grouse flew up beside the road or quail trotted in front of the horses' feet. Songs of rare warblers echoed from among the giant trees. It was, indeed, a rare treat to see nature in her habiliment before it was torn away by man's rapacity.

The Frenchman wondered why he met no wagons hauling ore, coal, or lumber and, at last, inquired of the superintendent. The war had caused a drop in prices; it did not pay to ship anything at present, was the reply. At noon, they emerged into a vast clearing. On a treeless knoll, which rose near the brook, stood the spacious residence of the agent. It was built in the latest French style of architecture, with a Mansard roof and tall windows.

The entrance, which was imposing, led into a large hall, on one side of which was an open fireplace with an imported marble mantel. Tall mirrors in gilt frames were between the windows; the walnut furniture was upholstered in silk and plush. Several oil paintings hung on the walls. In the tremendous clearing, which stretched as far as the timberline on the tops of the ridges on all sides of the mansion, were piles of earth, ore, and coal, showing the locations of the mines. Great skidways of pine logs were stacked along the roads; stumps, lops, and tops were everywhere. There were many dilapidated workmen's shanties, most of which looked to be uninhabited.

A butler had opened the carriage door and carried the young Frenchman's luggage into the house. There was an imposing staircase with walnut banisters and a red carpet, up which the youthful visitor was led to his room. It was a vast apartment with a mahogany four-poster bed in the center. There was very little furniture besides, only what was absolutely necessary. On the walls hung framed engravings of Queen Isabella and her mother, Christina. The butler deposited the baggage on the floor and threw open the shutters of one of the big windows. It offered a superb panorama of endless ranges of mountains, culminating in the knob-like head of Mount Pipsisseway.

But there was a loneliness to everything which the young Frenchman, globe-trotter that he was, could not understand. He longed to get away; he feared that he could not summon enough interest to make his mission a success. Accompanied by the Scotch superintendent and several of his factotums, visits were made to the mines, ore banks, and logging camps. There was plenty of available material, but it looked to be going to waste. Yet the heavy operating expenses still ran on.

After a couple of days on the 'Scootac, a trip to other parts of the domain was proposed. This time they were to visit the famous Black Forest, where the highest-grade timber stood. When they came to the railway, a train was readying to start for the east. Hubert could scarcely restrain himself from climbing on board, abandoning everything for his will o' the wisp love. He traveled up Lick Run with his associates, passing many lumbering operations. Rafts were being built for the fall floods, and logs were piled on the banks to be rolled in at high water. But these activities, it was explained to him, were on other people's lands. The royal forests were located on both sides of the Coudersport Pike, leading over to the waters of Salmon Creek.

Fine as was the timber on Tangascootac, it was exceeded in every way by what the young Frenchman saw in the Black Forest. The hemlocks and pines grew to the height of nearly two hundred feet, bare of limbs to a height of over a hundred feet, straight as gun-barrels, and as thick together to use the woodsmen's expression "as hair on a dog's back."

The night was spent at a hunter's cabin in the primitive little village of Haneyville, where Hubert suffered more than ever from the pangs of heart-hungriness. About midnight, he woke up to hear some pitiful cries, like a woman in distress, in the dense wood across the road from the house. It sounded like his own heart giving vent to its misery. He endured it as long as he could. Then he dressed, went downstairs, and woke a teamster who slept in a bunk in the kitchen. The fellow, who was a Swiss-German, growled when the youth shook him, eventually sitting up.

He listened to the plaintive cries for a minute or two; then he laid down grumbling about it only being "that damned hellgrammite of bender." Hubert divined that the sound came from some animal, so he returned to his room rather sheepishly. In the morning, he mentioned the subject at breakfast.

"It might have been a panther," said an old timber skidder who sat opposite him at the table, "only it's the rarest thing when they utter a sound this early in the year."

Several days were spent in the Black Forest, and then the young man said he would have to go to Harrisburg for a few days before beginning his actual work at the properties. His spirit was compelling him to renew his search for the illusive beauty he had seen at Millersburg. He went as far as the capital, then turned about and remained two days at Millersburg without adding to his hopes.

Returning to the 'Scootac, he remained until shortly before Christmas, preparing a report and reorganizing the system of management, working as hard as he knew how. But he did not forget a trip to Harrisburg, which he took soon after this time, and another stay at Millersburg only deepened his anguish. He returned to the wilds only to make similar trips east in January, February, and March. In his stolid way, the Scotch superintendent chided the lad for having a girl somewhere; otherwise, he could not grasp why he would want to take so many tedious car rides.

In April, he decided to visit Philadelphia, feeling that a big city might ease the burden of his heart for a few days. But he felt lonelier there than ever, although he was in the center of the gay life at the Girard House. It was toward the middle of April when he boarded the morning train at the main station of the Pennsylvania Railroad, bound again for the wilderness.

The winter had been long and hard, but a few signs of returning spring were apparent east of Harrisburg. Jonquils, or as they are called in the interior, "Easter flowers," were trying to unfold their yellow heads in garden corners and old graveyards, dandelions were out in profusion, and the sunshine was expanding the buds of the magnolias. Spice bushes were a gleam of gold; the brown hillsides were dotted with snow-like patches of Juneberry and wild cherry blossoms. The leafless woods had carpets of bottle-green skunk cabbage laid for them. When the car windows were opened, a sweet odor of grass wafted in, the snatch of a robin's or a flicker's song, or the metallic notes of the *hylodes* in the bogs. Yet it was an uneventful journey, at least as far as Harrisburg.

After leaving there, the young man's heart bounded with joy; he was on sacred ground. He wondered where his fair one could be, eight months had passed since he had seen her, and their eyes had met! Like a wall between him and his heart's desire, the First Mountain loomed before him; as the train moved through it, in the Narrows, he realized that even barriers like that could be passed. There was an old family burying ground near the shore of Paxton Creek with the graves of the slaves more humbly marked outside the pale. They were shaded by mammoth chestnut trees. This had impressed him every time he passed it; it seemed ever the same as his own inscrutable fate.

The afternoon was becoming more golden and clearer cut as Stony, Clark's, Powell's, Armstrong's, and Wiconisco Creeks wore passed. His

MODERN LOGGING SCENE

heart beat fast when the last was crossed over. He could see the old buttonwood tree under which he had often sat, waiting for the trains to
whistle.

The usual stop was made at quaint old Millersburg; he could see the
swarthy agent on the platform putting on the mailbag, the merry throng
greeting or God-speeding their friends. Then Liverpool hove in sight
with its great body of dead water, which the natives called the "Irish Sea,"
and the little town on the distant shore, and just beyond the western
slopes of mighty Mahantango Mountain, the curious little village of the
same name. Then the beautiful oak shaded Mahantango Creek came into
view, with Halcyons darting over the smooth waters, symbols of peace
and the golden hour. On one side were the sun-kissed mountains, the
other side the broad, brave river frowning anon for lack of similar favors.
Great grey clouds banked themselves against the sun, even shutting it off
from the favored summits.

A few red rays of sunset, then all was over as far as the day was concerned. Dusk set in quickly, for the newly born spring day was tiring.
Mahanoy Creek, deep, sullen, and intense, was crossed; a wild swan was
flying down it, and a pall was settling like a coming storm. Cattle moved
uneasily toward the overshoots of the big red barns. The wind swayed the
streamers of a precocious-leafed weeping willow near an old log house.

The portly, immaculately attired conductor rose in his seat and
languidly pulled the signal cord with his gloved hand. "Fisher's Ferry,"
he called out once, scorning to repeat the name because of its lack of
importance as a station stop. It had become quite dark. Just as the train
slowed, Hubert Le Grand looked out of the car window. The lights were
being lit in a dignified old stone house, which stood on the riverbank.
There was a flash and a gleam of warm,

yellow light; several faces stood clearly revealed by it. A young girl
with clear-cut features, ash blonde, broad-faced, slender, beautiful, was
gazing out of a rear window, which opened upon the blowy, night-swept
river. Wonder of wonders! Jumping from his seat, Hubert Le Grand
pressed his face against the sash. It was the girl he had seen and loved the
year before who had left the train at Millersburg. Gathering his overcoat,
stick and portmanteau, he lost no time leaving the train at Fisher's Ferry.

XIII

HUGH MITCHELTREE

(A Story of the Genesee Fork)

WHEN HUGH Mitcheltree, cursing and yelling, was carried off by six Indians in full view and range of the terrified garrison of Pomfret Castle, a fort built for defense against the savages on the headwaters of Upper Mahantango Creek in what is now Snyder County, it was generally supposed that he was taken to some secluded grove to be scalped and tortured to death, much as crows fly with a chicken to a mountain top where they can pick it to pieces unmolested. But far from such being the case, he was not killed at all.

This stalwart, red-headed Irishman had left the fort one evening and crossed the little creek which flowed beside it to fodder his cattle which he kept in a log stockade on the opposite bank; back of the cattle pen was the forest, which also extended to the rear of the fort. While he was feeding the animals, the Indians were crouching at the edge of the woods. As he emerged from the enclosure, they rushed forward from both sides, closing in on their victim and picking him up on their powerful shoulders as though he were a sack of flour. Mitcheltree called loudly for assistance, as but fifteen minutes earlier, he had left ten sturdy frontiersmen armed with rifles in the fort. The men appeared at the gun holes but were apparently too panic-stricken to shoot. The captive added curses to his repertoire of yells, but nothing could flinch the warriors in their purpose of carrying him away.

After the captors had vanished from sight in the dense timber at the rear of the fort, the valiant defenders came out, looking around wildly, and brandishing their firearms. They loosed their dogs, which took up the trail, but this accomplished no purpose, as the frontiersmen refused to follow them. The winter night soon closed in on the scene, and the garrison of Pomfret Castle huddled about their blazing fire, apparently more anxious to keep warm than to rescue their fellow guardsman. As no commissioned officers were present at this deplorable piece of cowardice, this true story might never have been known had not several of the men revealed it themselves when they became very old and childish, long years afterward.

Hugh Mitcheltree belonged to a numerous family who had arrived in central Pennsylvania from Donegal in Ireland about 1740. At the time of Hugh's disappearance in 1756, he was in his twenty-first year. His father, known as "old Patt" was dead, but his mother, Catherine, who was an unusually forceful woman, his brother, "young Patt," and other brothers and sisters afterward raised quite an outcry over the Indians' audacity. But even they did not know that he had been carried off without a single shot having been passed in his defense.

To avenge his probable death, the Mitcheltree boys, seven in number, became an unofficial band of Indian fighters, shooting down any Indians whom they encountered during their wanderings in the forests. "Young Patt" Mitcheltree was considered one of the most expert riflemen of his generation and was feared by the savages. In appearance, he was different from the lamented Hugh, being small and dark, with piercing steel grey eyes. He was said to resemble his mother's family, the McGuigans. Young Patt catechized the garrison, but they declared they did not know the identity of a single Indian concerned in the dastardly act. They knew who most of the "bad" Indians were who frequented the Shade, Jack's, and Firestone Mountains and had names for them, but Hugh's kidnappers could be none of these. They described them as six very tall, very dark-complexioned warriors dressed differently from any Indians they had ever seen. They seemed to have no guns but carried scalping knives in their belts. It was all over so quickly, and the hour was so late that their shots went wide; they solemnly averred.

Old Mother Mitcheltree became possessed with the idea of finding her boy; she could talk, think, or dream of nothing else. She believed that he was being held for ransom, but until her death, when she was over eighty-six years of age, no news, direct or indirect, had come in. She liked to talk to an old German witch-doctress, Granny Seebold, who lived on the Susquehanna near New Buffalo and always reassured her that her boy was alive and well. But in time, the rest of the family, including young Patt, concluded that Hugh had been done away with. His disappearance formed an absorbing topic of conversation as time went on, and it began to take its place in history.

When children wanted to go out after dark, their parents frightened them by saying they would be carried off by Indians "like Hughey Mitcheltree." In that way, the captive's name became a household word; he became more famous than if he had served his time in the rangers for the defense of the colony and then retired to a hum-drum life on some remote hill-top farm.

As to the actual fate of Mitcheltree, it is preserved by the Seneca Indians, whose ancestors carried him away, and by a few of the old settlers in the Black Forest, who heard it from their parents and grandparents. The actual story began over a year before the young man was kidnapped. At that time, he was living on his mother's farm, which was close to the west bank of the Susquehanna, at the present village of McKee's Half Falls. The Mitcheltree homestead, a commodious log structure, stood on the left side of the old stone tavern, famous in later days when run by "Jumbo" Karstetter for its chicken and waffle suppers.

On the trail which followed along the river, emigrants, soldiers, travelers, packers, and Indians were constantly passing. Many delegations of distinguished natives were among the numbers on their way to or from visits to the provincial authorities at Philadelphia or Harris's Ferry. They were mostly protestants against the usurpation of their lands by the settlers, and generally, their attitude eastward bound at least was decidedly belligerent. In many cases, they were flattered and bribed by the Indian agents and Quakers in power, so they assumed a milder air when working their way homeward. Sometimes they traveled in canoes or bateaus, but many made the long journeys on foot.

There was a great elm tree, bigger than the historic one at Shackamaxon, which grew over an eddy, famous for its shad fishery, across the trail from the Mitcheltree abode. Some even said that the family name had been originally

Mitchel, but the Indians and others had referred to stopping so often under the "Mitchel tree" that the compound name had resulted. At any rate, the huge, wide-spreading elm was a favorite resting place for the traveling Indians during the mid-day heat. They often slept there from about ten o'clock in the morning until sunset and resumed their journeys in the cool of the evening.

The Mitcheltree family were always on friendly terms with the tribesmen, especially big burly Hugh; this impressive-looking youth had a shock of stiff red hair, pale blue eyes, a big nose, full lips, and a freckled face. He was as strong as an ox; even in his teens, he weighed two hundred pounds, filling out his frame very well, for he stood over six feet tall. All the Indians liked him, and his name was passed on among them as a particularly fair-minded and honorable man.

Among the Indian embassies which passed down the trail was one headed by a skillful Seneca diplomat named New Arrow; in later years, he was famed for his polished addresses to Presidents Washington and Jefferson. He was an intimate friend of the mighty chieftains, Cornplant and Red Jacket; with a dozen almost equally illustrious of his tribesmen, such as Young King, Little Billy, Seneca White, Tall Peter, and Henry Two Guns, he visited Philadelphia to protest against some atrocities committed against his people by the settlers. The wives and sisters of some of the Indians accompanied them. They were men and women, all magnificently attired, wearing feathers, beads, gold nose and earrings, and varicolored blankets.

One day they stopped for their siesta under the Mitchel Tree. In the party was New Arrow's beautiful sister, Princess Sasapah, or The Firefly. At this time, she was a girl of about eighteen, rather slim and under medium size. But she was graceful and sprightly and possessed a beautiful pair of black eyes and an expressive countenance. She was always tastefully dressed and wore red bird wings in her hair. She was what might be called a "wideawake," for while the other Indians were sleeping, she was looking about her. She noticed the big red-headed Irish boy and fell violently in love with him. In every way possible, she made glances and sought to form his acquaintance, but he was as shy as a faun and could not be captivated.

The princess was piqued and heartbroken but said nothing to her party, with whom she resumed the easterly tramp at sundown. But she thought of naught else but the huge "strawberry blonde" during the entire sojourn in Philadelphia, which lasted several months.

It was fall when they started homeward, having been mollified by gifts and promises, as well as liberal entertainment. New Arrow and Young King, the two wisest of the party, secretly felt that they had been hoodwinked, as after they left the Quaker City, they "took stock" and found little else but glittering generalities in their packs. Some of the Indians and their women had acquired a taste for liquors and marched along in maudlin fashion, not knowing or caring whether or not their mission had been successful. The only actually happy and hopeful person in the whole aggregation was the sprightly Sasapah. As she neared the Mitchel Tree, she began humming an old Seneca love song.

The Indians, with so little to show for their long absence, were in no hurry to arrive at their homes, so they gladly accepted the princess's suggestion that they spend a day under the giant elm. It was a bleak, windy day, and yellow leaves were blowing about, so they built several small fires to warm themselves. Again, Sasapah saw Hugh Mitcheltree, seeking to charm him with every artifice that nature had given her. But the husky Irish lad only blushed and skulked away back of the log barn. In his heart, he too was smitten, but as he knew not a single word of the Seneca dialect, he considered that becoming acquainted with nothing to say would only make him seem foolish.

This time Sasapah had a hard task in keeping back her tears when the march began again. She feared that she would never more see her red-headed youth. Everything she had wanted since childhood had been given to her; she wanted the Irish boy because he seemed hard to get. She was even thinner than when she had first rested under the big tree. She had difficulty eating and sleeping; her romance weighed so heavily upon her. New Arrow noticed her altered appearance but attributed it to homesickness and the change of water and food. She sulked most of the time, also flying into violent tempers. All these were signs that she was in love, it was like the clucking irritability of a hen that wants to set, but her brother was too dense to comprehend. But he had his own troubles.

It would be hard to face the Council of Chiefs with a report consisting of what this Quaker said he would do and what that Quaker said would never be done again. When they reached the headquarters on the upper reaches of Tiadaghton, Sasapah was so weak and miserable that she could barely walk. Soon after arriving home, she took to her couch, sinking into a kind of stupor or trance. Medicine men and wise men were summoned, who declared that she had caught "tide-water fever." They gave her all kinds of drastic medicines and sweated her in a bank of clay, which all but killed her.

When she realized that she would succumb to Such misdirected treatment, she confessed to her brother, New Arrow, of whom she was very fond, that she was in love with an Irishman. She described his looks and that he lived in the log house which stood across the trail from the big elm where they had rested going to and coming from Philadelphia. She must have the youth brought to her; else she would surely die.

New Arrow said that it would give him pleasure to meet her wish. The big elm was in the territory of the Lenni-Lenape, who were often unfriendly to the Mingoes, but he would send a band of selected warriors to capture the red-headed boy. He sent for George Silverheels, a young brave who had been in the party, and asked him if he recalled any such big fiery-headed youth. The Indian said he did; the lad was Hugh Mitcheltree, whose mother owned the elm, or Mitchel Tree. New Arrow, therefore, chose Silverheels to lead the party of kidnappers. They were cautioned to move through the country carefully and not make their presence known to the settlers or Lenni-Lenape. They were to locate the youth at his home, or wherever he might be, and wait until a good chance arrived to capture him alive. They were to do this even if they remained away a year, but they must bring him back in that time without harming a hair on his head.

It was a difficult errand, but the sagacious braves who made up the party were sanguine of success. Their departure reduced Sasapah's malady to the point of convalescing. She was up and about within a week afterward, actually beginning to hum love songs again. She was confident of having her lover brought to her; she wanted to be healthy and good-looking to charm him. Every night she dreamed about him; he was such a superb creature that in her fancy, she called him Sissilijah, or the Powerful-Buffalo-Who-Butts-Against-and-Breaks-Everything-to-Pieces, as typifying his massive animal strength. Sasapah idealized him in no end of ways. She was in a delirium of love, which grew more intense as the time drew near for the kidnapping party to return.

Meanwhile, these Indians, under George Silverheels' leadership, had plenty of excitement. First of all, they blundered into a camp of Lenni-Lenape on Pine Creek, a branch of Karoondinha. A skirmish occurred in which they killed three of their enemies, including the chief, One Kalasunay, and George Silverheels himself was badly wounded in his left thigh. The injury left him lame to his dying day, which occurred many years later when he was nearly one hundred years old.

This made it necessary to move with greater caution than ever, and they hid in the Seven Mountains in Coxe's Valley for a month before it was safe to venture forth again. They had to leave that remote fastness because they were seen by some land prospectors who opened fire on them, wounding another of their party seriously, and they escaped into the inaccessible thickets of Green's Valley, hiding there for another month.

When at length they reconnoitered about the Mitchel Tree, they learned that their prize had left home, having volunteered to join the garrison at Pomfret Castle. Hugh was a thrifty lad, for he took his cattle with him and tended to the animals in the pen that he had built across the Mahantango from the fort during his periods of inactivity.

George Silverheels and his party wasted most of the summer waiting for a chance to seize their prey, but the Irish boy seldom went from the fort unattended. When he went out to feed his stock, he was usually guarded by a dozen eager men inside. So much time elapsed that Silverheels decided to send an Indian back to Princess Sasapah to tell her of the difficulties encountered, but that the young man had been located and would be eventually taken captive without any shedding of blood. This Indian was shot at three times on the way, but he seemed to bear a charmed life as he reached the princess in safety, telling her his cheering story. She sent him back with a message of confidence to his chief.

Winter was coming on, and Silverheels and his aides were becoming desperate. Mitcheltree must have had an inkling of danger; otherwise, why was he so timid in his movements? At various times, the skulking kidnappers could have captured every other member of the garrison. One night, when they were sick and tired of waiting and hiding half-starved in a strange country, surrounded by enemies, they resolved to carry their prey away by sheer force in full view of the garrison. Even if a few of their party were shot, it would be better than to lose their man altogether and be executed upon return to the princess empty-handed.

When Mitcheltree went into his cattle pen to do his feeding, they watched him until he came out, then they made a sortie, picking him up in their brawny arms in full view of the dumbfounded garrison. To their even greater surprise, not a shot was fired as they carried the prisoner away, shrieking and yelling for help within the trajectory of every firearm in the fort. The garrison was so taken aback by the bold conduct of the strange-looking abductors that not a man of them could fire his gun. It was like "buck fever," a disease experienced by many huntsmen and descendants of these hardy guardians of rights and liberties upon seeing their first antlered stag in the forest.

As soon as a quiet nook in the woods was reached, the captive was bound and gagged, then taken to the Mingoes' camp in the Shade Mountains. There it was explained to him that he was to go on a long journey to the north. If he went willingly, his pinions would be removed but not his gag. If he wanted to make trouble, he would be carried bound and gagged the entire distance. Mitcheltree was game under any circumstances and quickly declared his intention of acting decently if allowed to walk freely on the journey. He had a jolly way with him that the warriors liked, so he became a prime favorite on the long tramp to the big Mingo encampment on Tiadaghton, near the mouth of Upper Trout Run.

Near the journey's end, the gag was removed, and Silverheels confided to him that he was expected to marry an Indian princess so as to put him in the proper frame of mind. Quick as a flash, the Irish boy asked if she was the beautiful maiden who wore the red bird wings in her hair, whom he had seen on two occasions at the rendezvous under the big tree near his old home. The meaning of his capture had dawned on his intuitive Celtic mind.

Silverheels answered in the affirmative, which greatly pieced the future bridegroom. He danced about and walked twice as fast as before.

When they were within twenty miles of Sasapah's home, a runner was sent on ahead to acquaint the princess of her lover's coming so that she could array herself for the occasion and have a feast in readiness. When breathless, the Indian told her the good news, she was beside herself with joy. Adjusting the red feathers in her coal-black hair, she insisted on walking several miles down the trail to be the first to greet him. She waited under another giant elm, which grew close to the bank of Tiadaghton, building a fire to warm her pretty pink hands.

Toward evening, Mitcheltree and his escort hove in sight. Sasapah gave a little scream of joy and rushed forward, throwing herself in her stalwart lover's arms. The youth shouted in sheer happiness. The scene, as described afterward by Silverheels, was said to have been so affecting that all of the Indian braves broke down, weeping like children.

Sasapah and her lover walked back to the big encampment, hand in hand like two happy children. Silverheels and the others filed on ahead. It was late at night when they reached the settlement, but watch fires were blazing, and all the villagers, old and young, were out in gala attire. Several carcasses of elks were roasting, and at the royal fireplace, panther chops, a special delicacy, were being spitted. When the happy company appeared, a great shouting of "Joh Hoh, Joh Hoh," an Indian exclamation of joy, made the woods ring. Then several maidens advanced, forming a circle about the lovers, dancing and singing touching love ditties. The great chief, New Arrow, embraced his new brother-in-law and led him to the feast. The whole night was spent dancing, singing, shouting, and eating.

The next morning, Hugh Mitcheltree was adopted into the tribe, and in the afternoon, his marriage with Princess Sasapah was solemnized with great pomp and ceremony. He took the name of Sissilijah or the Powerful-Buffalo-Who-Butts-Against-and-Breaks-Everything-to-Pieces. The union was a happy one. A number of children were born. Sissilijah became an Indian in everything except coloring. He was one of the greatest hunters of his day. When the settlers and trappers threatened to preempt the fertile patches of ground along the clear waters of Tiadaghton, he moved with his family to the Genesee Fork of the same Creek, which was in the depths of the Black Forest. There he was seldom seen by the settlers. The few who did encounter him in the wilderness called him the "Pale Indian." As he grew older, he shunned the neighborhoods where they might frequent and, in every way, sought to prove that he belonged to the Indian race. But some say that toward the end of his life, about the year 1816, he stained his sunburned face to make it look darker and traveled on foot to New Buffalo, where he visited the grave of his mother in the old Presbyterian cemetery near the "dreamy Susquehanna."

XIV

GEORGE SHOVER'S PANTHER

(A Story of Little Miller Run)

I T WAS on Christmas Eve that the residents of Haneyville became aware of the existence of a "painter" on the Long Mountain, which formed the divide between the waters flowing toward Tiadaghton and to the Susquehanna. It was a strange visitor and, very unlike Kriss Kringle, that calm, clear, moonlit night in 1864. Far out on the very comb of the bold ridge, the lovesick brute poured out his anguish to the wilderness. By midnight, everybody in the little hamlet was wide awake. The young men and half-grown boys crawled into beds together, already planning hunting trips.

So used to the legend of the Pennsylvania lion's ferocity, the women and children covered their heads with the bedclothes. To the old men, the weird cries brought back memories of other days when they fought panthers and wolves for the supremacy of the Black Forest. Until the morning star grew dim, the panther's song continued, sometimes stopping for half an hour to await an answering call, only to resume again in a sadder key which seemed impatient toward the end. How another panther had gotten into this country which was beginning to teem with lumbermen and hunters, was a puzzle to the old men who listened to it. It had either been driven south by dogs or had some inkling that a mate existed in the Alleghenies or the Bald Eagles.

At any rate, it had taken its stand, determined to find a companion if one existed in the endless ranges of mountains which undulated one behind the other in interlocking lines fading into a dim line against the southern sky. But barely had the panther finished his wailing when several bands of hunters, carrying rifles and holding bulldogs on a leash, were leaving the settlement for the northern ridges in the stillness of that Christmas morning. It was a picturesque scene, to be sure; the tall pines and hemlocks which still grew close to the northern side of the Coudersport Pike were weighted down with snow, the cottages and fields were white, the dark figures of the hunters, who cracked the frosty covering with their boots. That and an occasional jaybird's nervous cry were the only sounds that broke the wintry silence. But the huntsmen found no satisfaction on the ridges. The four parties formed in the Conaway, Packard, Lovett, and Glover families operated independently but did not locate even the panther's tracks.

A light skiff of snow had fallen at daybreak, but even that ought not to have obscured the footprints so completely. It looked as if the panther's cries had come from mountains still further north and had been amplified and reverberated by the calm of the atmosphere and the high altitude. The hunters returned to their homes to eat a belated snack long after dark, having missed their weighty Christmas dinners.

One hunter, Moses Button, remained in a shanty on the slope of the Long Mountain all night. All the nimrods and their families were on the *qui vive* that night, thinking they would be able to locate the exact spot from which the plaintive cries emanated. But the panther was silent. There was no sound except toward morning; a steady wind swayed into doleful music, the shaggy, ice-laden boughs of the original pines and hemlocks. Nothing further was heard from the panther for over a week, to be exact, until the night of the second of January. The good people of Haneyville had about concluded that the animal was a "wanderer," a type of panther with no fixed abode which traveled north and south at all times of the year. These were said by the old hunters to be somewhat smaller in size than panthers which remained in the vicinity of dens or caves on some particular mountain.

On the night in question, two young men, Francis Dyer and Johnny Angevine, who resided five miles beyond Haneyville near one of the sources of Young Woman's Creek, had been calling on two young ladies, sisters, whose home was at the foot of Grindstone Hill about three miles east of the settlement. They left their friends' cottage at midnight, the night being bright and frosty, driving a horse hitched to a small, old-fashioned bobsled. About a mile beyond their starting place, they passed a small clearing, in which stood the ruins of a lumberman's camp.

Just as the clearing receded from the view, the young fellows were startled by the loud cry of a panther, coming from a thicket by the roadside. The dry limbs cracked as the enormous creature sprang into the road behind them. The moon shone brightly down among the opening treetops as over the snow-covered road, steep and icy, the trembling horse hurried the sled along. Deeper and further the forest closed up behind the frightened lads, leaving, in their opinion, little chance to reach Haneyville in safety. Turning their eyes backward, the approaching form of the huge panther could be seen within almost a stone's throw, leaping along at a rate that corresponded to their own. The silence of the woods, the sounds of the horse's feet, the crunching of the sled runners on the frozen snow, the terribly distinct yells of the pursuing animal breaking in upon the surrounding gloom, and their own defenseless condition made a terrible impression upon the young fugitives' minds.

They shot down hill after hill, around curve after curve, without uttering a sound or hardly drawing a breath, expecting every moment that the sled would be racked to pieces on some projecting stone or that every spring of the panther would enable him to overtake them. For over two miles, the panther's chase continued, giving, as it advanced, its clear, appalling cries at intervals of every minute. When the hill leading to Haneyville was reached, they urged the horse up the ascent at a gallop while the panther slackened his speed perceptibly and ceased his shrieks, which induced the belief that the chase was abandoned.

When they emerged from the solitude of the woods, and the open fields and buildings of the tiny settlement were apparent, the boys gave way to a shout of triumph, which to their dismay, hardly had the echo died away when it was answered by the panther's wild scream which literally froze their blood, coming from the forest behind them."

They reined their tired and steaming horse in front of the primitive tavern stand at the crossroads, kept by "Dan" Haney, and called loudly for assistance. The startled landlord poked his head out of an upper window, pointing his rifle at the boys in excitement. Talking both at once, they told him their story, and he invited them to put up their horse in his barn and remain all night. He dressed and helped them unharness, all the while saying, "Honest to Goodness, I hadn't heard of anyone seeing a *painter* around here except this one since 1850 when John Hamilton ran into an old she one and six cubs crossing the Pike at the head of Chatham 's Run."

The next morning, the old man repeated the boys' adventure to a crowd in the store, and it was decided to renew the hunt. Late that afternoon, Moses Button's dogs came close upon the panther on the ridge north of John Lovett's farm. There was some terrific caterwauling indulged in by the brute to frighten his pursuers, which the Lovett family and Button heard distinctly. It had its effect as the dogs dropped the trail and galloped back toward the fields with their tails between their legs. It was with difficulty that their owner got them to take up the scent again, but when they did so, the panther had escaped. An hour or so afterward, Button came upon George Shover, who lived on Little Chatham's Run, who had several good dogs, and who had heard the panther screaming near his premises a night or two previous.

The two men decided to join forces and remain in the woods until they killed the monster. But by the next night, as no tracks were found, Button decided to return to his home for some provisions, as the small game did not seem abundant, and he became cold and hungry. George Shover had just come upon the tracks the morning after when he met Jake Zinck with his dogs out on the same errand. Jake was well-provisioned, so they set out together, following the huge tracks all day, crossing many ridges. Toward evening they came into the waters of Little Miller Run, which flows through a rocky gorge that some enthusiasts have compared to Watkins' Glen in New York State and empties into Tiadaghton near Waterville.

The tracks were so fresh that it looked as if they were close to their quarry. They got their rifles ready, expecting an almost momentary meeting. But to their disappointment, the tracks began leaving the hollow, leading up the steep side of the mountains. It was hard climbing, especially through laurel and hemlock thickets banked with snow. Near the brow of the steep cliff were several rocky caves, and into one of these, the tracks led. They urged the dogs in, thinking they might dislodge the brute, but the animals only went in a short distance and came out again.

BULDING A SLIDE   (Corbett, Pa.)

The hunters got down on their hands and knees, pushing the dogs ahead as they entered. They soon found out the cause of the trouble. The cave was a shallow affair, the main opening ten feet from its mouth being a deep hole about large enough for a human being to crawl into, which apparently descended to the center of the mountain. It would have been cruel to drop the dogs into the hole, as they could not have gotten out if hard pressed by the panther. It would have been foolhardy for the hunters to have descended into the chasm, as the brute might have sprung upon them in the darkness. Yet there was no telling how long the animal might remain underground. Hunger alone would drive him out.

Zinck suggested blocking up the mouth of the cave and starving him to the point of forcing him to make a dash for liberty. But George Shover did not care to waste time while the brute's appetite was augmenting. He wanted more immediate results. He remembered his father telling him that in the old days on the Rocky Branch of Babb's Creek, the first settlers had smothered many wolves by lighting smoke fires at the mouths of their dens. This method had effectually rid that region of wolves, as the smothering was generally done during the breeding season. After the animals were dead, the hunters crawled into the caves and drew out the carcasses of the she-wolves and sometimes as many as a dozen pups at a time. They skinned the dead animals, sold the hides, and collected bounties on their scalps.

Shover mentioned this scheme to his companion who received it with approval. There was a great deal of laurel on the mountainsides, including many dead bushes, which had been killed in a recent forest fire. This would create a terribly foul-smelling smoke, well calculated to send a panther to his reward. There were also many dead tops and stobs, relics from windfalls and fires strewn about, making a wide variety of fuel to select from. The fire was built well inside the mouth of the cave by piling up wet wood with the naturally smoky laurel. Shover touched a match to it. The smoke which quickly arose was nauseating in the extreme, so much so that it was difficult to continue blocking the cavern's mouth. But at length, the task was completed, done so well that hardly any smoke escaped. Then the hunters built a cozy lean-to at the foot of the mountain, spending the night around a crackling campfire. The men determined not to leave the spot with their prize within reach.

The news of the panther had doubtless spread by this time to Swissdale, Hardscrabble, Caldwell, Richville, Charlton, and maybe to Jersey Shore, which would mean that scores of hunters would go on the warpath immediately. If they found the tracks and the blocked-up cave, they would dig out the dead panther and refuse to give it up to the rightful owners upon their return. Early the next morning, a fresh snowfall occurred. The hunters had a hard time keeping their fires going, and the lean-to frequently threatened to fall in through the weight *of* snow on it. But the nimrods were thankful for the blizzard as it would discourage the "town" hunters; it would leave them to finish their task unmolested.

All through that day, with the snow coming down heavily, Shover and Zinck waited patiently and all that night. The next morning it was bitterly cold. The dogs were taken to the blocked-up entrance to the cave, where they sniffed about in such a courageous way as to indicate that the panther was not crouching inside the barriers. But it was decided to wait until after dinner before opening the aperture. The snow had commenced falling again when the two men started the re-opening work.

A terrible odor of stale smoke rushed out as they ripped down the logs; it was surely enough to stifle man or beast. But they worked away with a will and soon had the opening clear. Inside were the still smoldering embers of the laurel fire but no signs of the panther. The dogs rushed in ahead and began sniffing around the hole leading into the cavern's lower chamber. For a moment, the hunters imagined that the "painter" was still alive. But as the dogs were so anxious to climb down into the depths, this could not be the case. Shover and Zinck climbed into the hole, finding that it descended to a depth of twenty feet, below which was a long, low apartment. They lit matches and, by their fitful glow, perceived the lifeless body of the giant panther.

From the size of the tracks, they had been led to believe that the animal was extra-large but stretched out on the cavern floor, it seemed to be as big as "all outdoors." Peacefully it lay there, like some huge cat asleep. Evidently, it had died without a struggle as its eyes were closed, and the expression was calm. Shover stooped down and lifted the big, heavy head with his hand. The lower jaw fell open, revealing that there were very few teeth; the animal was a very old one. In addition, the men noticed that the hair was very grey; "as grey as a bat," said one of them; it was white under the throat and along the belly; it had none of the fulvous or orange color so conspicuous on the coats of panthers taken in their prime. The tail was very long and thick, with a band of white near the tuft of heavy, black hair at the extreme end. The body was still warm; a slash with a knife drew blood from the throat; death had come not long before. The ribs were noticeable, showing that it had eaten very little lately. It was evidently waiting to be killed or to die, as in its toothless state, it could not be very terrifying even to diseased fawns or birds.

Though it was a male, the probabilities were that most of its wailing was caused by hunger rather than love. That also explained why it approached so near to human habitations.

The hunters talked and speculated over their grand trophy for over an hour before they began the severe work of lifting it up to the main room in the cave. It was about the toughest undertaking they had attempted in a long while. Thin as it was, the panther weighed at least two hundred pounds. The head, paws, and tail hung like lead weights. Despite the cold weather, the hunters were sweating freely when they landed the carcass at the cavern's mouth. Then they rolled it down the mountain to their campfire, where they carefully skinned it. They took along the skull to preserve it as a souvenir and did not cut off the paws with the huge, worn-away claws. They were surely two of the happiest men in the entire Black Forest, perhaps in the Keystone State that night.

There was absolutely no fat on the carcass, and the flesh was practically dried to the bones. How much more the brute would have weighed when in good condition was a problem to the hunters. As it was, he was little else but bones and muscles. However, they cut a few chops out of the ribs, determined to make the triumph complete by tasting the meat of their victim. Soon, half a dozen chops were broiling over the cheery fire.

While the preparations for supper were in progress, the dogs jumped up with their bristles on end and commenced to bark fiercely. Pretty soon, the gleaming eyes of two large hounds appeared back of the campfire, followed shortly after by a whiskered man in woodsman's garb. Both hunters recognized the visitor at Hiram Laffery, a character who lived several miles further down Little Miller. Though a drinking man and, at times, a cantankerous fellow, he had worked up quite a clientele among Williamsport hunters and fishermen whom he boarded and guided through the woods on their outings. He knew, in reality, very little about woodcraft or hunting, but he did so much talking that words passed for wisdom with the " tenderfeet."

He could hardly believe his senses when he saw the huge hide of the panther, which Shover and Zinck explained had been killed on the mountain directly above where they were camping.

"Man alive," ejaculated Laffery, "had I but known that there was a 'painter' in this valley, I could have made a fortune inviting some of the rich sportsmen from down country to come out and kill it."

Then his face darkened, and he pulled out his flask and took a big drink to hide his disappointment. Then he offered the flask to the hunters, but they declined with thanks. The whiskey made him more talkative, and he told about a rich Williamsport banker who doubted that a single panther was left in Pennsylvania. He had bet him a hundred dollars that there were still a few in the Black Forest and the Seven Mountains and would give half that amount to anyone who would help him win that bet.

"But man alive," he rambled on, "here these boys kill a painter and the biggest one I ever saw in my life only within three miles of my home, I had been hearing dogs barking for the past two days, which was unusual in such bad weather, and this evening I could stand it no longer. I had to come here and find out what was going on."

Then he drank more whiskey and ate three of the six panther chops. He wound up inviting the hunters to come to his cabin.

"I'll treat you right, just like I do the 'High Zekes' from Williamsport and Muncy."

The hunters were glad to sleep under cover for a change; their faces burned from exposure to the elements, and they felt like taking off their clothes and washing. So, the three men carrying the hide, the skull, and the hunting paraphernalia wended their way down the dark ravine, followed by the dogs. Laffery was living alone at the time, but there were occasions when he employed a housekeeper or relative to help him. There was a cheery fire in the stove, about which the men were glad to warm themselves. They sat about it until after midnight, swapping hunting stories and jokes, during which time Laffery consumed much whiskey. The host got the hunters out of bed early the next morning, and they could see that he was much the worse for his tippling. His eyes were bloodshot, and he had little to say except to swear loudly when he burnt the coffee and let the pan of ham fall off the stove.

The breakfast was a wretched affair, and the two guests wondered if this was what the Williamsport magnates were forced to endure. If so, they paid dearly for their sojourns in the woods. After the meal, the nimrods announced that they would be starting for their homes immediately. This aroused Laffery from his drunken torpor, and he asked them if they would sell the panther hide.

"Not for a mint," replied Shover decisively.

"I'll give you fifty dollars cash for it," answered the guide. "Then I can win that hundred dollar bet with the 'High Zeke' and make a lot besides drawing folks here to see the last *painter* killed in northern Pennsylvania."

The hide was lying on the floor, as Laffery had just finished measuring it. It stretched out to eleven feet from tip to tip, almost a record hide. Joe Snyder's panther, killed on Young Woman's Creek in 1858, is said to have measured eleven feet six inches, and a panther killed near Newry, Blair County, by Solomon Boos in 1873, measured eleven feet three inches. A New York State panther killed in Herkimer County in the forties by Joe Wood also measured eleven feet three inches.

"You won't sell me that hide for fifty dollars?" said Laffery eyeing the hunters critically.

Both of them answered that they would not. Shover was reaching down to roll it up when the angered guide picked up an ax that stood beside the wood box and, with a vicious swing, cut off one of the paws. "There, damn you both. I've fixed that hide, so you can't sell it to anybody."

This was too much for Zinck, and striking out, he hit the malicious shack-dweller a sharp blow with the back of his hand, drawing blood from the whiskered lips. Laffery would have fallen on the stove had not Shover caught him in his arms. They laid the fellow cursing and bellowing on his couch, from which he was too drunk and maudlin to move.

Gathering up the hide, the skull, and their rifles, the two hunters departed, slamming the door on their unsociable host. By evening they were back at the head of Chatham's Run, where they tossed a Continental penny, which Zinck always carried as a "pocket piece," as to who should receive the mutilated hide. Shover won it, but it had been previously agreed that the loser should get the ears on which the twelve-dollar bounty would be paid, the skull, and the severed paw.

When he returned to his modest home with his grand prize, Shover had a great ovation. He had a rug made from the skin, which was kept in his family for many years. After his death, it was admired by a traveling man from New York State and sold to him for fifty dollars. Evidently, Hiram Laffery had offered good value for it. Zinck preserved the skull and the severed paw, and they are said to be still in his home on the hill back of the town of Oak Grove.

XV

THE TRAMPER
(The Story of a Famous Lost Boy)

THE WIND was howling, and the snow was beating against the doors and windows of the old halfway house between the Germania settlement and Galeton. It was such a terrible night that the landlord, old Daniel Osch, did not care to go to bed. Instead, he sat in his stocking feet by the big, white-washed stove in the barroom. The low-ceilinged room was lit by a single kerosene lamp, which stood on a bracket back of the bar; there were four other lamps in the room, but these were only lighted on Saturday nights or when trade was especially good. A pair of many-tined stag horns hung above the mirror, and on one side of it was a framed lithograph showing Johnstown before and after the flood of 1889; on the other side was a framed engraving of the ancient German city of Bonn.

It was not to be expected that there would be any visitors on such a wild night. The old settlers and the trappers were snowed up in their forest-hidden cabins, and the big hemlock camps which had lately opened in the neighboring ravines only kept a few skidders and loaders working during the winter months. A new but passing prosperity had come with the opening of these camps. Hundreds of reckless spenders were among the loggers and bark-peelers, who made business brisk while the operations lasted, then, when the last log was peeled, like the Arabs, stole silently away, leaving desolation and forest fires in their wake, and the financial ruin of the permanent inhabitants of the Black Forest.

Old Osch was figuring this out in his slow but German analytic brain and thinking of his boyhood days in the old country where a tree was planted for every one cut down, where there were no forest fires, and the lumbering industry was permanent, building its sawmills of brick or cement, and not of slabs or culls. Lumbering carried on by the Potter County natives on a small scale was calculated to last indefinitely, even without replanting, but by big corporations, it meant waste, ruin, unhappiness for all except the Buffalo millionaires who controlled it. No wonder he glanced with his small, dark eyes at a poster lithograph of William J. Bryan, under which someone had facetiously scribbled "No Trust." The Nebraskan, of all American statesmen, had seen clearest the evils of monopolies, but it would take several generations before the public would realize that they had been unmercifully buncoed into allowing "big business," which spelled backward means serfdom for the individual, free rein.

Amid his ruminations, there came a loud rapping at the barroom door. At first, the old German thought it was hail, charged with a particularly insistent gust of wind, and prepared to take no notice of it. But it kept up again and again, louder and louder. Someone was outside, sure enough. He glanced at the clock which hung above the picture of Colonel Bryan; it was half past eleven. Nobody in that "neck of woods," as he always called it, came out that late for a first drink. They often enough stayed until closing time, but they always began imbibing early. It was unthinkable that a traveler could be on the road in such a fierce storm; no liveryman in Galeton, Germania, or Gaines would let a team go out.

He sat and thought a moment more. Then he got up from his chair, walked slowly to the door, and unbolted it. As he flung the door open, the wind whistled fiercely, and a spray of snow and sleet rushed in, almost sweeping the ponderous Teuton off his feet. For a moment, he could see nobody outside. Then through the storm appeared an unkempt figure, covered with snow, which caked to his face, hat and garments. As if pushed by the gale, he rushed pell-mell past the landlord into the barroom, where he settled himself in the armchair by the stove.

Old man Osch threw his weight against the door, closing and bolting it. Then he turned around, wishing the stranger good evening. By this time, some of the sleet had thawed off the individual's face and clothing, and one could see what he looked like. He was a fair-haired, blue-eyed young man above medium height with clear-cut, sensitive features. His arched nose was particularly fine, but his face was half-hidden behind a ten days growth of beard. He looked very cold and pale, so the proprietor slipped behind the bar and poured out a tumbler full of whiskey without being asked for it.

"Take that," he said. "I don't know who you are yet, but this will do you good."

The stranger drank it down at a single gulp, after which the color came to his lips, and he seemed more composed.

"You asked me who I was a bit ago," he said, eyeing the landlord cautiously. "I don't quite know myself; I have always been called Charley Stamler, but I have every reason to believe that my real name is Charley Carson. I think that I am the person who, as a boy, was kidnapped years ago from my home in one of the suburbs of Philadelphia."

Old man Osch looked at the man in surprise. Was he talking in good faith, or was it the whiskey talking?

"I have had my ups and down," the stranger resumed. "I have been a newsboy and a farmhand in Ohio, a deckhand on the lakes, a strike-breaker at Homestead and Pittsburgh in 1892. I marched with Coxey's Army two years ago; I was a waiter in an oyster house at Baltimore, worked on a coaster, and finally beat it on the trucks from the Bowery to Rochester, and have been tramping it ever since; folks told me there was lots of healthy work in the Pennsylvania lumber woods. They tell me I have tuberculosis."

The landlord was interested in the recital of the young man's varied career. Such ne'er do wells often turned up in the Black Forest, but they seldom made good loggers or peelers. But if this man was ill and wanted to do the right thing, there might be a chance for him. But he first explained to him that there would be no work on a large scale until the last of April when the park-peeling began. Most of the logs from the previous summer's cutting had been skidded to the railways and trails, and only a small crew needed to load the cars and sleds. No hardwood would be cut until the tracts had been cleaned off of hemlock, when a different set of jobbers, who worked in winter, would take it up.

"I'd work here for my board," said the stranger, "willingly, until it came time for me to get a chance in the woods."

Landlord Osch always dispensed with his handyman when business grew slack in the fall, but here was a chance to try a man on the lowest wages he had yet paid. So, he told the stranger that he would give him a trial, and if he proved satisfactory, he could remain two months until April, when the peeling began and when his regular hostler, who lived over on Lyman's Run, would return. The stranger was delighted. He got up and shook the landlord by the hand,

"You have saved my life," he said.

"Tell me one thing," said the old man before he showed his new helper to bed. "Do you really think you are the lost Charley Carson?"

"I do not think it, I am sure of it," the fellow replied. "I wrote letters and offered to come in person and prove my case, but I could get no replies. I put my evidence in the hands of lawyers, but I could not fight the case right with no money. It is a long story; sometime, I'll tell you all about it."

The stranger was not a failure in his new position. He worked hard, even in the kitchen and laundry, which pleased the landlord's thrifty wife. When the bark-peeling season opened, the regular helper, though he was an old soldier, became imbued with the idea of making better pay driving a team in the woods and sent word he was not coming back. The stranger asked to remain and got the place on the same terms as his predecessor. During the summer months business was lively, for, in addition to the hordes of bark-peelers and jobbers, the hotel was daily thronged with peddlers, agents, traveling photographers, patent medicine men, and all kinds of fakers in general—the lumbermen's camp-followers, as well as many trout fishermen.

During the rush season, an Indian girl named Armanie Doxtater was engaged to assist with the housework. She was a pretty girl of nineteen, slender, with large, dark blue eyes, which with her rather pale complexion denoted the usual admixture of white blood. No sooner did she arrive than Charley Stamler, the helper began to spruce up his appearance. He went to Galeton one evening, where he had his blonde beard trimmed to a fashionable point, and bought a straw hat, new shoes, and a new suit of clothes.

He was a gentlemanly, almost good-looking chap when well-dressed, and he began to pay marked attentions to the Indian girl, who seemed to like him in return.

This little undercurrent of romance helped to pass away the summer pleasantly. Old Osch was waiting all the time for his protege to tell him why he felt sure he was the lost Charley Carson, but never again did he open his mouth on the subject. Evidently, he had been nervously tired the night of his strange arrival in the storm and talked more freely as a result, and besides, his loquacity had been helped along by that tumbler full of whiskey. Daniel Osch was inquisitive and could not rest easy until he heard more of the Charley Carson story. He reminded the helper every few days of his promise to finish the narrative, but the only answer he could get from him was a polite rejoinder that he would tell it later on.

The old man hit upon the plan of imparting what he knew to Armanie, asking her to wheedle it out of the stranger. She was a modest girl, and while the queer story interested her, she never got enough courage to put the question to him. Old Mother Osch brought it up several times, even at the dinner table, but could gain no satisfaction. But as long as it remained untold, the old landlord determined to hold on to the stranger, as it made him feel that he was harboring someone of consequence.

When bark-peeling was about over for the season in October, Armanie returned to her parents' home, which was also on Lyman's Run. The stranger felt her loss keenly; it was as if the spirit had left the place. Twice a week, he made the journey to see her. The tram road for logs took him most of the way, but he had to make the long walk back at midnight. Though the distance was long, it was not unpleasant through the avenues of sweet-scented, newly peeled logs. But he always seemed much happier the days after he had been to see her.

Old Mother Osch whispered to her husband and intimates "that it was going to be a match." As she had no children of her own, she was much interested in the strange romance. Of course, she said she knew nothing of the hired man; he might be a jailbird of some kind from the cities. She was sure that there was some mystery about him. If he was sure of being the lost Charley Carson, why did he not continue hiring lawyers and enforcing his claim? He might very easily be the famous kidnapped boy, as he had every indication of gentle birth. But all this gossip resulted in nothing. When the rabbit, squirrel, and bird shooting season set in, business at the halfway house began to grow brisk again. The old woman regretted that she had let Armanie go, but the hired man made himself so useful that she soon ceased complaining of overwork.

Parties of half a dozen sportsmen, with their dogs, came to the hotel nightly; they were convivial fellows, those hunters, drinking much of the excellent beer brewed in the neighborhood and tipping liberally for every favor received. Some of them indulged in more drinking than hunting, and it was a wonder that when they did shoot, they did not kill one another. The bibulous gunners could be appeased if the game was served to them for supper after their fruitless days in the woods as it was before the passage of any of the wise laws forbidding the sale of game. Landlord Osch would engage half a dozen local pot hunters to keep the table supplied.

One night toward the middle of October, a dozen rabbit hunters spent the night at the halfway house. They lived near the New York State line and came into the Black Forest to hunt every autumn. Although they had had a very successful day, they preferred to eat the rabbits the landlord served, as they wanted to take their own "kills" home as trophies. As a special delicacy, a northern hare, a very rare animal, was the *pièce de résistance* of the feast. The dining room was on the hotel's second floor; in warm weather, the meals were served on a porch, which opened out from it, and gave an excellent view of the forests and mountains and the purling, babbling brook below. It was a cold night, and the small stove barely heated the large, high-ceilinged apartment. It was illuminated by a couple of small lamps on the walls, and one with a green glass shade stood on the supper table.

A stuffed grey fox or Colishay ornamented the mantel shelf. The hunters were ravenously hungry after their strenuous day in the brisk mountain air and drank a round of whiskey before the meal had been announced. During the supper, they drank much beer, which they poured out in tumblers from two large cut-glass pitchers. A cat, yellow like a panther and with one black spot over its eye, was playing about the room with a spool. It reminded one of the hunters, so he said, of a black-eyed panther that was a terror to the first settlers on Eleven Mile Run nearly a hundred years before. He added with great gusto that his grandfather had shot it, making a lap-robe out of the hide.

After the feast, all the gunners began to feel sleepy, slouching down in their chairs and laying aside their cigars. Suddenly the cat dropped the spool and, with a yell, bristled up and ran under the table. At the same time, the most wide-awake member of the party jumped up from his seat, shouting, "See that pale man over there? Who is he? Where did he come from?"

And as he spoke, he pointed to the door, which in the summertime led to the porch where meals were served but which was now kept locked. All the men looked around. Most of them saw a white figure resembling the hired man standing against the closed door. As they looked at him, he faded away; he seemed to go through the keyhole as he vanished. Having heard the commotion, Landlord Osch and his wife rushed into the room, finding their guests in attitudes of greatest agitation. They told the old couple as best they could what had happened.

Osch shook his head. "It could not have been Charley Stamler; he left here before dark to visit his girl on Lyman's Run, and I do not believe in ghosts."

"Neither do we," chorused the hunters, every man wanting to go on record for his materialism. But they were frightened half to death, nevertheless. As quickly as they could, they hurried down the narrow stairs to the bar to brace themselves for the night with whiskey straight.

When Mother Osch was clearing off the table, her foot touched the cat, still crouching beneath it. She dragged the frightened animal out, but to use her own words, it was "scared stiff." The hunters were too nervous to want to go to bed early and kept fortifying their nerves with more liquor. They kept the landlord back of the bar until a few minutes after the official hour for closing. For once in their lives, they were thankful that they had to sleep two in a bed. But the night passed uneventfully; not one of them saw a ghost or even heard a rustle.

When old man Osch came downstairs at daybreak, he looked about for his hired man, whom he usually found building the fires. He waited until his wife came on the scene and then started on a search. The man's bed had not been occupied; if he had come back, he had not gone to his room. He went out to the barn, the chicken house, the hog pen, and the cellar, but there were no signs of his helper. He thought of the little restaurant building over by the creek, where above the door was the modest sign, "Soft drinks, ice cream, light lunch for sale here." It was only open for business during the summer months. It would be extremely unlikely that the man went into such a flimsy structure on such a cold night, but he decided to go there anyhow.

The building had been closed for nearly a month; the wooden shutters were upon the windows. When he reached the door, he found it locked, with the key sticking in the keyhole. Upon opening the door, he was greeted by a foul, musty odor, as all unventilated apartments give forth.

As his eyes became accustomed to the semidarkness, he could make out a pair of feet raised aloft behind the counter. Going closer, he found the body of a man, with his head wedged under the counter, literally standing on his head. Not wishing to disturb the body alone, he hurried back to the hotel, calling for his guests, who were lounging about the cold stove in the barroom waiting for breakfast to be announced. Hatless, they walked with him across the poplar-dotted yard to the little restaurant beside the brook. They followed into the gloomy storeroom, where they saw the awful spectacle behind the counter.

The bravest one of them, a man named Albert Adams, brushed by the others and, catching the corpse by its feet, dragged it out on the center of the floor. When he turned it so that the face would be upward, they all recognized it as the hired man, Charley Stamler, and as the apparition that had appeared to them in the dining room. Several of the men gave way to a shout of terror. It was a trying situation.

Then the question arose about how the dead man got into such a peculiar position behind the counter. Adams said that the head was tightly cramped between two boxes of empty soda-water bottles; it was with difficulty that he extracted it. During the discussion, Mother Osch appeared on the scene; she wrung her hands with grief when she learned of the tragic fate of her favorite helper, especially since he had died with his secret untold.

It was decided not to examine the body further until the coroner could be summoned. A neighbor was dispatched for the official with a speedy horse and buggy, returning with him in the late afternoon. The hunters who had lingered around the premises all day were used as jurors and witnesses. The coroner happened to be a practicing physician, so he made a critical examination of the dead man.

There were no signs of foul play or self-destruction. He had apparently met his death from apoplexy or heart failure due to losing his balance while leaning over the counter. From the body's appearance, death had occurred about nine or ten o'clock the previous night. That was when the hunters saw the specter in the dining room. Several of them turned pale when they heard this pronouncement.

While they were conferring over the peculiar affair, Armanie Doxtater appeared on the premises wild-eyed and disheveled. She had failed to receive her expected visit from her lover; all night long, she had dreamed horribly about him. White and ghost-like, he had appeared before her bedside six times. She was sure that he had met with foul play. When she saw the body lying on the storehouse floor, she threw herself upon it and had to be dragged away. Her grief, primitive and genuine, brought tears to some of the unsentimental hunters grouped about the room.

The coroner tried to get her to compose herself so she could tell what she knew about the strange man. She said that he had been very reticent concerning himself, except to say that Stamler was not his real name, that his name was Charley Carson. When she had asked him if he was the hero of the famous kidnapping of twenty-odd years before, he had been silent a while, then whispered that he felt that he was, but refused to say more. Then the girl started to tell about the deceased's many good qualities, finally breaking into hysterical weeping.

The coroner brought up the question Landlord Osch had mentioned earlier in the inquest, about finding the storehouse locked with a key on the outside. The old German maintained that he had made no mistake about it. But it was hard to believe with all the indications pointing to death from natural causes.

The only solution to it was that the man had died outside and had been put in the storehouse by someone who had afterward locked the door. Finally, the coroner asked the landlord, who usually kept the storehouse key.

"Charley had it," he said. "He put up the shutters and locked the door at the end of the season, and I forgot to ask him for it."

The verdict was that the man had come to his death from heart fail-ure, which was induced by an apoplectic fit.

"That's all right enough," said Albert Adams that evening, as he leaned against one of the pillars of the hotel porch, pulling his long, blonde mustache, "but it doesn't explain where he met his death or how he got in that storehouse in such a cramped position with the door locked on the outside."

XVI

LITTLE RED RIDING HOOD
(Story of the Packet-Boat Wolf)

OLD MIKE CURTS, who spent most of his life in the Black Forest, hunting and trapping wolves, used to tell the story of how he killed the famous Black Wolf, which was wont to follow the packet boats every night, which plied between Williamsport and Lock Haven. From him, as well as many others, including the chief actress herself, has come the remarkable tale of the Little Red Riding Hood of the West Branch.

It was during the early forties that the "packet-boat wolf" was first noticed. In those days, wolves were becoming scarce in the West Branch Valley, the bounty hunters and the poisoners having pretty well succeeded in driving them to the fastnesses of the Black Forest to the north and the Seven Mountains to the south. Ten years previously, they were numerous, coming down into the fields to play or commit small depredations.

The venerable Jacob Quiggle, who died on the eve of his ninetieth birthday in 1911, often told how his father would go at sunset to the back door of his home near Pine Station, Clinton County, and imitate the barking of a wolf. It would be answered from the summit of the Round Top, first by one wolf, then by two, by four, and so on, until the entire pack was yelping in chorus. If he continued his imitations long enough, the animals would descend from the mountain and come to the edge of his fields, the bolder ones approaching almost to the farm buildings.

One time the youthful Jacob informed his parents that his little brother, his sister, and himself had been followed to school and back every day by a big, brown dog. The shrewd pioneer became suspicious of

BOLD HUNTERS (Norwich, Pa.)

the "dog" and accompanied the children the next morning, armed with his trusty rifle. He found a shaggy, brown wolf waiting on the path in a wood not far from his home. The animal was lying, his paws stretched out, his tongue lolling and panting, just like an ordinary dog. Despite the tearful protests of the children, he shot the wolf dead.

During the forties, what wolves remained in the West Branch were scattering individuals, the big packs having been killed off or sought safer localities. It began to be noticed that a wolf was following the night packet boat; the animal was using the old Indian trail, which ran along the tops of the Bald Eagle Mountains. It took up the trail soon after Williamsport was left and did not give it up until the mountain at the right side of Castanea Gap, near Lock Haven, was reached. From its remote situation, it could make out the boat in the valley below by its gleaming lights. Every time a Gap was neared, the wolf would give out some unearthly howls, which often would seemingly be answered by every dog in the deep valley. During the summer months, when the days were long, the wolf was seldom heard from, although it was presumed he followed the boats nightly, as on stormy nights, he barked as usual.

Many causes were assigned for his bold and unusual conduct. The chief one was that he was charmed by the lights. Others were that hunger drove him on or that the moving boat looked like some edible animal. Some declared that it was no wolf but a spook; even though it made huge tracks in the snow. In the beginning, the farmers and hunters of the valley were too occupied otherwise to kill this lone wolf. It apparently did no harm; there were troublesome beasts nearer home, which must first be exterminated. As time passed, the "packet-boat wolf" became so well-known that several hunters coveted the distinction of killing it.

These brave nimrods posted themselves along the path on the mountain summits waiting for the wolf to trot past and be shot. They were always disappointed to see the packet boat go by in the valley beneath and then, a few minutes later, to hear the wolf barking on the crest of the next mountain beyond. These hunters waited night after night with no better results. It seemed like wasting time, so they gradually dropped the quest. However, many traps were placed along the trail, which the sagacious wolf always managed to dodge. Poisoning was tried with no success. If the wolf was as hungry as so many claimed, it was strange he would not touch choice bits of veal and mutton deeply impregnated with strychnine. Other animals and birds took the bait readily enough; dead foxes, skunks, hawks, owls, and buzzards were found near the poisoned meat.

On one occasion, when a large band of young men was out on the mountain west of Aughanbaugh's Gap, driving deer with their dogs, they noticed the packet boat coming up the valley in the distance. They quickly formed a human cordon across the mountain's top and sides. They thought the wolf would have to turn back or go through them. Much to their anger, they heard the familiar barking after the boat had passed, coming from the extreme end of the mountain to the west, where it dips into Kearns's Gap.

The wolf seemed to bear a charmed life, and when hunters got together, all agreed that no one had ever seen the animal. Perhaps it was a different wolf every night, one very young hunter ventured. If it was, then the mountains were teeming with them, which was surely not the case then, to judge by the number killed each year.

Many liked to hear the packet-wolf at night, among them the great jurist Ellis Lewis, who often traveled to Lock Haven, then a growing lumbering center as well as the seat of justice of the new county of Clinton. But the wolf had many more foes than friends; consequently, through its own alertness, it managed to survive.

In September 1847, occurred a memorable flood in the West Branch. The canal was torn out in many places, especially at the canal bridges over Tiadaghton and Chatham's Run. Traffic was temporarily suspended while bands of sturdy Irishmen toiled to restore it to normal condition. Some alarmists said that it would take until winter before the packet boats would be running again, so formidable seemed the piles of logs and drift which choked the canal bed, to say nothing of the washouts at the bridges and locks.

The impatient public that must travel soon caused the old stages to be requisitioned during the interval. These aged vehicles once so conspicuous along the "river road" were dragged out, cob-webbed and creaking, from their shadowy retirement in a shed back of the Union House in

Williamsport and, after a little greasing and varnishing, traveled as well as ever, though they had been out of commission for over ten years. Such is the ultimate triumph of good material! These stages ran by day, as the roads were too poor to risk the danger of a breakdown on some lonely stretch after dark.

When the packet boats were not running, nothing was heard of the black wolf for some time. It was predicted that the flood would be his undoing, that he would come down into the valley to investigate and meet his death. Some children living near Adam Carlsson's, afterward M'am Smith's old halfway house, claimed to have seen a huge, black animal swimming the river late one afternoon. It came ashore not far from where the ruins of the old Chatham's Run High School building are now, shook itself, and scampered up the bank and into the woods at the foot of Hulings' hill to the north of the highway. Settlers in the Black Forest, especially several families living at the sources of Upper and Lower Pine Bottom Runs, reported seeing a black wolf of enormous size lurking about their premises.

Soon the story went the rounds that the packet boat wolf had gone to the Black Forest; in the future, he might trot along the tops of the Alleghenies instead of the Bald Eagles. Work on the canal progressed much faster than the "calamity-howlers" predicted, and in the "Squaw Winter" appeared to be ready for traffic again. This was pleasing to shippers, who had a great accumulation of lumber and grain to send eastward. It also pleased the traveling public, who preferred the calm and comfort of the boats to the rattle and dust or mud of stage riding. And there were almost as many who wished for the return of the packet-boat wolf as they did for the packet boats.

Over in Nippenose Valley, not far from the gates of the majestic Sanderson estate of "Lochabar," lived an estimable family named Steyne. They came originally from Berks County but had been established in their abode on Antes Creek for two generations. Jacob Steyne, the husband and father, was a successful farmer and stockman. He turned his attention mostly to sheep raising, producing larger animals than most of his fellow breeders. Pasture was scarce during the summer months, especially on a small farm where there was so much stock, as a result of which the Steyne cattle, numbering nearly a score, were driven every morning out on the mountain road which leads to Bastress, where they would find plenty to feed upon on the shady highlands.

Caroline Steyne, then a girl of about nine years, usually drove the animals out on the mountain, as it was only a short distance from the farm. She was of good size and sturdy and never knew such a thing as fear. Often when she went to fetch the cattle homeward in the cool of the evenings, she was accompanied by a younger brother and sister. The children all loved these excursions into the land of laurel and rhododendron, where there were tall pines, splashing cascades, and dark, mossy paths. The cattle were liberally supplied with bells so that they could be heard long distances. But as evening approached, they generally wended their way off the highest eminences, being oftenest found waiting patiently along the Bastress Road.

Out on the summits, a few brown bears and wild eats still lingered, but these creatures hardly ever molested livestock and never troubled human beings. A little girl named Phoebe Armpriester, who lived on the present site of Nippeno Park, once wandered into the forest where she met with a huge, brown bear, which took good care of her until she was rescued by her almost-frantic father a few days later.

Little Caroline loved the woods and all wild nature. She often saw deer on her rambles; they appeared to be friendly with the cattle. Foxes often crossed the road in front of her; once, she saw one destroy a yellow-jackets nest by flopping its tail on the aperture of the hive attracting the insects and then knocking them to the ground, devouring them. Rabbits, squirrels, porcupines, and woodchucks scarcely moved at her approach. Ravens were plentiful, croaking among the mature yellow pines on the high tablelands. There were still a few strutting heath-cocks, and numerous wild turkeys, ruffed grouse, and bobwhites. The great blue herons and brown bitterns waded in the fern-banked pools. Cardinal birds, wood thrushes, and rare warblers sang in the deep woods. As if fearful of being seen, the shrill-voiced blue jays darted from tree to tree through the dense foliage. She especially loved the sad notes of the upland plover. Often the wild pigeons' nests could be seen among the wide-spreading beeches. Wildflowers of all kinds abounded, and huckleberries, dishberries, and wild gooseberries grew in profusion in patches where the timber had been cut away. It inspired a sensible, impressionable childlike Caroline, who appreciated her daily visits to the wilds as the modern child does an art gallery or theatrical performance.

One evening, the last part of October, when she started out, she could feel that the air was becoming much cooler. She loved this time of the year, with its intimation of a change of seasons. She noticed places on the mountainsides where the sun had shone at this hour earlier in the summer but was now obscured in shadow. As she walked along the steep road, she broke off stalks of the withered Joe Pye weed or stooped to pluck the dainty Blue-wood asters. The deciduous trees were tinted with the colors of the rainbow.

High up on the mountain road, she could hear the melodious cow-bells; the cattle were far from home this evening. They had to go further out on the summits to get pasture as the season progressed. Several times the energetic little girl called to her brother and sister to walk faster; she hated to leave them out of her sight in the advancing gloom. There was very little sun left except on the mountain tops; the gorge up which the road wound was now the color tone of dusk.

As they climbed higher and higher, they neared a clearing where once an early settler's home had stood. Often the cattle waited for their drivers in that spot, as there was much clover among the grass, and cool shade from the ancient "wild" apple and plum trees, planted there in Indian days. In the stillness of the autumn evening, it was a quaint spot, pastured smooth, with dry mullein and milkweed; sumac with reddened leaves was growing near where the stones of the old foundations raised their heads.

As Caroline, her little brother, and sister passed along the road; they noticed a large, black object seated on its haunches under an apple tree. It could not be a calf from its attitude, yet it was too big to be a dog. The trio eyed it critically, and then Caroline told the others to remain where they were until she went closer and saw for herself.

Bravely she walked across the field toward where the monster sat watching her. When she got close, she saw that she was literally walking into the jaws of a giant wolf. The creature was coal-black, with great brown bars running around it; evidently, it had not yet gotten its winter coat. Its head was large and broad, with narrow, pointed ears. The eyes were round and somewhat bloodshot, the mouth cut far back, and cruel, white teeth protruded. The chest was broad, the forelegs heavy and powerfully muscled. It made no move, even when the little investigator turned to leave the spot. She wasn't in the least afraid; she had the courage to face a dozen wolves. This was the first live wolf she had ever seen.

Her father, and his next-door neighbor, Mike Curts, had killed many brown wolves, fetching the hides back from their expeditions to be cured before selling them. During the past winter, an exceptionally well-coated wolf hide rested on her smallest brother's cradle. Wolves were nothing new to her; she had heard of their ferocity and hideousness ever since she was old enough to understand. But this wolf was bigger by far than she had ever seen; in color, it was most distinctive.

With admirable calmness, she returned to her little companions and told them to go home, that she would fetch the cows alone. At first, they demurred, but she explained that the beasts were far away, that it would make them very tired to climb to the crest of the mountain. She watched the two little people as they toddled down the winding road, hand in hand. When they had reached the high road, she resumed her way up the mountain in search of the cows.

As she left the vicinity of the old clearing, she looked back over her shoulder; the wolf was still sitting there. When, nearly an hour later, and it was almost dark, she came back with the drove of lowing cattle, the brute was still resting under the apple tree. He made no move to molest cows or child. In passing the wolf, Caroline affected an air of nonchalance, and she even stopped to pick a spray of late asters directly opposite where he sat. When she had gotten the animals to the high road in safety, she threw some pebbles at them, urging them into a trot, which she kept until she caught up with her little brother and sister.

It was quite dark when the party turned into the narrow lane which led to the Steyne cottage. "What makes you so late?" asked the little cowgirl's father when she turned the cattle over to him.

Caroline looked him squarely in the eyes, saying that she had met with a giant black wolf at the old clearing on the Bastress Road.

"And you didn't run?" said the good man, almost incredulously.

"We surely did not," replied the little girl, because if we did, all would have been lost."

Steyne went into the house and told the story to his wife, who became much agitated. He asked her to milk the cows, then took down his favorite rifle from its rack and strode out of the house. Calling his dogs, he repaired to the home of his neighbor, Mike Curts. This worthy wolfer swung his trusty rifle over his shoulder, called for his dogs, and accompanied Steyne to the home of another neighbor, John Phillips. Like a snowball rolling downhill, the hunting party gained in numbers. It was joined by Jesse Hughes, Jacob Youngman, Alanson Stevens, Adam Greenlee, Peter Brosius, and others. Among them was a pack of at least twenty formidable-looking dogs.

As they marched through Antes Gap, swinging their tin lanterns, they looked like soldiers headed for the field of battle. The fall *hylodes* serenaded them from the grass as they tramped along. They wended their way to the old clearing on the Bastress Road, where the dogs soon took up the scent, although the wolf was nowhere to be found. The trial led up the steep face of the mountain, the baying of the dogs making sweet music in the crisp night air. It was a hard climb, and several of the old-fashioned lanterns were dropped and extinguished. There were a few stars visible but no moon.

On the mountain's topmost peak, the dogs seemed to have cornered their victim. They drove it around and around the narrow point, alternately howling with pleasure or pain. When the hunters got to them, the wolf had evidently broken through the line of its tormentors and headed for the level tableland to the east. There, if it outran its pursuers, it would have to break into open country in Mosquito Valley. But it had no such intention. After leading the dogs on a merry chase for five miles straightway, it doubled on its tracks, coming back in the direction of the hunters.

John Phillips, who had been a member of the party of deer slayers who had formed a cordon across the Bald Eagle Mountain a year or so previously, suggested that the huntsmen now spread out, and every man make an effort to stop the wolf's progress through their line. They were on a vast open plateau, where the timber did not grow thickly; it was carpeted with ferns and huckleberry bushes; objects were discernable even on a moonless night. It was very cold on that height, almost like a night in mid-winter.

Nearer and nearer came the wolf with the angry hounds close at his heels. The hunters primed their guns, wondering who would have the lucky shot. As it came in sight, it was headed to go between Jesse Hughes and John Phillips. Both were expert shots and had killed many wolves and panthers; they did not calculate to miss. They had arranged to fire ahead at the brute's head so as not to endanger one another. On it came, magnified in the uncertain light to the size of a horse. It would have given "buck fever" to any but experienced nimrods. Hughes and Phillips both fired at thirty feet. They thought they heard a snort of pain, but the brute still advanced. The dogs were but a dozen feet behind. As it passed between the two hunters, they struck at it with their rifle barrels, dealing it heavy blows on the back. As it passed out of sight, it seemed to redouble its speed. It darted down a steep ravine that cut its way along the big mountain, eventually joining Wi-daagh's Creek Hollow, noted for its cool breezes, which comes out at the public road near the site of the present stone woolen mill.

There was nothing for the hunters to do but scramble down the circuitous gorge as best they could. Part of the way, they had to walk over the slippery stones of a running brook and bend over to avoid the low-hanging boughs of the ancient hemlocks. All the lights were lost or extinguished by this time. The hunters were stumbling and tripping; some were swearing. The dogs were following the trail bravely, so they must back up their faithful canines. It was now the time that the older hunters called "the hour between dog and wolf." There were streaks of dawn above the mountain they had just left when they saw the Antes Gap road. The dogs were barking loudly; it sounded like the wolf had been brought to bay.

As the hunters crossed the road, a sorry looking, torn, and exhausted lot, they could see two thin trails of blood, side by side, in the sand. There was also blood on the worm fence on the far side of the road, over which the wolf had leaped. Beyond the fence was an open field with a few old apple trees. A dense fog had risen from the creek; it was difficult to see far ahead. The hunters were almost upon the dogs and the wolf before they saw them. They could only judge the distance by the terrific racket. In the grey morning light, they could make out the wolf, propped up against one of the apple trees, his forefeet bloody and helpless, biting and snapping at the hounds.

Already several of the dogs appeared to have had enough of it; one of them had both of his long ears chewed off. But the wolf, game to the end, was evidently determined to die fighting. Mike Curts, the first man on the scene, leveled his rifle at the monster's skull and fired. There was a loud report, and when the smoke and vapor lifted, the wolf lay dead among the on-rushing dogs. It took the combined strength of all the hunters to beat the hounds off and prevent them from tearing the carcass to pieces. It was rescued and laid out in the field before skinning and measuring. From tip to tip, it came to three inches under six feet. Its estimated weight was one hundred pounds.„

The hunters examined it carefully, noticing that in addition to Curts' bullet, it had been shot through both shoulders. These were the bullets put at it by John Phillips and Jesse Hughes; had they not hit, doubtless, it would have eluded its pursuers. With both fore-shoulders broken, it had run down the precipitous mountainside, across a four-foot fence, keeping on bravely until pain and disabilities compelled it to make its last stand by the old apple tree.

John Phillips looked at it, saying, "Boys, we have made a great kill; this is surely the famous packet-boat wolf." Then he shook Mike Curts by the hand, telling him that he deserved deathless fame for speeding the deciding bullet. The other hunters grouped around the lucky man, overwhelming him with congratulations.

Curts shook his head, saying that the real credit was due to little Caroline Steyne, who had given the alarm.

That night, when the Williamsport-Lock Haven packet boat made its initial trip after the repairs to the canal consequent to the great flood, no barking wolf followed its lights from the distant summits of the "dark and somber ridge" of the Bald Eagles. All was still except the melancholy *hylodes* in the tall, twisted acacia trees by the towpath. Night followed night, but the packet wolf was never heard again. He had ended his life of mystery fighting gamely like a black knight.

XVII

THE CURSED WOODS
(A Legend of One of Nature's Blights)

W E WERE riding along the outskirts of the Black Forest one afternoon in the early autumn. The original forest grew close to both sides of the road for a long distance. The giant hemlocks and beeches towered seemingly to the Blue Dome, the dark green of the former and the paler green of the latter producing a marvelous, tapestried effect. The pure air, the breath of the forest, swept across our path in every ravine, through which little streams, newly born, meandered, their courses checkered by fallen, moss-covered logs.

Beneath the giant trees was a mysterious purple light, not unlike what one sees in old cathedrals in France and Italy, where there is much medieval, richly tinted stained glass. The ground was carpeted with moss, with here and there tufts of delicate ferns, and in the deeper recesses grew the porcelain-like beech drops. In the soft light, it was only in keeping that the songs of the birds should be subdued. Once, we heard the solo of a Blackburnian warbler and, on several occasions, dimly the echoes of the wood thrush's exquisite choir. On one occasion, a porcupine ambled across the road some distance in front of our horses, looking like some dignified sacristan.

We felt ourselves in Nature's Cathedral, which, like many other cathedrals, was only too soon to be leveled by the ruthless hand of man. If ancient churches must fall to make room for improvements, what chance has a forest, remote from appreciative persons, who at most are a small and sometimes un-influential class? But it is a great pity nevertheless that future generations, and most of the present generation, must regard the Black Forest as a tradition, with only a few published descriptions and fewer photographs as proofs that it actually existed.

Fortunate, yes blessed, is the writer of these lines, though born in a great city, to have spent considerable time and been in a measure able to appreciate Nature's Cathedral, the vast and limitless, the inspiring, the soft-lighted and sweet-scented, the ever happy, the vanished forever Black Forest of Pennsylvania.

As we rode along, we came to several small clearings, in which stood log cabins and log barns. The dwellers in these modest abodes worked in the lumber camps, also raising potatoes and hay to sell to the lumbermen. In the fence corners were some original chestnut trees, saved from the demolition of the surrounding woods, great slim-boled monarchs, sending up shafts a hundred feet, unmarred by branches, culminating in graceful, umbrella shaped tops. These big trees were laden with the green burrs, as it was before the days of the chestnut blight. In those days, it seemed unthinkable that suddenly a whole race of trees could be literally swept off the face of the earth, and man powerless to stop it. The axe might do it, but never an invisible insect!

As we rode further on, the gilt clouds of the golden hour succeeded the bluer coloring of the afternoon sky. We came near a strange-looking area on the brow of a hill. For a stretch of fifty or sixty acres, all the timber on both sides of the road was dead. The white, barkless trunks were in strange contrast to the living, propitiating green of the growing trees. It was like the skeleton at the wedding feast or the graveyard of the Black Forest! As we drew nearer, we saw the remains of a little clearing, with the rotting foundations of a cabin, a half-fallen-down chimney, and out-buildings, but all strangely barren and devoid of berry-bushes, sumacs, Virginia creepers, and fireweed, the usual complement of ruins in these parts. About the buildings were a few broken stobs of ancient apple trees. It looked like a picture of desolation, no wonder the property had been abandoned.

Yet the somber has always had a charm for the writer. Just as he would always stop at old graveyards to decipher the inscriptions and ponder over the lives of the interred, this dead forest, this dead house, this dead ground, peculiarly appealed to him. He reined up his horse Trident, gazing intently at the solemn scene.

All was silent until a red-headed woodpecker began banging like a trip-hammer at the silvery trunk of one of the dead hemlocks. It looked as if some beetle or blight had ravaged the forest, and the dwellers in the humble home at its edge, overcome by the awesomeness of death, had moved away horribly depressed. Even the death of trees and flowers can affect some of us. Or perhaps a forest fire had killed the trees, and the dwellers had fled for their lives, never to return. Or perhaps they had given up their lives fighting the flames at the edge of the clearing. There were no signs that the buildings had been burned; if fire was the destroyer, a rain or backfire must have stopped it before the buildings were reached.

These and many other thoughts puzzled the writer as he sat on his faithful horse that calm September evening. But there was no immediate answer until that night when a stop was made at Dyer's comfortable boarding house at the headwaters of the East Branch of Young Woman's Creek. There the writer met an old friend, a Grand Army man, who knew the woods well, and whose active mind teemed with legends and anecdotes of the long ago. He was the only person at the supper table aware of the story of the dead timber and the abandoned clearing. Most of those living along the Pike did not possess memories long enough; perhaps some of them, imbued with the materialism, which was soon to sweep away the Black Forest, didn't care.

After supper, a stroll was taken along the rocky road from the Dyer home to the Pike while the old soldier unraveled the mystery. It dated back to the dark days of 1832, when the United States Government, urged on by the "big business" of that time, made a treaty with the Menomonies, a tribe of Indians living near Green Bay, Wisconsin, by which five hundred thousand acres of land were purchased from them as a future home for the Senecas and other Indians, residing in New York State. It was stipulated that the New York Indians should be removed there within three years, or their right to it would be forfeited, and it would revert to the United States.

This, it was hoped, would induce them to sell their reservations in New York to the shrewd land grabbers on easy terms. The Senecas paid no attention to the treaty. They were satisfied with their old homes, where they had been so happy, and cared nothing for the forfeiture of lands they had not purchased and did not want. In the hope that they might be brought to change their minds, a supplementary article was procured, by which the time for their removal was left to the discretion of the President. In this way, matters remained until 1837.

About this time, the magnates who desired to obtain the Indians' lands in New York became impatient and sent a band of hired agents to bring the matter to a head, by bribery or otherwise. One of these agents afterward said that he had paid one chief two thousand dollars cash and gave him a lease at nominal rental during occupancy of the farm on which he lived, on the consideration that he used the best of his exertions and endeavors to secure a treaty such as the land company desired, which would ensure the speedy removal of the Indians. He was promised further pay at the time of the removal. Another chief, upon the removal, was to receive five thousand dollars cash.

As a result of bribery and the debauching and making drunk of the chiefs, several signatures were secured ratifying the treaty of removal. Among the signers were ten Indians who had been made chiefs illegally for the special purpose of signing the treaty. Six actual chiefs whose signatures appeared solemnly swore they never signed it nor authorized others to sign it on their behalf. But the signatures of a majority of chiefs, real or fraudulent, were never obtained. But the result was, as expected, the Senecas were crowded into a narrow reservation, stripped of their best lands, and humbled to the dirt.

The Indian who was to receive five thousand dollars in cash when the Senecas were compelled to part with their choicest lands clamored for his pay, but it was not forthcoming. He was told that matters had not turned out quite as were expected, that the land company owed him nothing. As a traitor to his people, he had "burned his bridges," and now he would not even have enough money to leave the country. He was ostracized, his life threatened; the only thing left was to get away. The fat, well-paid agents of the land company sneered at him and finally threw him bodily out of their office in Batavia when he became too loud in his protests.

In his fall down a flight of steps, he broke both legs. His squaw and his sons carried him into the center of a swamp, where they nursed him until he could get about again. After that, he was a wretched cripple, hobbling about with two heavy staffs. On his first re-appearance in the village, he was set upon by two half-breeds in the employ of the land agents and beaten into insensibility. That was an invitation, without words, never to come to town again. His sons found him more helpless than ever, lying by the roadside the next morning. Men going to and fro from the settlement had seen the unconscious figure but offered no help. Let us be charitable and say that they thought he was a drunken Indian, a sight common enough in those days.

Robbed of his high estate, the renegade chief went by the name of Billy Bowlegs on account of the crookedness of his limbs after his accident. But he must not be confused with the Seminole Chief Bowlegs, who was a very different sort of person and a leader in the uprising of 1812 on the Georgian frontier.

The sons of Billy Bowlegs, in some manner, became the owners of a very dilapidated-looking horse, a travesty on the equine race, blind of both eyes, and minus ears and tail. It had been mutilated by some previous Indian owner in a drunken orgy but survived its hurts for many years. On this, the crippled chief was mounted, like Hudibras, and started for the "free country" in Pennsylvania. Poles, like shafts, were affixed to the horse, and it drew a kind of travois loaded with household utensils. The old squaw and the sons marched alongside, forming a curious looking "cavalcade."

Most of the traveling was done by night to avoid ridicule or interference. Two Indian dogs of the ancient, grey-colored breed accompanied the party to ward off attacks from the night-prowling canines of the settlers, whose homes they necessarily must pass. And the Indian dogs, with their wolfish aspect and small, erect, pointed ears, were a match for any dog of European stock, no matter if they were twice their size. This party followed the Genesee River to its source, climbed over the ridge, and moved southerly along the Genesee Fork of Tiadaghton.

At about the present site of Galeton, they left the creek, continuing south, until they found a comfortable location along the Coudersport Pike, then in the course of construction. They camped near a sweet spring, finding hunting and trapping good. When the Pike was completed, they pre-empted a log cabin, which a gang of Irish laborers had occupied. Only enough trees had been cut out of the forest to make room for the structure, but the two young Indians soon set to work making a field of tillable size about it. This they planted with apple, peach, pear, and plum trees, which they carried from Coudersport, having obtained them in exchange for furs.

Nobody seemed to claim the land on which they were living. Settlers with whom they talked said it could be bought for fifty cents an acre if the rightful owners could be found. At that time, if it had private ownership, it was being sold and re-sold for taxes. Nobody wanted such remote, mountainous land. Hemlock timber had no value, besides the Black Forest was so far from the market. James David and his son Flavius surveyed some of this land for the first time, about 1865, several years after Billy Bowlegs had gone to his future state.

Like Red-Jacket, with whom he had once been on terms of intimacy, the crippled chief held to his Pagan faith. He believed in the Gitchi-Manitto or Great Spirit, with a host of lesser divinities and a reward for the spirits of the brave. But his beliefs were not very coherent, and neither did they form a very active part of his everyday life. He was of a sullen, taciturn disposition in his later years, very different from his sons.

The boys became fast friends with the stage drivers and packers, who generally watered their horses at the spring at the clearing. This brought them in touch with travelers and traders, who bought their furs without taking them to Coudersport or Jersey Shore. To attract attention, they always kept bear, panther, wolf, fisher, fox, and deer skins nailed on the cabin and the outbuildings. Many persons not otherwise interested would see the hides and want to buy one or two of them as souvenirs of their trip through the Black Forest. Occasionally the boys guided parties on hunting or fishing expeditions, but in those days, the region was too remote to be known by many city sportsmen. When panthers, wolves, and elk could be killed in the "Elk Forest" in the Pocono Mountains, and bears, wild cats, deer, and even wolves were still abundant in the Blue Mountains, hunters from Philadelphia, Harrisburg, Lancaster, and Reading did not find it necessary to take a long journey like to Potter County in search of game, big or small.

Billy Bowlegs hated the sight of all strangers, but especially white men. He might have had a lingering fear of being dispossessed or the

"LAST RAFT" AT LOCK HAVEN, 1914

unforgettable memory of the chicanery and violence he had suffered at their hands. Indians occasionally spent a night at the cabin upon invitation of the boys or the squaw, but they were mostly Pennsylvania natives, who were ignorant of the land steals in New York State. To these, the old chief was courteous but had little to say.

When New York Indians appeared, the entire family tried to conceal their identities. They might have been murdered in their sleep had the truth been known. The old man was too decrepit to do any farming or wood-cutting but took the greatest pride in his little orchard. The altitude was favorable for fruit culture, and abundant birds, scales, and insect pests were unknown in those days. The chief pleasure was in trimming and grafting and digging about the roots of the growing trees. Some Indian apple trees were found along Rightman's Creek, being transplanted with excellent results and other varieties grafted on them.

The old savage was very happy in his wilderness home. He forgot about his wrongs when he saw no white men; he was leading a new life, as it were. His greatest joy was looking forward to the year when his trees would bear for the first time. While the peach trees had already blossomed, the others would all bear fruit at about the same time. But he was impatient, waiting for the time, often cursing and swearing when rainy days came, which passed slowly.

With no education, he had no mental resources to ease his irritable disposition. He had been born for a life of activity and leadership, which had been denied him by being a traitor and a cripple. He had been in his mountain retreat for about eight years when the season for the fruit crop drew near. The previous winter was long, and he was never so exacting and cantankerous. He was always cursing the slow passage of time, going into paroxysms of rage at every snowfall, which might delay the coming of the bluebirds. His sons often camped in the forest, ostensibly to trap, to get away from him; the old squaw was worried into a state of prostration.

With the coming of the bluebirds, the shad-cocks, and the shadflies, the old man was somewhat more composed. The boys entertained him all they could, carrying him in a litter to Rightman's Creek, where he could see them catching the mammoth suckers with their hands. But he was hard to divert. All he could talk or think about was blossom time and his prospective fruit crop. His father and grandfather had been famed for their orchards; it was one of his grandfather's plantations that General Sullivan cut down during the expedition into the Iroquois Country in 1777.

In what appeared to be an early spring, the blossoms came out in all their loveliness. Surely, they would be followed by an immense crop for such young trees if climatic conditions were favorable. The aged Indian literally lived in his orchard, watching the various colored, sweet-scented blooms with the concern of a parent. He always carried a shotgun, killing every bird that drew near his precious trees. In that respect, he was a precursor of the silly generations of white men who slaughtered the birds, their best friends, when they visited their orchards and gardens to devour insect pests.

One evening, while the blossoms were at their height, the sun went down unusually silvery and cold. The old man sat by the red glow of his open fireplace while the north wind blew down the chimney and whistled about the house's eaves. Outside, the giant hemlocks swayed and creaked with ominous cadences. The Indian was too cold and shivery to worry about his trees; his squaw and sons feared to mention the subject to him. During the night, the wind ceased, but a heavy frost occurred. When the old man looked out of doors in the morning, the ground was white; when the sun came out, every blossom was killed by the black frost.

It was then and there that old Billy Bowlegs lost his self-control. Cursing and screaming, he ran out into the orchard as fast as his long staffs would permit. He hurled imprecations and anathemas against the Gitchi-Manitto that permitted such a blight to occur. He shook his staff at the Heavens, stamped his lame feet, and exerted himself so much that he became dizzy, sinking to the ground in a heap. The frightened family, awed by the old man's blasphemy and violent actions, stood quiescent in the doorway until they saw him fall. Then they rushed forward, picking him up tenderly, and carried him into the house. They pried open his whiskered lips and poured a pint of whiskey down his throat. When he came to himself, he spoke not in a spirit of thankfulness but with a renewed torrent of profanity. This he kept up all day long until he sank asleep, exhausted at nightfall. When he woke up the next morning, he was too weak to leave his couch, though his mind seemed more rational.

He attributed the unseasonable frost which had killed the blossoms to the curse put on him at the time he had betrayed his tribesmen to the land thieves but not to his long-continued practice of profanity.

"But I still have the trees; in another year, I'll have blossoms again" was the extent of his philosophy.

But even that was not to be. By some strange phenomenon of nature, the trees were killed at the same time as the blossoms. The leaves shriveled, and no new ones came out again. By autumn, the trunks and branches were dry and brittle. The old Indian suffered keenly from this added disappointment. He wandered the orchard every evening, cutting off twigs, hoping to find signs of life somewhere. When he returned for supper, he stormed and swore, eating little in his excited condition.

Once, he was so angry that he threw a cup of scalding coffee over his faithful squaw's breast and shoulders. In a civilized community, he would have been locked up; in the Black Forest, he could act as mean as he wished until the end.

In the next spring, a few apple trees sprouted out at the roots, but most of these died away during the dry spell in August, despite the old man's valiant efforts to keep them watered. When he saw that his work was in vain, he turned his thoughts to the big hemlock timber, which stood on three sides of his clearing.

"Boys," he said to his sons, "someday those trees will make a fortune for us. Go out and stake off a hundred acres; when we have been here twenty-one years unmolested, it will be mine in the sight of the law."

There was considerable foresight in this, as settlers were beginning to take up homesteads along the Pike, and there was an increasing demand for lumber. Several Irishmen, who had helped build the road, had remained, and after ten years had improved farms of which they could be proud; now Swiss, Germans, and New Englanders were coming. The boys blazed the trees on what they approximated to be a hundred acres, chuckling to themselves over their father's sagacity.

"Someday," said one of the youths, "the old man will get five thousand dollars for this timber, or just as much as the damned land agents in York State cheated him out of."

Years passed, and no claimant for the hundred acres appeared. Billy Bowlegs, under the name of William Green, took title to the tract at the courthouse in Coudersport, He was eighty years old, but it had paid him to be patient; his impatience had been punished in the past. He had long since given up his hobby for fruit trees and, of later years, had turned his attention to garden-truck and bees. The latter the Indians used to call the "white men's flies." One by one, the tracts of land along the Pike had been taken up and cleared; those further back had passed into the hands of big lumber companies in Williamsport and New York State. There were a dozen small sawmills on the Pike between Jersey Shore and Coudersport.

One summer afternoon, a ponderous German, who was buying up hemlock lands for a tanning company, stopped at the old man's home. He liked the looks of the thrifty body of white hemlocks, which adjoined to the north a much larger tract that he purchased the year before at a tax sale. In fact, it gave him the right of way to the Pike. He priced the Indian's timber but said he would not sell it without the land and buildings, all of which he held at five thousand dollars.

The German offered him three thousand, which he accepted on the condition that his boys be given the job for peeling the bark the following summer and that a cash rental be paid for allowing the camps and stables to be erected on his clearing facing the pike. All this, he figured, would bring the total up to the five thousand marks. That night was the happiest the old man had spent since the days before he had become a traitor and exile.

The big job was to be opened the following spring, and he would have cash for his timber, work for his boys, rent for his ground, and he might raise some potatoes and hay for the woodsmen and their teams.

During the dry spell, which lasted from early August to September, he noticed that some hemlock trees were becoming brown. He sent the boys to investigate; they reported that a beetle was working under the bark. Every tree seemed to be affected, they said.

The old man's confidence in the future turned to alarm. Every day he looked at the forest back of the house; the trees seemed to the browning before his eyes. By autumn, some of them had lost their needles entirely. During the winter, the disease, or whatever it was, progressed. By the first of April, when the German returned to close the contract, every tree was doomed. Among the hard, dry trunks could be heard the "boom, boom,

boom" of the strong bills of the pileated woodpeckers or weather cocks. Although the work of the hemlock beetles is plentiful enough today, the German tannery man had never seen the like.

"What is the cause of it?" he asked with wonderment in his voice.

"Shall I tell you the truth?" replied the old Indian, with a sob in his voice. "They are cursed woods; I sold out my tribe to land thieves thirty years ago; I have had no luck since."

The old squaw, peeling potatoes inside the kitchen, hobbled to the back door. "Billy may have been a traitor, but I don't think he meant any harm; his bad luck came from another reason. He was always cursing and swearing and blaming the Heavens, and none can prosper who do that."

XVIII

THE SCREAMING SKULL
(A Ghost Story of the Pike)

THERE IS a universality to psychic experience. Readers of Ingram's *Haunted Houses and Family Legends of Great Britain* will remember the tale of the "screaming skull" of Bettiscombe House, near Bridport, in Dorsetshire, which made an awful racket every time it was moved from its favorite resting place on a window-ledge. There was a story of another screaming skull current on the Coudersport Pike a score of years ago, which had many points of similarity to the English legend.

This proves that all legends have had a common origin or that there are as definite laws in the unseen, not understood world as in the physical world, the laws of which mankind is slowly growing to understand. The writer of these lines would like to believe that there is an unseen world that someday will be laid before us after we have grasped the facts of the world, we see about us. And he has had intimations of such a world; otherwise, he could not seriously attempt preserving stories such as these.

But even apart from ghost stories, there is a current parallelism between all legends. In his *Extinct British Animals*, Harting speaks of a soldier in Ireland, on his way to take passage for England, who had to pass through a wood, and being weary, sat down under a tree, opening his knapsack, which contained some victuals and commencing to eat.

Suddenly he was surprised by several wolves coming toward him; he threw them some scraps of bread and cheese until all was gone. The wolves made a closer approach to him, and he knew not what to do, so he took a pair of bagpipes that he had, and as soon as he began to play upon them, all the wolves ran away as if they had been scared out of their wits. The soldier, disgusted, cried out, "A pox take you all; if I had known you had loved music so well, you should have had it before dinner."

A month ago, the writer visited Treaster Valley, Mifflin County, to secure some verification of one of the legends contained in this collection. Among the many interesting persons, he met was one man whose father had been a great wolfer in the Seven Mountains.

This man stated that once when the old gentleman in question was a youth and courting the girl whom he afterward married, he was followed one night by several black wolves. They pressed him so closely for such a long distance that he determined to ward them off somehow. He backed up against a tree and began throwing pieces of smoked meat to the brutes, which he had with him in a basket. When it was all gone, the wolves made a closer approach, and not knowing what to do, he picked up a stone and began striking it against the blade of a scythe that he was carrying. As soon as he began this, the wolves all ran away as if scared out of their wits. The woodsman said, disgusted, "The plague take you all; if I had known you liked that sound so well, you should have had it before dinner."

But to return to the screaming skull of our own Black Forest. For a few short weeks in the early fifties, a lone highwayman named Mark McCoy plied his trade on the loneliest parts of the Coudersport Pike. Like William Brennan, the hero of the Irish folk song "Brennan on the Moor," McCoy only robbed the well-to-do or the packers; he was said to have made presents of money to the poor, especially to wretched tramps and emigrants who toiled their weary ways along the forest-hidden highway. How the young man got into this precarious occupation was a mystery, although some hinted that an unhappy love affair in his home county of Northumberland was responsible.

As he was a handsome, well-set-up fellow, this seemed hardly believable to the class of people whose basis of love and marriage was external attractiveness. But there must have been other causes. McCoy had been left an orphan when he was one year old; he was brought up by strangers who were wholly out of sympathy with him. He had served a term in jail before appearing on the Pike, although the sentence was received for having beaten an aged farmer for whom he worked. The quarrel had arisen because the old man remonstrated with him for cruelly treating one of his farm horses.

Though good-looking, the highwayman possessed a forbidding countenance. He had ash-colored hair, brown eyes, always scowling, a somewhat colorless complexion, and a stubby, brown chin beard. The upper lip, which was clean shaved, was contracted and hard. Physically, he looked powerful, and he knew no fear.

His first victim was a wealthy lumberman from Williamsport, driving up the pike with his body servant to inspect some pineries he owned on the highlands above Hyner Run. On a high hill, a short distance beyond what is now the Lebo place, where the wind has swept for centuries through an open grove of gnarled yellow pines, the highwayman, masked and booted, appeared from behind a hunter's shanty, pointing a brace of pistols at them. The magnate and his servant threw up their hands with alacrity and submitted to removing all their belongings, even their coats and vests. Then they were ordered to turn about, drive back to Jersey Shore, and give the alarm. When they arrived, and the constables came out on the pike, there was no trace of the knight of the road.

At the time of the committing of this robbery. McCoy had no particular headquarters. He had started up the pike aimlessly a week before like so many others had done as if somewhere in the boundless wilderness was a Promised Land. The ease with which he committed his crime tickled his pride, and he determined to try again. He walked in a northerly direction over the bleak, wind-swept plateau until night began settling down. By that time, he had come to a steep ravine, which led down into one of the branches of Slate Run, probably the South Fork.

The slopes of the mountain were covered with a dense growth of white pine and hemlock, and it seemed an interminable distance to the creek, which he could hear, but not see, flowing through the bottom. Although the hour was not late, it was pitchy dark where he was and growing cold, although it was in June. Halfway down the mountain, he came to a path that led in a circuitous way to the valley. He was delighted to find it, as it evidently led to some habitation. No matter who would be living there, he was sure of impressing upon the good people the necessity of keeping him for the night. At length, as he neared the creek, he was apprised of his approach to the dwelling by the harsh barking of a dog.

As he came out into the open, he could make out the lines of a small log cabin in the center of a clearing of possibly five acres, which extended on both sides of the brook. A red light, like a beacon, glowed in the windows and shone on the waters of the sullen, swift stream. An improvised bridge consisting of a giant hemlock felled across the water and led him to the modest dwelling. The dog rushed at him savagely, being apparently unused to strangers, and he had just enough time to pick up a stake at the yard fence to beat it off. Defending himself with his stick in one hand, he knocked on the door with the other. It was opened after some hesitation by a very attractive-looking young girl whose eyes met his squarely as she stood before him.

Instantly he was charmed by her, feeling as if he had known her always. She was dark and slender, rather tall, with jetty black eyes and a peculiar cast of features, the nose being aquiline and turned up a trifle at the end, the lips pale and pitifully thin. He told her in as few words as possible that he had lost his way on the mountain and would like to be accommodated for the night. Without hesitation, the girl motioned for him to enter. The room was almost dark, save for the rosy glow of the fire, which cast fantastic shadows on the walls and floor. Once inside, the girl lit a rushlight on a table by a window, enabling the unexpected guest to look about him.

A very old man and a very old woman sat on chairs by the windows. The woman arose from her seat, but the man did not stir a muscle. He was a grand-looking old gentleman with a massive head covered with stiff white hair; his features were prominent and boldly cut; he was a picture of Andrew Jackson in his latter days. McCoy looked at him closely and noticed that the patriarch was blind.

"'Please excuse me for intruding so late in the evening," said the stranger, "but as I was telling this young lady, I became lost in the forest and appeared here quite by accident. My name is Mark McCoy, and I come from down country, near Sunbury. I am a timber prospector by occupation."

The old woman said that she was glad to be of service to a bewildered forester while the old man muttered something, probably to the same effect. Then the young girl said that the old couple were her grandparents, Burkheiser by name, and that they had moved into the Black Forest from Berks County five years before. Her mother, she said, had been dead for many years, but her father, who was the old man's only son, had been killed by a falling log on Tiadaghton a year previous, and that her name was Ava Burkheiser. With all these explanations, friendly relations were established, and the girl set about to prepare supper for the guest. McCoy could be pleasant when he wanted to be and thanked the family for their cordial greeting, adding that he would pay them well for any trouble he might cause them.

During the supper, the old woman, who was naturally a talkative soul, and saw few strangers with whom to exchange ideas, told more of the family history. She had never ceased regretting leaving her comfortable homestead near Probst's Town in Alleminga, in Berks, for this lonesome life in the wilderness. Her son Adam, the father of Ava, was a great hunter and had killed much big game on the Pinnacle, the highest point in the Blue Mountains near their old home. The growing scarcity of wild animals had made him desirous of moving into a wilder country, so he had induced his parents to sell everything and come with him to the Black Forest. He had been very successful as a hunter, killing as many as fifty bears in a winter. But they never saw anybody; there was not a human habitation in the eight miles between their cabin and the pike, except a hunting shack across the hill, where lived a little hunch-backed Indian named Seneca White. This Indian was middle-aged and infirm but the greatest hunter in three counties. He visited them occasionally; they were always glad to see him, and he played so well on the flute.

Early the next morning, McCoy returned to the pike, waiting all day for some fresh victim, but none appeared. On the second day, he met and held up a band of five constables, who were out looking for him with a warrant obtained by his first victim, the Williamsport lumberman. That night he arrived at the Burkheiser cabin as unconcerned as if nothing had happened. He hid his weapons and disguise in the woods so that if the place was entered and searched, nothing incriminating could be found. He was deeply in love with Ava and flattered himself to think that his ardor was reciprocated. He kept away from the pike for several days, returning at length to hold up a well-to-do peddler.

These robberies were kept up at intervals of three or four days for several weeks to the growing terror of the traveling public. He never molested the mail wagon or, as stated before, poor people. Consequently, the outcry against him was slower at developing than it otherwise might have been. He made presents to some poor travelers whom he could have robbed. Some nights he laid out among the ferns, but generally, Ava was the loadstone that drew him back to the humble cabin. He paid so liberally for his entertainment that no questions were asked.

One afternoon he encountered a young attorney from Smethport, who was on his way on horseback to Williamsport. The youth was carrying a large sum of money to pay some back taxes on some unseated lands in Lycoming County. He had been fully warned about the highwayman but laughingly declared he could take care of himself. On his saddle, he carried loaded pistols in holsters, and his keen eyes scanned the road with the unconcern of a brave man. But out of the dense hemlocks came the order to throw up his hands. Instead, he dug the spurs into his big bay horse's flanks and started down the road at a gallop. As thus far McCoy had never let a person escape, he shot after the fleeing horseman. One of the bullets went through his back, coming out at the breast, but the young lawyer gamely held his place on the saddle, riding on. The hemorrhage was so intense that he welcomed the sight of a house. He drew rein before the cabin of Horatio Nelson, and as he did so, losing his balance and falling to the turf. The woodsman and his good wife rushed forward and picked up the poor fellow, carrying him tenderly into the house. He had never spoken and soon lapsed into unconsciousness, dying two hours later.

Back at the scene of the shooting, the knight of the road became possessed by the feeling that he had killed his man. It was a rash act; it would put the arm of the law after him so strongly that there would be no escape. He would have to leave the country; the west always had a fascination for him; he would ask Ava to marry him, and they could go to the Mississippi Country and take up a homestead. As he walked over the desolate highlands toward his sweetheart's cabin, all these thoughts passed through his head. He strode into the house with utter unconcern and laughed and joked all through the supper.

After Ava finished her work, he invited her to go with him for a stroll. It was a calm, lovely evening, and the sunset's red rays lingered long above the feathery tips of the old hemlocks. At dusk, the whippoorwills commenced their songs, continuing until the moon rose above the forest. Then all was still, save for the occasional lament of a killdeer. McCoy waited until it was time to walk back to the cottage before declaring his love. He told the girl that he had decided to go to the west, where there were greater opportunities, and that he would like her to marry him and go along. He would have departed days before; only he could not go without her. Without waiting for an answer, he caught her in his arms, giving her a tight embrace and many kisses.

As gently as she could, Ava wrenched herself free and stood facing him in the moonlight. She looked like a spirit, with her white frock and so slim and pale in the moonlight. With a firm voice, she said that while she deeply appreciated his wanting to make her his wife, she could never marry, let alone leave her grandparents. McCoy tried to take her in his arms again, but she backed up against the fence. He tried to explain to her that he would gladly pay the expenses of bringing the old couple to the west and would make them a comfortable home if only she would marry him. He dared not say he would marry her and remain in the Black Forest, for he knew only too well that the authorities were on his trail.

But Ava shook her head and said it was time for her to get to bed. The lover asked her if she cared for him, to which she answered that she did, but not enough to marry him and leave her relatives.

The bold highwayman was humbled completely and could not bear the thought of spending the night in the cabin. With a voice full of emotion, he bade her goodbye. Taking several gold pieces from his pocket, the proceeds of one of his hold-ups, he handed them to her for the old folks to pay the balance of his board and lodging.

"I want to show my appreciation for the kind way in which I have been treated here," he said sadly as he turned away. He came back after he had taken a few steps, asking the girl to make up a lunch for him, as he would be several days in the forest. To this, she gladly assented, and he went with her to the kitchen while she prepared it by the flickering gleams of the rushlight. It was placed in a little oaken basket, which she said that old Seneca White, who was a clever basket-maker, as well as hunter and musician, had fashioned.

Then he clasped her hand and left the cabin. The girl watched him while he crossed the foot log over the run, the moonlight streaming down on him. He was a man of mystery, and she was glad he was going away. Once more in the forest, McCoy followed the path halfway to the top of the mountain and then left it and headed in a westerly direction. By morning, he would turn north and get to New York State as directly as possible. There he might climb on the steam railway train unobserved; it would take him to the western country.

But at daybreak, he was filled with an irrepressible desire to return to Ava's cabin. He found that he could not live without her. He would ask her to marry him, let him go west, and make a home for her. He would live alone until her grandparents died, then she could join him if her sense of duty would not let her go now. He tried to fight against this inclination to return; his conscience told him that it was a foolhardy move; surely the sheriff's posse would visit the cabin and be on his tracks, as they would hear of a stranger having been harbored there.

It was a silly surrender after making good his escape. But love was stronger than the sense of self-preservation. He turned back. Sometimes his heart was heavy; at other times, it was glad; it seemed like there were two personalities alternately ruling his nature. He traveled slowly, as he did not wish to reach Slate Run before dark. He would come into the creek at its headwaters and slip up as close to the cabin as he could without being observed. If only that dog would not bark. But he had been told it always barked when a night-prowling bear or wolf came near the premises. It might not cause a commotion.

The whippoorwills had ceased their sad songs, and the moon was rising as he neared the spring where this branch of Slate Run had its source. It was a pretty spot where a jet of clear water as thick as a man's arm gushed from out of the moss-grown rocks. Large stones had been piled up on either side of it for seats. It was an ideal resting place on a summer's day, overhung by giant hemlocks.

As he neared the spring, he heard voices. Could it be the sheriffs and constables conferring over his escape? He listened intently; it was Ava's voice; he knew it well, and another's, hardly like a man's way of talking, yet not a woman's, so squeaky and so strangely accented.

In the dead silence, he heard these words distinctly from the lips of his beloved: "That stranger wanted to marry me and take me west; I told him that I could not leave the old folks; in truth, I could not leave *you*. You are the only love I will ever have."

McCoy's heart stood still, and like a ghost, he crept nearer to the awful spot. A quivering shaft of moonlight revealed the couple to him. There was the frail, beautiful Ava, clasped in the arms of an ill-favored, undersized Indian with a foxlike face and long dark hair hanging about his eyes.

The rejected lover had an impulse to shoot them both, but he recalled his hasty move the day before when his killing a man had probably made him the fugitive he now was. He put the pistol back in his belt, then took it out again. Creeping close to where the lovers stood, he waited until a moon ray illuminated the scene. Then he fired once, twice; there were two piercing shrieks, followed by a dog barking. Then all was still again, and he hastened up the mountain path.

On the summit, he turned south and started toward the bleak upland where the aged yellow pines swayed their knotted branches in the night wind. Bathed in moonlight, they looked like a regiment of ghosts. When he reached the hunter's shanty on the pike, he loosed his rope belt, tying it in a noose about his neck. Then he climbed up in the old yellow pine, which grew back of the hut, straddling one of the branches. He fastened the rope securely about the branch and dropped off into space. As the noose tightened about his throat, voluntarily or involuntarily, a piercing scream like that uttered by his recent victims broke from his lips. It echoed and re-echoed among the pines. Then all was silent, save for the night wind singing with the old pines. All night long, the dark figure dangled from the tree, the hands swaying and gesticulating in attitudes almost alive, the moonlight giving weird, hideous expressions to his face.

Shortly after dawn, an armed body of men recruited in Jersey Shore and along the pike, rode close to where the corpse was hanging. One of the horses shied, which was how it came to be discovered. The posse dismounted, grouping themselves about the frightful effigy. Among the party was a sheriff and coroner, the latter official just having come from the Nelson cabin down the road, where lay the body of the murdered attorney from Smethport, shot in the back. A struck jury was formed, and it was decided to bury the suicide at the foot of the tree on which he had hung himself. He was cut down, and his pockets were searched. Two hundred dollars in gold and silver coins were discovered, besides various papers which had belonged to his victims. The highwayman of the pike had died like a coward because he feared arrest, they all averred, as they buried him in a shallow grave, dug principally with a rusty potato hook, which they found in the shanty. But the real reason, the heart reason for his death, was not known until days afterward, nor his name and identity.

That autumn, when Levi Trexler, the owner of the shack, appeared on the scene with his dogs intent on chasing deer, the savage animals dug up the highwayman's skull. The hunter had heard of the suicide and burial of the outlaw and laughed when he saw the skull, with the brown chin beard still growing on it. He nailed it above the cabin door as he would with a catamount's head. That night he was awakened by a piercing scream, which woke the echoes of the lonely mountaintop. He pulled his wolfskin robe over his head, swearing softly in Pennsylvania German.

The dogs set up such a terrific uproar that, at length, his courage returned sufficiently to get out of bed to club them into silence. As he went out of the door, the skull, evidently broken loose by the wind, tumbled down, striking him on the top of his bald cranium. With a yell almost as terrible as the one which had roused him from his slumbers, he ran down the road as if pursued by demons until he fell exhausted in the deep sand. He lay there until morning, when two of his hunting comrades, who were on their way to join him at the camp, found him and dragged him to the shack. The visitors picked up the skull and buried it in the desecrated grave. That night the dogs dug it up again, and once more, the piercing scream resounded over the desolate upland. The three hunters were frightfully alarmed, abandoning the camp at daybreak.

During a sudden thaw in the depth of winter, a packer's team became mired near the abandoned shanty, and the good fellow determined to

NEW ORDER OF THINGS

spend the night there. In walking around the cabin looking for pine knots to start a fire, he noticed the decaying skull. Picking it up in a spirit of jest, he hung it by one of its eye-sockets on the stump of a broken-off branch of the ancient pine tree. During the night, the man was aroused by a horrible yell, which sent him from his bunk as if hit by a bullet. He ran out of doors but could see nothing. He sat the remainder of the night in his wagon and, at daybreak, forced his team ahead, almost cudgeling the horses to death to get away from the ghastly surroundings.

In the springtime, a party of fishermen decided to spend a night in the hut. They saw the skull hooked to the pine tree and knew the story of the place, but all agreed that they were not afraid. During the night, they were put in a state of panic by the horrid scream that frightened many others. They decided to leave at the first signs of dawn, but before doing so, one of the party took the skull and pitched it away as far as he could among the sweet ferns and huckleberry bushes.

Some children from a party of emigrants, who had stopped at the spring across the pike from the shack for their mid-day meal, found the skull and ran laughing with it to their elders. The superstitious Germans ordered the little folks to return it to where they had found it. Instead of doing so, with childish perversity, they set it on the doorstep of the cabin. There it remained unnoticed until a timber prospector came to the shanty for the night. With a show of unconcern, he tossed the skull on the shanty roof. At midnight, the hideous scream resounded upon his ears; he sprang from his bunk and ran out, hurrying along the road, puffing and wheezing until daylight eased his fears.

During November, Horatio Nelson and his wife were going to a corn-husking party to be held at the home of another old settler, William Green, who lived several miles up the Pike. Out of curiosity, they stopped to look at the scene of the highwayman's suicide. The good woman, with her native intuition, noticed the grinning bearded skull resting on the shanty roof.

"Oh, Horatio," she called, "it's an awful shame to keep that fellow's head there, arch murderer though he may be. Let's give it a decent burial."

The hardy pioneer had promised to loan the Green boys a grubbing hoe and had it with him, so this was an easy matter. While he was hooking the skull down from the roof, the wife noticed the torn-up, dilapidated grave beneath the pine tree. She pointed it out to her husband and told him to dig the grave deeper. The skull and the bones were re-interred in a deep pit, and heavy stones were laid over the remains so that they could not be dug out by dogs or wild animals.

And to this day, although the grave is well known, no more has been heard of the screaming skull.

www.ingramcontent.com/pod-product-compliance
Lightning Source LLC
Chambersburg PA
CBHW030518020726
47494CB00004B/1139